The Little Cornish House

BOOKS BY DONNA ASHCROFT

Summer in the Scottish Highlands

The Little Village of New Starts

The Little Guesthouse of New Beginnings

Summer at the Castle Cafe

Christmas in the Scottish Highlands

If Every Day Was Christmas

The Christmas Countdown

The Little Christmas Teashop of Second Chances

Donna Ashcroft

The Little Cornish House

bookouture

Published by Bookouture in 2022

An imprint of Storyfire Ltd.
Carmelite House
50 Victoria Embankment
London EC4Y 0DZ

www.bookouture.com

ISBN: 978-1-80019-353-6
eBook ISBN: 978-1-80019-352-9

To Mel and Rob Harrison of Goodman Fox
For your big hearts and generosity

1

Ruby Penhaligon laid her head against the train window as it chugged its way through the Cornish countryside, past winding wooded valleys and golden sandy bays offering teasing glimpses of the azure sea. She pressed her nose to the glass just as the tip of the hill that marked the start of her destination came into view, and suddenly she wanted to bounce on her seat. The journey was familiar and reminded Ruby of when she'd made the same journey with her mum for their holidays in Indigo Cove years before. She let out a long breath as her head filled with a hundred memories – good and bad – and her chest compressed as if an elephant had sat on it. It was the strangest thing, brought on whenever she thought about her mother or wayward dad. Sometimes, losing herself in the comfort and familiarity of spreadsheets during her daily life as an accountant helped to relieve the pressure. But recently she was finding it harder to ignore.

Ruby took her mobile from her pocket to check through her emails and answer a few, trying to distract herself. When that didn't work, she returned her phone to her handbag and leaned her head back on the window as her eyes traced the rolling green hillsides, admiring the bright pink foxgloves and the fluffy wild rabbits bouncing in the corner of a field. She took in a few long breaths, encouraging herself to relax. Ten minutes later, the train chugged into the small station at Indigo Cove and Ruby immediately spotted her grandmother on the platform, looking anxiously at the carriages. Lila Penhaligon had obviously only just finished teaching a pottery class because she wore one of her trademark smocks smeared with clay, bright purple Doc Martens boots, and her hair had been swept into a bun littered with the random tools she had a habit of filing in her 'do'.

'Cooee!' Lila shouted as the doors slid open, and Ruby hauled her large black suitcase out before being enveloped in a warm hug.

'Nanou!' She called out her childhood name for her grandmother, surprised when her eyes pricked with tears.

'It's been over a year – that's way too long not to see my only granddaughter!' Lila declared, grabbing Ruby's suitcase before she could stop her. At sixty-eight, Lila was fit and remarkably spritely – with long, lean limbs and exquisitely smooth skin.

'I'm sorry it's been so long,' Ruby murmured, feeling guilty. 'I've no idea where the time's gone.'

'You've been working too hard, pet,' Lila soothed. Ruby followed as the older woman marched quickly along the short platform, which was lined with an array of oak barrels filled with a vibrant sprawl of red, pink, green and yellow summer flowers. 'The car's parked out front – I thought you might like a quick jaunt through the village to catch you up. We've got a few more shops since you last visited; a lot has changed. We'll have a meal at home this evening and then there's a meeting with Indigo Cove's answer to Neighbourhood Watch. You'll meet a handful of the villagers there.' She winked. 'We're gathering in The Beach Cafe on the harbour – that's new too – so you'll get to meet a few of my favourite people.' Her grandmother spoke at a million miles an hour, which made her Cornish lilt even more pronounced. Ruby jerked to a stop as they exited the station. Lila's beautiful green cabriolet Volkswagen Beetle, which she often referred to as Beatrix, sat in the no parking zone. 'We're just heading off!' Lila blew a noisy kiss to the ticket inspector, who was frowning at the car. Ruby helped her Nanou swing the suitcase into the back, and climbed in just as Lila fired up the engine and squealed out of the space.

'I really appreciate you coming to help out for the next few weeks,' Lila shouted above the wind, zooming out of the station and taking a fast left, which Ruby knew would lead them towards the harbour. Years ago, Indigo Cove had been a thriving fishing community. Now a few of the older residents still worked out at sea, but the village was more of a busy tourist hub, flanked by wildlife conservation areas and a plethora of companies offering boat trips and water sports along with award-winning restaurants – thousands of people flocked here in the summer months. 'I've not got that many bookings at the moment, so it won't be too busy, which means you'll have plenty of opportunities to let your hair down. Maybe you'll even have time for a holiday fling – it's been yonks since you had a boyfriend!' Lila yelled as they reached the top of the hill.

'It's not been that long,' Ruby murmured, calculating exactly how many months it had been since she'd last dated, realising it was over fourteen. Then she forgot everything and a spontaneous smile crept across her face as she got her first uninterrupted view of Indigo Cove. The vibrant greens and blues of the sea always took her breath away, despite the number of times she saw it. Lila followed an open-top bus down the hill, past the quaint rows of cottages painted in pastel pinks, yellows and blues – each with baskets and pots of multicoloured flowers strewn around their windows or doors.

'As I mentioned, I need help serving cakes and cream teas, assisting the clients when we're doing lessons, driving them to and from The Beach Cafe at lunchtime. I've a widower booked in from tomorrow – his granddaughter has rented a cottage by the harbour and paid for a full four weeks of lessons. Apparently, he'll benefit from getting out of the house.' She winked. 'There's also Gabe Roskilly who runs the brewery. You'll know of it,' she said when Ruby looked at her blankly. She'd made a point over the years of staying away from the locals, preferring to steer clear of anyone who might be friends with her estranged father. 'The Roskilly Brewery, just outside the village – it's been in their family for generations?'

'Nope.' Lila looked disappointed when Ruby shook her head.

'You'd remember him if you'd met.' Lila fanned herself enthusiastically. 'He's been coming to the Pottery Project whenever he can – he's working on some special edition tankards for the brewery centenary. He's got big plans, and there'll be a party in three weeks, which you're invited to, of course.' Lila winked at Ruby again before her eyes darted back to the road. 'I'm also expecting a teenage boy that a friend of mine who works at the local secondary school asked me to tutor. I'm told he's a talented artist, but he's not so good at connecting with others, so we'll have our work cut out. Other than that, there's a couple who've just moved to Indigo Cove, a Mr and Mrs Harris. I know you'll help me make everyone feel at home.'

'Do any of our students have pottery experience?' Ruby asked, taking a deep breath of sea air.

'Gabe is a complete novice – we'll have to see about the rest.' Lila let out a small whoop as they reached the bottom of the hill – here the road curved around the small harbour which was sprinkled with hundreds of boats. The beach was layered with smooth white sand, and there were people dotted across it, some walking, some lounging on bright rectangular towels. More couples and families sauntered along the pavement, a few staring into the front windows of the bustling array of shops.

'This has changed a lot,' Ruby said, her voice growing husky as she took in the scene, ignoring the dull thud of pain that hit her chest as she remembered walking along the seafront with her mum on their holidays years before.

'You barely made it out of bed when you came last year; it's no wonder you've missed all the new stuff. I hope you avoided the prawn sandwiches on your journey this time?' Lila raised a blonde eyebrow, making Ruby chuckle. Last April, she'd arrived with her best friend Anna Lovejoy for a long weekend with her grandmother, ready to celebrate at the annual Indigo Cove Spring Carnival. Anna had been on one of her frequent relationship breaks from her long-term boyfriend, Simon Green – and Ruby had been determined to take her friend's mind off the stormy romance. Instead, she'd spent most of the time in bed throwing up with a bout of food poisoning – while Anna had painted the town all the colours of the rainbow, and a few dozen more. Since the trip a lot had settled in Anna's life; she was back with Simon permanently and they had a beautiful baby girl called Maisy.

'I went for a safe cheese salad today.' Ruby grinned.

'Then you'll be fine for our meeting.' Lila followed the road round past a large wooden-fronted building with a long glass window facing the sea. Chrome tables and chairs had been set outside, laid with starched linen tablecloths, wine glasses and sparkling silver cutlery. 'That's The Oyster Bar, our new seafood restaurant. The chef's French and tourists come from miles away to try his dishes. The food's exquisite.' Lila waved at a couple walking along the high street, before dodging in front of the bus, making the driver honk his horn. She blew him a kiss before taking another fast right, up a long hill flanked by tall grass and pink wildflowers. Ruby rested her head back on the seat and took another deep breath of sea air, shielding her eyes from the bright sunshine. Everything smelled so good here, so different from London. She should have come earlier, stopped putting off her visits. Then again, she'd been determined to avoid seeing her dad who'd been making frequent visits to the area and had only recently returned for a long stint in his regular bolt-hole, Spain.

It took another five minutes before they arrived at the Pottery Project, which was set in six acres of semi-wild moorland with a small lake and mini enchanted woodland that Ruby used to play in when she was a child. The pottery studio was located in a pretty converted brick barn with one large room Lila used for teaching, a small kitchen area, toilets, a clay storage space, and a separate room where she did all the glazing and firing in the kiln. Next to that, positioned on the far side of the cliff, sat The Little Cornish House where her Nanou lived. The house offered spectacular views of the sea from two of the three bedrooms, kitchen and sitting room. Ruby's eyes filled as she took in the pretty buildings, and her mind flooded with a million memories of her mother and all the wonderful days they'd spent holidaying here. Then Lila screeched to a stop in the drive, spraying pebbles left and right. Two cats who were sprawled on the stones bathing in the sun leaped to their feet and scampered behind the house.

'Sorry, Lemon and Ginger!' Lila sang after her pets, who were named for two of her favourite cake flavours. She grabbed Ruby's suitcase from the back seat and marched to the entrance of the cottage before Ruby had even opened the passenger door. 'I put you in your usual room – the one with the best view.' Lila beamed as she opened the front door, which she hadn't bothered locking. Few people strayed out of the village in this direction unless they were hiking along the cliffs. The hallway was painted bright white, but it smelled a little musty, and Ruby frowned as she followed her Nanou inside. To their left was the entrance to a large lounge with a dark parquet floor, a big pink rug, a sofa, and a hodgepodge of artsy chairs that had been angled towards sliding glass doors which showcased the spectacular view, as well as a stunning array of Lila's pottery sculptures. An open fire to the right of the room was laid with wood; to the right of that were a couple of bookshelves stuffed with crime and romance paperbacks, interspersed with various pottery and art tomes. A heavy sideboard along the back wall displayed various pieces of pottery – some created by Lila; some of her prize treasures which she'd collected over the years, including pieces from famous potters she admired. There were a few bits Ruby's father had made, including a delicate mug he'd created when he was just thirteen. Ross Penhaligon was a good potter and loved showing off his skills, but he was too lazy to put the time in to be truly great. It was the story of his life: her dad had always been more interested in his quest for fast, easy money than in building anything – and that had included a proper relationship with his daughter and wife. A lone red bowl sat in pride of place next to his mug, and Ruby recognised it as the last piece she'd ever crafted – she'd made it in the second year of a Ceramics degree, after which she'd vowed to give up pottery for good. She paused for a moment, tempted to wander into the room and run her fingers over one of the pieces, but then Lila headed towards the bedroom at the far end of the hallway where she'd be sleeping, and she followed.

Halfway up the hallway, Ruby paused beside the door that led to the study, where the musty smell grew stronger. She opened the door and peered inside, alarmed at the spray of dark mould that had spread across the corner of the far wall, curling the wallpaper and turning the edges of the carpet black. 'What happened here?' she asked, stepping further inside and wincing.

'We had a hole in the roof,' Lila explained, waving her hand. 'The water was streaming down the wall for months. I made a gorgeous piece of pottery to interpret the flow, it looks just like a waterfall,' she added wistfully before frowning. 'I didn't think the leak was a problem, but it got into the plaster and bricks.'

'You didn't mention it,' Ruby said sharply. She hadn't visited, but made a point of ringing her Nanou every week.

'I didn't want to bother you, love. Besides, it's nothing to worry about.' The older woman shrugged and swiped her hands on her smock, dismissing the subject. Lila had always been very bohemian in her outlook, with little patience for practicalities outside the pottery studio. 'Someone from the village has plugged it, but I need a proper roofer to finish the job and a builder to look at the damage to the bricks and plaster. Apparently, it needs doing before the winter or it'll get a lot worse.'

'Have you claimed on your insurance?' Ruby asked, guessing the answer would be no. But she could sort that while she was staying here.

'Someone in the village called them for me, but, apparently, I'd let the policy lapse. I've restarted it now, but they won't cover the damage and I've not got the cash to pay for it myself.' For the first time, Lila looked a little perturbed. 'Would you like some tea and cake?'

'What about your savings?' Ruby asked, confused. She did her Nanou's accounts and knew the pottery studio hadn't been thriving, but the older woman had invested over the years – she had plenty saved for rainy days and leaky roofs.

Lila pulled a face. 'I loaned some money to your dad...' She turned away when Ruby widened her eyes.

'How much?'

'All of it,' Lila muttered.

'Why would you do that?' Angry words shot from Ruby's mouth before she could stop them. 'You know you can't trust him!' Something clawed at her throat, the bitterness a tangible thing as fury heated her blood. As disgust for the man who'd as good as killed her mother took hold. For almost twenty years, Ross Penhaligon had dipped into their lives whenever the mood had taken him before disappearing again, sometimes for months. Her mother had spent her life working hard, keeping a roof over their heads, stressing over every bill, while her father had abandoned them to pursue a mythical fortune that had never materialised. In the end, it had all been too much, and the gentle woman who'd done nothing but love him had died of a fatal heart attack after suffering for years. The doctors had called it a tragic complication, but Ruby knew her mum had finally had enough. Knew her father was responsible.

Ross was nothing like her Nanou. The man had inherited all of Lila's free love and bohemian spirit but none of her loyalty or heart. Ruby had spent the years since her mother's death ensuring she'd never be like him. It's why she'd chosen to be an accountant – because it was a safe career you could rely on. And it was the reason she'd given up pottery for good. She knew it wasn't logical, but she didn't want to have anything in common with the man. She also knew it upset her grandmother, but even for her she couldn't relent. 'Where is he?' she snapped.

'Still in Spain, but I've not heard from him for a couple of weeks. Don't worry yourself,' Lila soothed, turning to pat Ruby's hand. 'I'll figure something out. It's been very quiet at the Pottery Project recently. I used to have a long waiting list, now I'm lucky to scrape five students a month. A rival potter set up just outside the village, and they're a lot better at advertising than me. Or maybe my lessons just aren't what they were.' She paused. 'I've been wondering whether it would be better if I gave the place up. I can't bear to see it so empty. Perhaps it needs some new blood...' She swirled back through the hallway towards the entrance of the kitchen as Ruby followed. 'I'll make us some tea and cake.'

'Nanou!' she pleaded. 'A hot drink and slice of cake won't fix this.' Her grandmother had always waxed lyrical about their properties – as if they had some kind of cosmic ability to fix all of life's woes. 'You can't give up the Pottery Project. It's your livelihood, your home. You love it here. I don't understand...' Ruby would never comprehend how Ross Penhaligon managed to wind women of all ages around his finger as if they were thin strips of cloth. Dishonest, deceitful, unreliable, unprincipled, fickle and as slippery as an eel. If she shared any genes with that man, she could only hope her body had somehow ejected them in an act of self-preservation.

'It's fine,' Lila said again, marching into the large yellow kitchen and putting the kettle on, pointing to a fresh, spongy lemon cake on a glass stand on the counter. 'Hungry? I made it especially. There's soup later, but you know my mantra – *always eat dessert first!*'

'Sure,' Ruby said, working hard to calm her voice. She wouldn't take her annoyance out on her grandmother anymore. But whatever happened while she was staying, she'd track down her errant father and make him pay back every penny – ensuring her Nanou could keep the Pottery Project she loved so much.

2

Gabe Roskilly swiped a hand through his sandy blond hair as he glared at the tyres of his shabby black Volvo 4x4, looking around the car park of his family's brewery to see if the culprit had decided to hang around for a laugh. He'd been working in the brewery's small office all day – battling with the email system, which had developed a sudden case of Gremlins and reformatted their latest newsletter, adding in a load of gobbledygook before spewing it to their whole database. Gabe still had no idea what had caused it, but he'd received a flurry of complaints before drowning his sorrows in a mug of black coffee when one hundred and two people had unsubscribed. Now, when his crap day was almost at an end, he'd come outside to discover all four tyres on his car were as flat as the breakfast pancakes he sometimes bought from his favourite cafe in Indigo Cove.

Gabe went to kick one of the tyres – because hell, why not – wincing when Sammie, his one-year-old pocket beagle, trotted over to join him and cocked his leg. Rex, Sammie's slightly plumper brother, scampered after, sniffing one of the other wheels before whining.

'Yep, we're not going anywhere.' Gabe sighed, putting the

large keg of Deep Water Ale he was carrying onto the gravel, waving Sammie away when he jogged over to sniff the rim. 'Leave it,' he ground out. 'We've talked about not peeing on the merchandise before, remember? Do you want to go to doggie detention school?' The dog sniffed again and went to relieve himself somewhere else, which Gabe considered a win in the circumstances. Sammie was the bad boy of the two dogs, the yin to Rex's angelic yang. How two brothers could be so completely different still baffled Gabe. They'd shared a womb, had been to the same training classes, ate the same food...

'What happened?' Jago Thomas, head brewer of the Roskilly Brewery, sauntered down the steps at the entrance to the large wooden building that fronted the business. He was still wearing his green steel-capped wellies and black overalls, and must have been boiling in the full heat of the sun. He scratched his dark hair, squinting at the car.

'Someone let all the tyres down,' Gabe complained, kneeling to take a proper look.

'To misquote Oscar Wilde – to lose one tyre may be regarded as a misfortune, to lose four...' Jago's brows knitted. 'On top of the scratch you found along your passenger door last week and all the things that have been going missing from the car park and inside the shop...' He looked pointedly at the entrance.

Gabe stroked the rough stubble on his chin. He'd forgotten to shave; there always seemed to be so much to do in the morning. His tummy grumbled – had he skipped lunch again too? 'It's not just here. There's stuff happening all over the village. It'll be teenagers playing silly pranks.' He'd been a teenager once, hadn't he? He might even have stolen a traffic cone in his day. He winced, trying to remember that far back. To the days when he'd had the time to lark around and laugh...

'Didn't you say someone keeps banging on the door of your

cottage at 3 a.m. and running away?' Jago asked, clearly unwilling to let the subject drop.

Gabe puffed out a breath. 'It's probably just the boyfriend of one of my brother's latest conquests making himself known. The dogs saw them off all four times.' And Sammie had proceeded to bark for an hour and half, which meant his neighbours were now out for his blood. 'I'll call the garage. Then I need to work out how to deliver this.' He frowned down at the large silver keg.

'Where is the elusive Aaron Roskilly?' Jago asked idly. 'Can't he do it?'

'He's out. He worked late, but didn't come home last night and hasn't made it in yet.' Gabe sighed. 'I've tried his mobile a few times.' He ground his teeth, fighting annoyance. Being angry with his brother had never done him any good in the past. Aaron would turn up at some point with a cheeky smile, a convoluted excuse about rescuing some damsel from a burning car before galloping her on a white steed to Scotland, and Gabe would forgive him before he'd even finished the story. Because protecting Aaron was ingrained in his psyche – he'd even finished with his last girlfriend when she'd tried to come between them. 'Blood is thicker than water,' his father had always said, and Gabe tried to live up to that. Although some days it was easier than others.

'When do you have to deliver the beer by?' Jago asked, pointing to the keg.

'Before six.' Gabe checked his watch. It was past five o'clock already. 'I've got an early date at the Pottery Project. Then there's a Neighbourhood Watch meeting this evening.'

Jago frowned, his eyes scanning Gabe's face, the look of sympathy familiar but unnecessary. 'Exactly the night every eligible, single man of thirty-one dreams of...'

Gabe snorted and shook his head. 'Says the boring old man with a wife and two and a half kids.' He patted his stomach, feeling an unexpected twinge of jealously. 'Tell me your exciting plans?' he teased.

'Putting up bunk beds and getting jumped on by a two-year-old.' Jago grinned before swiping a piece of paper from his back pocket. 'Almost forgot. The hydrometer has somehow recalibrated itself.'

'Sh—ugar. How bad is it?' Gabe asked, gritting his teeth.

Jago scratched his head. 'Our latest brew is more alcoholic than my grandmother's elderflower wine – and that has me under the table after half a glass. I don't understand, it's never happened before. We'll have to chuck the lot, I'm afraid.' He looked concerned. Despite being thirty-two, a mere year older than Gabe, Jago had the expressions of a man twice his age.

'That makes no sense,' Gabe murmured, wondering how much it would set them back. 'What about the special brew for the centenary?' The brewery would celebrate its anniversary in just three weeks, and they'd planned a host of celebrations – not least a special beer along with bespoke tankards he was making at the Pottery Project. They'd been advertising the event for months, and Gabe was hoping word of mouth would take the brewery up another notch. He had big plans for the future, but these setbacks were in danger of derailing them.

'Everything okay?' Jago took a step forward, looking serious.

'Nothing I can't handle.' Gabe grimaced. Faulty equipment and flat tyres were just more problems in a long line of them. Just once he wished things could go right. Almost nothing had for the last two years. Not since his dad had died suddenly and left him and Aaron in charge of the family business – depositing a host of responsibilities and expectations on their shoulders. None of which his brother seemed remotely interested in.

Jago scanned his face and Gabe knew he didn't believe him, but instead of challenging him, he let out a long sigh. 'I'll drop the keg off if you hold the fort here. How will you get to Lila's?'

Gabe shrugged. 'My bike. I'll walk home with the dogs after

we close. I'll just need to find it in the shed, pump up the tyres. Hopefully, they're not flat too.' He glanced at the car again, wondering, not for the first time, why so many things kept going wrong.

Gabe heaved in a breath as he got to the top of the steep hill and climbed off his bike before pushing it onto the gravel driveway and steering towards the huge barn where the Pottery Project was located. He spent a minute catching his breath, wondering when he'd got so out of shape. It was still hot and beads of sweat slid down his face and the centre of his back, making him wish he'd at least brought a change of clothes.

Lila's car was parked in the drive, so he put the bike on the ground beside it and stood for a moment enjoying a rare gust of wind before sauntering to the door. A Frank Sinatra song was blasting inside the studio, and he suspected Lila had dragged out her record player and vinyl again. She often did when he came for his pottery lessons. Because 'excellent music inspires creativity', she'd told him. Not only that; her treasured tomato plants, which she kept on the windowsills of the studio, apparently thrived on the loud tunes.

'Hello!' Gabe pushed the door slowly, not wanting to startle Lila, and wandered inside. A woman was standing with her back to him at one of the tables wearing earphones, hypnotically sliding her fingertips into a wedge of clay. She was smoothing the edges, stroking her thumbs skilfully from side to side, forming a delicate angular shape. Her movements were slow and graceful, and Gabe stopped where he was just inside the doorway, transfixed. He could see the edge of her face, the way her nose turned up at the end as if she'd been born judging the world and finding it lacking. She had long blonde hair with a soft wave that tumbled down her back, ending in a series of gossamer ringlets. For some reason she made Gabe think of those ancient tales of mermaids who convinced sailors to crash onto rocks. She couldn't have been more than five foot three and was an attractive mixture of curvy and lean. He swallowed a wave of lust, wondering what had got into him, and took a step forward – just as Lila marched out of the storage area to the right of the room holding a wedge of clay and the tankard he'd been working on last night. She beamed when she spotted him and placed everything carefully on the table in front of the woman, then turned the music down.

'Gabe, you're here!' Lila walked up to give him a big hug, jabbing all kinds of pottery tools which were sticking out of her hair into his chest, barely missing his right eye.

He cleared his throat, glancing at the woman, who'd pulled out the earphones and squashed the clay she'd been working on into a misshapen ball before stepping away from the counter. Her expression was tinged with annoyance, but he had no idea if it was directed at him or herself. 'I'm sorry I'm late, car trouble. I know you'll want to eat before the meeting later.'

'That won't take long, we've already had dessert.' Lila beamed, moving backwards so Gabe could see the woman properly. 'This is my granddaughter, Ruby Penhaligon. She told me she doesn't think you've met. This is Gabe Roskilly.'

Gabe ignored the sudden tightness in his chest as the woman stepped forward and opened her wide grey eyes. She was prettier than he'd been expecting, and it took him a full half minute to respond. When he did, he had to clear his throat twice before speaking. 'Um. I don't think so. I'd probably have remembered.' He wiped his suddenly sweaty palm on his T-shirt before holding it out. 'You visiting?' Odd he'd not seen her here before.

She nodded and took his hand, her grip firm. Desire swept through him, and he wondered if Ruby had felt it too because she quickly untangled their fingers.

'Ruby's come to help while Ms Richards— Morweena,' Lila

added, when Gabe started to shake his head, 'is on holiday. You know she won that trip to Hawaii?'

'Yep, of course,' Gabe said, wondering why his throat still felt like it was closing up. Ruby was staring at him. He was used to that. He wasn't vain, but he knew women liked the look of him, had been on the receiving end of the kind of attention a six-foot-two frame and a moderately attractive face invited. His eyes dropped to her mouth as she gave him a baffled smile before jerking them up again, trying to regain control. What was happening here – was this some kind of mermaid mind-control?

'You'll be seeing a lot of each other, I expect.' Lila beamed. 'Ruby will be helping with the classes, making tea, coffee, refreshments. Gabe likes his drinks black and he insists on only eating chocolate cake. I've been trying to tempt him with something more adventurous. Perhaps you'll have more luck?' she added with a wicked grin.

'My mum used to make chocolate cake,' Gabe said huskily. 'It's nice to meet you, Ruby. Are you a potter too?' He tried to gather himself, nodding at the clay as Ruby shook her head.

'I'm an accountant.' Her voice was silky and did odd things to his insides.

For a moment, Gabe felt lightheaded. Women never had this effect on him usually. Then again, how long had it been since he'd been on so much as a date? Not since he'd finished with his girlfriend Camilla Munroe eighteen months earlier, after she'd accused Aaron of making a pass at her... Ruby ran a hand through her hair and his libido did a happy dance. He really had to get out more, to take a break from the almost endless stream of responsibilities and chores.

'You always know where you are with numbers. They don't let you down,' Ruby continued, her lips tightening. The words were heaped with a meaning Gabe didn't understand, but he nodded because he guessed she'd expect it – and he was hoping it might make her smile. 'Would you like anything before you start work?' Her eyes flicked back to her grandmother, leaving him feeling strangely bereft.

'Just some cold water, please.' *Maybe an icy shower to go with it.* Gabe cleared his throat again because it was parched. As Lila went to pick up the equipment he'd need, Ruby followed her.

Gabe tried not to watch but found himself mesmerised by each tiny movement, the way the soft material of Ruby's trousers moulded itself to her legs, how her hips swayed from side to side. She disappeared into the small kitchen, breaking the spell – leaving him wondering when he'd begun to lose his grip on his sanity, and exactly why Ruby had affected him so much.

3

Ruby's mobile chirped in her handbag as Lila slid Beatrix into a parking spot a few hundred metres down from The Beach Cafe. The sun was still high, even though it was now eight o'clock, but the air had chilled so Ruby grabbed a white cardigan, along with her handbag, as she got out. She checked her phone as her Nanou secured the car. Her best friend Anna had sent a photo of her daughter Maisy wearing a pink paper crown. The baby was lying on her front on a carpet, laughing as she tried to tug off the hat.

Exactly six months old today, Auntie Ruby!! Anna had typed, signing off the message with a couple of smiley face emojis and a few kisses.

I can't believe how quickly that's gone! Ruby typed quickly, frowning as she stared at Maisy's face. All that innocence – the irresistible combination of chubby fists and angelic snubbed nose. How could anyone walk away from that? It had been a mystery to her ever since she'd been old enough to learn her own father had left her mother for the first time a mere five weeks after she was born. Ruby swallowed a wave of irritation, wishing she could just wipe the man from her history. *After* she'd tracked him down and made him return her Nanou's life savings, of course. She'd emailed him earlier to demand he return all the money and included the word URGENT in the heading along with four exclamation marks. She knew she'd be checking her email hourly until she heard back.

'Come on!' her grandmother said, linking their arms as she marched them both to the other side of the road, so they could walk along the pavement that lined the harbour. Boats were bobbing on the fluffy waves as day sailors secured their vessels, and a few stragglers on the beach packed up buckets, spades and towels. 'That's our new cafe,' Lila explained, pointing a little further down the street as they passed The Pasty Place, which Ruby knew served the best Cornish pasties in the area, and a quaint corner shop which was obviously new because she didn't recognise it. The Beach Cafe was a pretty white-fronted building with metal tables and chairs set out on a small square patio which offered beautiful views of the sea, harbour and cliffs. The chairs had been piled neatly on top of one another and put to one side, signalling the cafe was closed. As they drew closer, Ruby saw movement through the striking glass window. Lila led her to the left of it, through the front door which let out a pretty tinkling sound as it opened. The inside of the cafe had been painted a bright sunshine yellow, and there were a number of tables and chairs here too. These were laid with chequered blue-and-white tablecloths, and a few had been pushed together to create a long seating area.

'Hello!' A woman appeared from behind the counter and gave Lila a hug. She had long black hair, which she'd tied into a bun, and her mouth was painted deep red, giving her features a hint of Snow White. She wore a long yellow floaty skirt and a dark blue shirt with a frilly white apron that finished the effect.

'Evening!' Lila declared, pulling back to tug Ruby forward. 'This is Ella Santo. She's run this gorgeous cafe for the last eleven months. This is my granddaughter.'

'I know all about you.' Ella welcomed Ruby with a soft Cornish lilt, enveloping her in a hug that smelled of freshly baked scones. 'I feel like we're friends already, Lila talks about you so much. I'm new to the area. I used to run a teashop in Newquay, until my no-good husband buggered off with the takings and my former best friend.'

'Oh, I'm so sorry,' Ruby said.

Ella shook her head. 'Good riddance, I say. I'm happier here in my cafe alone.' She swept a hand around the room.

'It's lovely to meet you,' Ruby said, as Ella pointed her in the direction of the long table which was piled with plates of cakes, scones, and steaming pots of coffee and tea. Lila had made Ruby eat a slice of lemon cake earlier, followed by soup with chunky fresh bread. Ruby had no idea how she'd find room for anything else, but the amazing fragrances filling the air made her determined to try. The door tinkled again, and when Ruby glanced up, the man called Gabe was standing at the entrance. Her stomach felt odd, like someone had dropped a handful of coins into the bottom of it. He looked better than when she'd met him in the Pottery Project earlier; he'd showered and run a brush through his sandy hair, although it was tussled again. He wore faded denim jeans and a grey T-shirt that had clearly seen better days, but on him it still looked like something out of a men's magazine. She found herself smiling involuntarily when his lips curved, wondering why her defences seemed to dissolve around him. She didn't normally trust good-looking men, a legacy from her father and all the hard life lessons he'd taught her.

Two small brown-and-white dogs were sitting at Gabe's feet, both on leads. One sniffed the ground, probably looking for stray morsels, coming up empty because the black-and-white tiled floor was sparkly clean. The other sat on its haunches with his dark nose sniffing the air. Gabe's green eyes fixed on Ruby, and she had to fight the unexpected rush of heat. It had been years since she'd been so attracted to a man – she had never felt her pulse race faster than a moderate sprint. Was this what they called chemistry? If it was, she didn't trust it. 'Handsome!' Ella welcomed Gabe with a hug and pointed him in the direction of the table. He raised an eyebrow at Ruby and pulled up the chair beside her, winding the dogs' leads around one of the legs.

'Nice to see you again.' His voice was naturally husky – Ruby had noticed that earlier and chosen to ignore the way it burrowed under her skin, setting goosebumps skidding across the surface. She dragged her gaze away and looked down, catching one of the dogs trying to chew on Gabe's chair leg. He must have noticed too because he let out an embarrassed cough. 'Stop, Sammie.' He leaned down and tugged the dog away, scratching his head. 'The reprobate is Sammie and this is the angelic Rex.' He pointed to the smaller dog, who'd already settled with his eyes half-shut. 'My brother Aaron was supposed to watch them, but didn't make it home.' Gabe frowned as the door opened and a weathered well-built man stumbled inside and waved hello.

'Welcome!' Lila said before turning to Ruby. 'This is Clemo Eddy, he runs The Pasty Place a few shops down.'

Clemo offered Ruby a large hand before pulling up the chair opposite. Ten minutes later, they all had a drink and something sweet set in front of them. Lila stood and clapped her hands, encouraging the table to hush. 'Welcome, everyone, to our biweekly Neighbourhood Watch committee, or what we prefer to call The Marples – in honour of Agatha Christie's Miss Jane Marple. We are a bijou group, but we have big plans.' Her eyes skirted the table, and she flashed a grin in Ruby's direction. 'Ella, are you okay to take the minutes?' The younger woman nodded, sipping from her mug of tea as she opened the black notebook on the table beside her. 'First on the agenda are the recent incidents of vandalism.'

Gabe nodded as one of the dogs barked. 'Someone let my

tyres down outside the brewery today. I didn't have time to add that to the agenda, but I reported it to the police.'

'Actually, they hadn't just been let down. They were slashed with something sharp.' Clemo bit into a slice of lemon cake and hummed with pleasure. 'I saw Jago before I came here, and he told me the garage called the brewery and told him they'd have to replace them all, but they'd drop the car back in the morning. I expect he didn't want to bother you with the bad news tonight.' He gave Gabe a sympathetic grimace.

'Slashed? Why would anyone...' Gabe looked stricken and Ruby felt sorry for him, wanted to reach out and place a hand over his, found herself almost doing it before she caught herself. But Gabe must have seen her intention because he smiled. A broad, wide grin that lit his face, hitting her somewhere mid-chest. 'Thanks,' he said quietly, looking genuinely touched.

'I'm sorry about the car,' she murmured, confused by her reaction. Perhaps it was all the sea air interfering with her common sense?

'I wouldn't mind so much, but the tyres were probably the best part of the Volvo. Sammie's been chewing his way through most of the interior.' Gabe looked down at the dog with a baffled expression filled with love. This obviously wasn't a man who walked away from his responsibilities, no matter how badly behaved it was. Ruby respected that, reluctantly felt herself softening towards him.

There was another tinkle at the door and everyone turned as a dark-haired man with an angular jaw and brown eyes entered the cafe. He wore an immaculate black suit with a starched white shirt and had the kind of bone-deep air of sophistication that came from genetics rather than practice. '*Pardon* for the delay,' he said in a soft French accent, searching out the top of the table where Ella was now glaring at him.

She jabbed a finger towards the empty seat at the other end

– as far from her as he could get. 'Mr Laurent, I think we'd all be shocked if you made it on time,' she said dryly.

'Call me Claude, remember?' The man deliberately ambled across the room and pulled up the chair before helping himself to a slice of chocolate cake, polishing a fork slowly with his napkin before scooping up a minuscule sliver. Ella watched him intently, her expression defensive.

'We were talking about the issues we've been encountering in the village,' Lila jumped in before the Frenchman could comment on the food.

Claude's lips thinned and he put his fork down. 'I have some new *vandalisme* to report. Some *imbecile* stole two of the chairs outside my restaurant last Thursday evening. A waiter found one at the far end of the beach with one of its legs ripped off. The other is still missing.'

'You need help fixing the broken one?' Gabe offered, but Claude shook his head.

'*Non merci*, it is not repairable.'

Ella picked up one of the forks from the table and began to fiddle with it. 'I lost some chairs too – they haven't turned up. Do you think it might be the same people?' She addressed her question to the table and didn't look at the chef.

'Chances are it is.' Clemo scratched his beard. 'Nothing's happened at my shop, but there's been a lot of unusual activity reported around the village over the last few weeks.' He nodded at Ella, who flicked to another page of her pad.

'I've been keeping a record. Not because I'm nosy.' She shrugged, looking embarrassed. 'People talk when they come in, so it made sense. We need to find out who's doing this before the season really gets going – we don't want to scare off any tourists.' She scanned the page. 'Someone tried to break into one of the beach huts a few evenings ago, but a lifeguard was walking along the beach and frightened them off. Also, somebody had a bonfire on the beach at the far end of the harbour on the same night and left a lot of litter scattered around.' She pressed a fingertip on the page, continuing to read. 'There are a few other things: bins going missing; fishing nets being tampered with; posters getting torn down – mostly small acts of vandalism, but they add up.'

'Especially when they're so rare in Indigo Cove.' Lila looked unhappy. 'I've lived here for the last forty-five years, and I've never known of anything like it.'

'Someone keyed my car last week.' Gabe's shoulders hunched. 'It's pretty beaten up already, so I wasn't going to bother mentioning it, but I noticed the scratch because it was deep and went across the whole passenger side.'

'Jago told me a couple of things have gone missing from the brewery shop too,' Clemo added. 'And you've been having visitors to your house in the middle of the night?' He looked concerned. 'A lot of things seem to be happening specifically to you.'

'A coincidence, it's just kids...' Gabe shrugged. 'The local youth club closed a few weeks ago because the couple who ran it moved away. I'm guessing that's left a lot of teenagers with time on their hands. Most of what they're up to is harmless fun.'

'Slashed tyres aren't harmless. Sure this has got nothing to do with Aaron?' Clemo's eyebrows met.

'Definitely not. He's still doing that design course online, so he's been really busy the last few months. He's made some new friends and...' Gabe looked unhappy. 'I don't know much about it all.' He picked up the mug of coffee he'd been nursing and sipped, effectively closing down the conversation. Ruby didn't miss Clemo's sigh. There was a story there; she'd have to ask her Nanou about it later.

'All the things happening around the village might not be a coincidence. It could be people targeting Indigo Cove for some reason,' Ella said.

'You've been watching too many crime series on Netflix.'

Clemo snorted. 'I think Gabe might be right, it's probably kids getting bored, teenage holidaymakers. If we can catch them in the act, we'll be able to put a stop to it.'

'How?' Ella asked.

'I was going to suggest we team up and do daytime and evening patrols. We might find some clues or just act as a deterrent,' Clemo suggested, and everyone around the table nodded.

'Good idea,' Lila said. 'Clemo, why don't you and I take some loops around the beach tomorrow? Claude, I'm guessing you won't have time to help patrol, what with the restaurant?'

He shrugged. 'I can take a stroll early evening before it gets busy.' His eyes shot to Ella, and he gave her a slow smile. 'Maybe Ms Santo would like to join me – we could try to find those missing chairs. I'll bring dessert...'

If looks could kill, Claude would be dead, Ruby guessed as Ella's face darkened. 'I'm sure your staff would appreciate a break from you,' she ground out. 'Five o'clock?' The chef nodded, his eyes sharp even after Ella deliberately looked away.

'Perhaps Clemo and I should join you, make sure no one gets hurt,' Lila joked, turning her attention to Gabe. 'Could you team up with Ruby please, love? That way you could show her around the village after one of your pottery lessons, and I'll have time to put your work in the kiln. It'll give you a chance to walk the dogs too?' She winked.

'I'm not—' Ruby was about to protest, but Gabe interrupted.

'It would be my pleasure – apparently, I'll get my car back tomorrow, so we could go to one of the beaches close to where I live. Someone in the brewery mentioned seeing a crowd of teenagers at Smuggler's Rest. Tuesday?' His lips curved as he turned to her.

Ruby closed her mouth. She didn't usually spend time with strange men, but it would be churlish to refuse. 'Sure,' she murmured. Spending time with Gabe would be fine – she knew herself well enough to know he wouldn't get past her defences. No one had before now...

It was late. Ruby pulled her pyjamas on and looked around the bedroom for something to do. Her laptop sat unopened on a grey chest of drawers positioned next to a matching wardrobe. She'd unpacked hours before and should be exhausted, but being in Indigo Cove always brought back uncomfortable feelings about her parents. Add that to her strange attraction to Gabe Roskilly and she was finding it difficult to settle – perhaps she needed to look at some spreadsheets; it was unlikely she'd sleep for hours yet. Maybe she'd take a midnight stroll around her Nanou's garden later?

Her eyes traced the bedroom. On the opposite side of the room to the furniture was a huge picture window which offered striking views of the cliffs and horizon. The moon was high and threw light across the lush lawn. She slumped onto the queen-sized bed and stared at the series of bright yellow daisies that had been embroidered into the duvet cover before her eyes slid to her small bedside table. The lamp was on, illuminating a photo of her and her mother, all dressed up for her tenth birthday, that had been taken years before. Ruby remembered the day as if it were yesterday. Her father had been in Spain pursuing another of his 'life-changing deals' and had promised to make it back for her party. She shut her eyes, slipping into the memory...

There were children everywhere, pots and bowls filled with half-eaten popcorn, crisps and sandwiches littering the table. A birthday cake in the shape of a pottery wheel, which Ruby's mum had spent hours making, was topped with pink candles. Ruby

had been up since 6 a.m., waiting by the door for her father to arrive from Spain. He'd been gone for months, but had called and promised not to be late, so she'd told her friends he was coming. She checked her new watch again and patted it to make sure it was definitely working. Her father wasn't just late – the party was almost over and some of the girls had started asking if her dad really existed. She squeezed back tears and placed a wide smile on her face, suppressing the hurt that was chewing its way through her insides. Her mother had grown paler as the day had progressed but was still grinning, so Ruby knew she had to be brave too.

'He'll be here soon!' her mum called out. 'He must have been held up at the airport. How about we put on some music while we're waiting?' Ruby nodded and encouraged her friends to dance, wriggling her hips, trying to giggle and laugh but almost crumbling from the effort. Then the phone started ringing. Her mother ran to pick it up and her face crumpled, but she nodded and faked a smile. Ruby stopped dancing and walked slowly across the sitting room, her heart sinking because she knew that smile meant one thing – her father wasn't coming, after all.

Then she watched her mother's face suddenly grow even paler, saw her place a hand on her chest before sliding slowly to the floor. One of the girls' mothers cried out and tried to assist her. Ruby heard shocked whispers from her friends as she ran up to grab her mum's arm.

She couldn't remember much more. Flashing lights from the ambulance, sleeping overnight at Anna's house, tossing and turning with worry and fear. Then the diagnosis – a minor heart attack. But Ruby had known better. Known her father was responsible. It had been the first nail in the coffin of their relationship, although it had taken many more years until she'd decided to exclude him from her life for good.

Swallowing a wave of emotion, Ruby shoved the photo frame onto its front and reached out to grab her mobile as it began to buzz.

'Anna?' she asked, grabbing her phone from where she'd plugged it in to charge. 'Everything okay?'

Her friend didn't speak for a beat, and when she did, her voice was filled with tears. 'No,' she wailed. 'I've just finished with Simon. It's over, Ruby. Really over this time. I've booked Maisy and me into a hotel. She's asleep, but it took her ages to settle. I don't know what I'm going to do now.' She broke off, weeping noisily.

'Oh Anna, I'm so sorry, that's awful.' Ruby sprang to her feet, her heart aching with concern. 'But why?' The relationship wasn't perfect, but this news was out of the blue. Ruby knew how much Anna cared for Simon, and could only guess how much this would hurt.

'We had a huge row – about Maisy.' Anna blew her nose. 'It's been coming for months. It came to a head today, I don't know why. Maybe because she's just turned six months.'

'What did you fight about?' Ruby asked, her pulse racing. 'Can't you both fix it?' Simon loved his daughter and he'd been by Anna's side from the moment she'd announced her pregnancy, which counted for a lot in her book.

'He's struggled with her not being his.' Anna sobbed noisily. 'He's been going on and on about adopting her, and when I finally said yes today, he said he'd changed his mind! He's worried the real father will come back on the scene. I couldn't believe it. I lost my temper and told him it was over.' She broke off, crying again before sniffing. 'I spent too many years watching your dad mess you and your mum about. I'm not going to have the same thing happen to my daughter.'

'Sorry?' Ruby squeaked, her heart hammering. She stopped

pacing, digesting the news. 'What did you say?' she asked again. 'Maisy isn't Simon's?' If she had a bottle of whisky nearby, she'd swallow a mouthful to get over the shock. 'What?' she repeated, reeling. 'If Simon's not her dad, who is? And why didn't you tell me this before? You know I would have helped with anything you needed.' Ruby turned to look back at the picture which was face down on her bedside table and shook her head. Had Maisy been abandoned by her father too?

'Oh God, I'm sorry, Ruby. I know I should have told you before. But I knew you'd insist on going after him and – that's complicated.' Anna paused, breathing deeply. 'Besides, Simon and I got back together, and he was happy to say Maisy was his. It was the perfect solution – it didn't make sense to tell anyone, even you. *Was* the perfect solution,' she reiterated with a hiccup. 'It's a good job Maisy is still so young – there's little chance she'll remember what's going on... although I've no idea what I'm going to do now. It's such a mess.'

'Are you okay? Is there anything I can do?' Ruby begged.

'There's nothing.' Anna gulped. 'I love you for asking, but this is something only I can sort out.'

'Oh Anna, whoever her dad is needs to step up and get involved,' Ruby soothed as anger started to build inside her. 'You know how I feel about absent fathers...'

'Oh I know, it's one of the other reasons why I didn't tell you. I knew you'd get upset and I didn't want to dredge up a lot of stuff for you. I shouldn't be telling you now, I'm sorry,' Anna murmured as the baby began to howl. 'I've got to go. Maisy needs me, and I have to clear my head, work out what I'm going to do with my life now.' She sniffed.

'But you need somewhere to live, you work for Simon's company...' Ruby shook her head as concern flooded her. 'Why don't you hop on a train and come here? I can help you to make a plan.'

'No – thank you, but I can't. If I come to Indigo Cove, it'll all still be here when I get back. I have to sort this out, somehow.' Anna blew her nose again as Maisy howled. 'I need to see to the baby and I'm exhausted. I just... I'm sorry. I had to talk to someone.'

'I'll call tomorrow,' Ruby promised, but her friend had already hung up. She frowned, glancing out of the window, and shook her head as the full implications of what Anna had told her took hold. What was Anna going to do? How could she help? All those months her friend had shouldered the weight of responsibility for her child while the errant father had got off scot-free. She could hardly believe it. She wished she could go back in time and offer her support. At least she could help now, maybe find the missing father?

But who was he? She searched her mind. There had been no serious boyfriends in between Anna's breaks with Simon. Ruby hadn't been aware her friend had even dated. She glanced at the photo frame again as anger knotted her chest. Whoever this man was, she had to find him. She'd get to the bottom of who it was eventually – and *he* wouldn't be allowed to desert Anna and his child. She'd track him down and make him take notice. Force him to be the father she'd never had.

4

'I still don't understand why we're selling.' Aaron turned to Gabe and shoved his hands into the pockets of his dark jeans, as he paced in front of the metal gate which marked the entrance to the large open field situated next door to the Roskilly Brewery. 'I don't think Dad would have approved.' He pursed his lips as he leaned on the top of the gate and gazed at the five acres of land that had belonged to the Roskilly family for over three generations. Sammie was out there somewhere, bombing up and down, dodging between the rows of poppies and wildflowers, probably terrorising wild mice – while Rex sat at the edge of the wilderness, calmly considering butterflies.

'Because we want to expand the brewery, remember?' Gabe said, fighting a pang of guilt. This was necessary, he knew that. But he still felt like he was somehow letting his family down. Perhaps even now his ancestors were glaring at him from a cloud, planning to hurl yet more bad luck in his direction? 'We can't afford to take out a loan to build another warehouse on the current lot, and this will free up enough cash for additional storage, more staff, maybe even a new truck.' God knows, they needed it – not to mention an upgrade of equipment which had started failing with a regularity that had surprised him. Hadn't it all been so much easier when his father was alive? He squeezed his eyes shut for a moment, wishing again that he still was. That he didn't feel so alone. 'I don't want to let go of this place either, but it's just sitting here. We don't have the resources or money to build on it ourselves... The bank doesn't want to lend us any more than we already owe, and the location means it's valuable. Cornwall land and property is hot at the moment; we need to cash in.' In the words of the estate agent Gabe had spoken to, they were sitting on a veritable goldmine – but the clock was ticking. In six months the whole market might have changed again. 'Once we list, we should have buyers queuing up... then we'll be able to take the brewery to the next level.'

'You could be crowned the world's most grown-up grown-up,' Aaron groaned, pressing his lips into what his father used to refer to as his 'man-pout'. 'You've got the word boring stamped into your bones. When was the last time you let your hair down, stopped trying to prop up the whole world?'

Gabe opened his mouth and closed it – he honestly had no idea, and wasn't that a kick in the gut? Not since he'd been dating Camilla – and when that had gone belly up, he'd been hurt and had found it easier to just focus on work.

'Where's the romance in your soul? We used to camp in that field, swim in the lake at the far end.' Aaron swiped a hand through his hair, ruffling it before turning back to lean on the gate to watch the dogs. His brother had always been the sensitive one, perhaps because he'd been so sick in his teens. Acute leukaemia – but happily he'd been one of the lucky ones and had been in remission since the age of sixteen. But Aaron had missed out on so much in the months before his diagnosis and treatment – school, friends, all the things Gabe had been able to take for granted. It's why he understood this was difficult. They'd both regularly come here with their dad, swum or kicked a ball about at the edge of the grass when Aaron had been up to it. It was the embodiment of all those memories. Gabe closed his eyes.

~

It was hot. Another beautiful day in a long summer filled with them. Gabe ran through the long grass after the ball his father had just kicked as Aaron sat in the shade of a huge Cornish oak. 'Come on!' Gabe shouted, booting the ball in his brother's direction, feeling frustrated when Aaron barely looked up. He ran and slumped beside him, catching his breath. 'You told me you were bored,' he whined. 'You told Dad you wanted to come...'

'I'm tired,' Aaron snapped, digging one of his new white trainers into the earth, covering it with dust. Gabe stared into his face. Aaron had pretended to be asleep when he'd crept into his room last night and tried to talk. They'd always shared secrets late in the evenings, caught up on each other's lives – but since his diagnosis, Aaron had shut him out. 'Dad likes you better now,' his brother said grumpily. 'Everybody does.'

'That's not true!' Gabe said, easing closer. He didn't miss Aaron's recoil but didn't know how to deal with the cavern that had opened up between them – which seemed to widen with every passing day.

'Susan Melrose fancies you and she used to like me,' Aaron moaned. 'You get to go on sleepovers – you're not missing school...'

'It's not my fault you're sick,' Gabe said softly.

'Or mine!' Aaron barked, looking up, his eyes bright with frustration. 'But why did it happen to me?' He shook his head when Gabe shrugged, and his brother's lips thinned. 'You don't get it, and you never will.'

The words hurt and Gabe searched for something to say.

'Let your brother rest, give him some space.' His father joined

them then, picked up the ball and kicked it back into the undergrowth. As Gabe rose and went after it, his dad patted him gently on the shoulder. 'He needs time, it's a lot to go through. We need to be patient, make sure he's happy and safe. He'll play with you later.'

'I'd rather play with my friends,' Gabe grumbled.

'Remember, blood is thicker than water,' his dad scolded. 'You need to take care of Aaron. He's not as strong as you and this hasn't been easy for him.'

It hadn't been easy for any of them. Gabe hung his head in shame because he knew the thought was selfish. He gritted his teeth, admonishing himself as he ran into the long grass. Then he heard the sound of feet behind him, and when he turned, Aaron was following, slower than before, but he was on his feet. Gabe made his steps sluggish, held back, so his brother could overtake. When Aaron got to the ball first and cheered, he knew he'd done the right thing, decided in that moment how things would be from now on. He'd be there for his brother whatever life threw at them, offer whatever he needed, so he could somehow make up for everything he was going through now.

Gabe let out a long sigh. So much guilt – would he ever be able to let it go? He patted Aaron's shoulder before leaning beside him on the gate, ignoring the heat from the sun which was burning a hole in the back of his neck. Was his great-grandmother's spirit spying on him now, giving him her legendary evil eye for even considering selling? 'I'm sorry we need to do this. I feel the same way. But we promised Dad we'd keep the brewery running – build on it and expand.' He swallowed. 'Do all the things he'd planned when he was still here...'

'But he's not here now.' Aaron turned to face him. 'Plus, it was his dream and *you* promised. I wasn't even there, remember. I was on a flight from Ibiza, trying to make it home in time.' His eyes flickered with something Gabe couldn't read. He shoved his hands into his pockets and his expression grew serious. 'Sometimes, I wonder if it would just be easier if we sold the whole thing. Made a new start.' He looked over Gabe's shoulder, and his eyes rested on the roof of the brewery, which was located a few metres to their right. 'If we're going to start breaking the property up, selling things off, maybe we should go the whole hog. It could be more valuable as a whole?' Aaron's face grew animated. It had been a long time since Gabe had seen his brother get excited about anything, and he wasn't sure whether to feel pleased or annoyed. 'Then we could relocate to somewhere cheaper, and you could start a new brewery of your own?'

'You didn't want to sell the field a minute ago,' Gabe said, measuring his tone. 'Now you're talking about giving up our legacy?' He could hardly believe Aaron had uttered the words. His gut felt sore, like someone had punched him. He'd slaved over this business, put so much into building it up, and their father had too.

His brother's face fell. 'Of course I don't mean it. I'm just considering all the options, thinking through the possibilities. You've put so much into this place, given up so much,' he echoed Gabe's thoughts. 'Perhaps it's just not worth it.'

'I'd do it again,' Gabe said gently. 'I agree – all the responsibility can get too much.' He ran a hand across his forehead, pressing into the skin at his temples where a headache was forming. It had been a long day already, and it was only twenty past nine. 'But I don't mind, not really,' he said, wondering if that was a lie. 'This brewery's our future. It goes back three generations. The Roskilly family are in the soil and air.' He reached up and slowly closed his fist, imagining grabbing all that history – wondering whether the weight of it might crush him one day. 'We'll give this to our kids, pass it to the next generation – just like Dad did for us.'

'For you,' Aaron said softly, the smile he delivered not quite reaching his eyes.

'For both of us,' Gabe said firmly. 'You're as much a part of this as me. You want to be, don't you?' Something stuck in his throat when it took his brother a full half minute to respond.

'Of course!' he said eventually, punctuating the sentiment with a nod.

Gabe checked his watch and turned to glance at the wide dusty track that led to the main road.

'Something wrong?' Aaron asked, straightening up from the gate.

'The estate agent was supposed to meet us here ten minutes ago,' Gabe murmured before grimacing. 'Someone booked a brewery tour this morning, and I've only got twenty minutes before I have to get back. No one else is free to run the tour. Unless you want to do it?'

'You're so much better with the customers.' Aaron shook his head as Gabe's phone buzzed in his pocket, and he pulled it out and quickly read the message.

'Mr Jones is going to be late – fifteen minutes.' He hissed. 'Traffic. That's just perfect.' He tapped the screen, started to reply. 'I'll see if he can come tomorrow.'

'Don't.' Aaron brushed Gabe's hand away from the phone. 'I can handle the meeting if you want to go to the brewery now? I owe you for disappearing yesterday.' He waggled his eyebrows. 'But beautiful women don't come along every day. I'm guessing it's just a case of showing this bloke the field?' Gabe nodded. 'I think I can manage that. I'll get the details and feed everything back to you. It's about time I did more around here – took some of the burden from your shoulders.' The words were a surprise. Since their dad had died, Aaron had rarely offered to help with the brewery more than necessary and Gabe had been waiting for a hint that he was finally taking a proper interest. 'If this Mr Jones asks anything I can't answer, I'll call,' Aaron added.

'You sure?' Gabe asked. 'Why the change of heart?'

Aaron shrugged. 'Let's just say you've convinced me.' He glanced back at the field as Sammie came flying out of the long grass, chasing a butterfly which soared high above his head. 'Leave the dogs. I'll bring them to the brewery after the meeting.'

'You'll watch them this time?' Gabe asked lightly. 'Because you know Sammie... He'll get himself into mischief if you take your eye off him for a second.' He watched the butterfly make a sudden U-turn towards the undergrowth, saw the dog thunder after it.

'Trust me,' Aaron said quietly, and Gabe nodded and turned to head back to the brewery, wondering why he had a sudden feeling of foreboding.

5

Ruby helped Lila open the doors to the Pottery Project on Monday morning. She hadn't slept well, and had tossed and turned as she'd stressed about her wayward dad, who hadn't responded to her email. Her worries had been compounded by Anna's news about her break-up with Simon and Maisy's biological father – and she was concerned about what her friend was going to do. She'd called Anna first thing, but she'd been in the middle of feeding Maisy and had promised to call later. The sun was out, and the skylights in the ceiling of the large barn-style room where the Pottery Project's studio was located channelled beams of light into the centre of the space, cleverly highlighting the main worktable where Lila would be teaching. Ruby was suddenly overwhelmed by a wave of excitement, and she forced the feelings down. She'd not worked on a pottery wheel since just after her mother had died, and had no intention of sinking her fingers into any clay while she was here. Yesterday had been an anomaly – she'd seen the block sitting on the counter and hadn't been able to stop herself. Once she'd started to craft, the call of the clay had overwhelmed her, the need to mould something out of it, to find the shapes hidden inside – until the spell had been broken when Gabe had arrived. She had no intention of repeating the mistake.

When Ruby had been eighteen, she'd applied to study ceramics at university and had been accepted. She'd loved her time at the wheel, the freedom of discovering shapes and forms, letting herself go. But soon after her mother died, her father had missed her second-year show at university, letting her down for the final time. It had been a catalyst, the moment when she'd finally admitted that having a relationship with him was damaging. So she'd closed herself off to everyone but Anna and her Nanou, choosing to keep her life simple and connection free. She'd switched her degree to accountancy – she needed security and something she could trust. She wanted to break all connections with her father and their mutual love of pottery was one. So what if the tightness across her chest – the need to break free – sometimes overwhelmed her? She was happy with her decision. She was safe.

'I've made tea and coffee and put it into flasks to keep warm. There are jugs of fresh milk and some mugs I hand-potted years ago. The croissants are already out for when everyone arrives at nine thirty.' Lila swept her silver-grey hair up into its trademark bun and poked a spoon-shaped tool into it, then grabbed a clean apron from a set of hooks on the canary-yellow wall closest to the kitchen. 'Ella's going to drop a batch of her scones in later, so we can offer mid-morning cream teas. As I mentioned, I've got four clients booked in this week.'

'Is that enough to break even?' Ruby asked, doing some quick mental sums.

'Not really.' Lila picked up another modelling tool and shoved it into her hair. 'But I tried advertising. Apparently, I need a "hook" – an old woman teaching pottery isn't enough these days. How are you today, my lovelies?' Lila said, kissing each of the tomato plants situated on the studio windowsill before turning to offer Ruby a beaming smile.

'I'm sure we can think of a way to bring in more clients,' Ruby said seriously, but her Nanou held up a hand.

'Don't bother yourself, love. This is my problem and it'll sort itself out.' Lila pointed to a row of tables to their right. 'Can you put some balls of clay out before our students arrive? About five hundred grams in weight and I think they'll need ten of them each. Use the scales on the counter.' She nodded when Ruby hefted a large bag of wet clay out of the storeroom and dumped it on the counter before slicing off chunks and weighing them. She followed up by wrapping cling film over each of the portions to stop them from drying out. 'I've laid out a selection of tools and towels and tested the wheels. I'm going to start everyone off making simple bowls, so I can get a feel for ability levels. I sent a questionnaire of course, but my clients sometimes misjudge or misrepresent their skills and experience. We'll work up to a cup and saucer later in the week, paint on one of the days, and do something more challenging next week if they all seem capable.' She pursed her lips, giving Ruby a thorough stare as if she were trying to read her mind. 'Feel free to work on something of your own – there's plenty of clay and you can pot over there during your downtime while I'm teaching?' She pointed to a pottery wheel in the corner. Ruby had crafted in that same spot hundreds of times when she'd been in her teens. She knew that's where Lila had taught her how to operate it for the first time. On rare days when her father had actually been around, they'd crafted there together.

'It's fine.' Ruby shook her head, swallowing a wave of longing. 'I've got plenty to keep me busy, I don't want to distract from your lesson by doing my own thing.' She felt a wave of guilt when Lila's face dropped, but she'd never really explained to her Nanou why she'd given up the craft. It was too painful – and Lila would never have understood. She'd always made too many allowances for her son.

There was a knock at the entrance, and a pretty young

woman carrying a baby who looked about the same age as Maisy strode in. The woman wore blue dungarees, and the baby had a matching outfit with a pink headband that held back a tumble of blonde curls. The woman beamed when she spotted Lila. 'Hello Ms Penhaligon, I think we spoke on the phone. I want to introduce you to—' She turned and stalled, frowning at the empty space behind her. 'Sorry!' The woman strode back to the doorway and leaned an arm on the frame to look outside. 'Grandad! You said you'd come today. You promised you'd give this a try. You can't carry on living like this...' She growled the words under her breath, obviously trying to be discreet and failing. A man's voice grumbled something unintelligible from outside. 'It's your Christmas present – it would be rude if you didn't at least give it a try! Besides, I've told you it's important to support local businesses.' She waved a hand and pointed meaningfully towards the workshop. 'Just one day, that's all I ask. You're on holiday in Indigo Cove with me anyway, and I've booked you into the Pottery Project for a month.'

They waited and watched until a man with salt and pepper hair and eyes as blue as gas-fire flames wandered into the room. He stopped a few feet inside, his bushy eyebrows knitting together. 'I'm not a child. I don't need to be entertained. Pottery lessons...' he moaned. He had a deep voice with a light Welsh accent similar to his granddaughter's, but any similarities ended there because he wasn't smiling and his expression was more peeved than anything else. 'You know how I feel about pottery,' he rumbled.

'Oh, we know. We just don't understand,' the woman said lightly, pulling a silly face at the baby, who giggled before grabbing her necklace and shoving it into her mouth. 'I'm April Brown, this is my grandad Gryffyn, and this is my daughter Harriet.' The baby gurgled and gave them a toothless smile.

'She's gorgeous,' Ruby said, stepping forward to beam at her. 'How old is she?'

'Exactly six months today, aren't you, poppet – conceived right here in Indigo Cove at the Spring Carnival last year. My husband's in the navy and he was home for a rare visit, so we decided to have a dirty weekend.' She winked at Ruby conspiratorially.

'My best friend's got a baby of the same age,' Ruby said, her cheeks warming at April's blunt admission as her head filled with Anna – and Maisy's mystery father.

'Too much information, April!' Gryffyn warned, striding further into the room and frowning at the equipment.

'Oops! Apologies, I've a reputation for oversharing, but I do so enjoy embarrassing Grandad,' she said affectionately. She glanced over to where he was standing by the back wall studying some of Lila's pottery, muttering under his breath. 'Grandad's not had a lot to get riled up about over the last few years,' she said, her voice morphing from teasing to gloomy.

'April!' Gryffyn snapped, spinning round to glare at his granddaughter. He wrinkled his nose. 'What's that smell?' he asked, turning towards Lila.

'Incense,' she said lightly. 'I burn some in the studio every morning to fill it with good vibes.'

Gryffyn's eyes widened and flicked to April, then he huffed and looked around. 'So, what qualifies you to teach me pottery?' he asked rudely, spreading his arms wide.

'Grandad...' April warned.

'It's okay, pet. It's a reasonable question.' Lila swiped one of the pottery tools from her hair and stroked it gently, turning to the older man. 'I grew up in Stoke-on-Trent and learned my craft from a potter who happened to live next door to my family.' Gryffyn looked unimpressed. 'When I was eighteen, I fell in love with an artist who was visiting him.' Her eyes glowed. 'I followed him to Spain and worked in Talavera de la Reina for five years with some talented ceramics artists from across the world, who finished off my education.'

For the first time, Gryffyn looked interested. 'I've seen some interesting work from that region. Why aren't you still there?'

Lila shrugged. 'The boy and I didn't work out, but I met my husband when we were both holidaying in Madrid, and we moved to Cornwall and set up the Pottery Project. I've been here ever since.'

'And your husband?' Gryffyn glanced meaningfully around the studio.

'He died thirty-eight years ago.' Lila folded her arms. 'Do I pass muster?'

'Of course you do, doesn't she, Grandad?' April said desperately.

The older man heaved out a breath. 'If you think you can teach an old dog some new tricks, I suppose... Not that I'll be any good.'

Lila's eyes twinkled. 'Let's get started and find out. I was going to set you all up over here.' She strode to where Ruby had placed the balls of clay, watching as Gryffyn paced the room, skimming a hand over the various pieces of equipment, frowning at the posters and pictures on the walls of the studio, until he came to a stop beside one of the pottery wheels on the opposite side of the room.

'If I'm staying, I want to work at this one.' He lifted his chin. 'I like the light. I like that I'll get a breeze from the door. I especially like the fact that I won't have to talk to anyone. I work alone and in silence.' He glanced back at April, and it was clear he was testing Lila – perhaps in an effort to get himself thrown off the course?

Ruby's Nanou studied him, her face twisted in concentration as if she were trying to solve a tricky puzzle. 'Sure,' she said eventually. 'You can move there, but I won't promise silence. My classes are noisy – I learned from my days in Spain that it inspires originality. Ruby, can you check the wheel is set up properly over there? There are refreshments in the kitchen.' She directed her attention back to Gryffyn. 'So you can help yourself while we wait for the other students. We're going to start by making a small bowl. If I recall correctly, your questionnaire said you don't have much potting experience?'

April's eyes widened and fixed on her grandad.

'That's right,' Gryffyn said, his face bare of emotion. Lila dipped her chin, but she didn't challenge him, even though it was obvious there was something odd going on. There was a slight smile playing at the edge of her mouth though, and Ruby guessed she was intrigued. Then she heard a noise at the front of the building, the sound of gravel as a vehicle pulled up in the drive. A hefty brown cat scampered in through the entrance to the studio, and a smaller beige cat followed closely at its heels.

'Good morning, Coffee and Walnut. Apt you should arrive now, as I've baked that exact flavour of cake for this afternoon!' Lila sang to the felines, as they shot towards the far side of the room where four fluffy round beds were located.

'Cats!' Gryffyn complained.

'I've four. You'll meet them all. They especially enjoy the company of old men. Something to do with their charming personalities, I suppose.' Lila grinned. April's chuckle turned into a cough, and she buried her face in her daughter's hair as footsteps crunched on the gravel outside. 'That'll be some of our other students, right on time.' Lila wandered to the door.

'We'll be off.' April went to join her as Harriet gurgled. 'I'll be back at five o'clock to pick you up,' she said to her grandad. 'Enjoy!' Gryffyn frowned and started to shake his head. 'Just try one day. It's about time you climbed back on the horse—' She stopped abruptly and flushed before disappearing through the door.

A man and a woman walked in a few seconds later – they were somewhere in their late fifties. Both looked terrified.

'Mr and Mrs Harris?' Lila stepped forward to greet them.

'Patricia and Ned.' The woman smiled shyly and hefted a

bulky handbag as it slipped from her shoulder before taking out a small cake tin from its depths. 'I bake when I'm nervous,' she confessed, handing it to Lila. 'But I'm excited to be here. We moved to the area from Dorset two months ago, and it's been difficult meeting new people. I've wanted to do pottery for as long as I can remember.' She glanced around the room, her eyes sparkling. 'I heard about your course and hoped this might be the start of a new chapter, perhaps a way to make some friends.'

'Anyone who makes me a cake gets my vote.' Lila grinned.

Ned stood beside his wife looking less enthusiastic, but he shook Lila's hand politely when she held it out.

'I've not done pottery before,' he admitted gruffly. 'I used to be a security guard. The closest I ever got to a studio was when someone broke into a gallery I was working for.'

Lila chuckled and patted him on the shoulder. 'I think you'll find this will be just as intriguing, and beginners are more than welcome here. In fact, you're not the only one...' She led them further into the studio and guided them to the tables where Ruby had put out the clay. 'Hang your things on those hooks.' Lila pointed to the far wall. 'There are refreshments in the kitchen, please help yourselves. Grab an apron, wash your hands, and choose a table. This is Gryffyn Brown.' She waved a hand at the grey-haired man as he headed out of the kitchen carrying a steaming mug and two croissants. Gryffyn flinched when Lila said his name, but didn't comment. He frowned at the couple and inclined his head. 'He's taking lessons here for the next month. Ned and Patricia are here for three weeks. I'm sure you'll be good friends. I like to encourage my pupils to get to know each other. Ruby will drive you to and from the harbour at lunchtime if you need a lift, so you'll get plenty of time to chat. I've booked you all a table in The Beach Cafe today.'

Gryffyn's cheeks puffed and he wandered back to his workspace, absentmindedly shoving croissants into his mouth as he found a shelf close to his table for his mug.

Someone by the entrance cleared their throat and everyone turned towards the door. A young boy with jet-black hair was standing with his hands in the pockets of his jeans, studying them, his mouth contorted into a sneer.

'Darren Dean?' Lila sidled up to greet him. 'My friend's told me you're a talented painter?'

'I'm all right,' Darren grunted, as Lila led him across the studio to an empty pottery wheel. 'If this is boring, I'm not staying.' He shrugged off his bag and dropped it onto a stool.

'I don't blame you.' Lila chuckled. 'Life's too short for dull. Why don't you grab an apron and get something to eat from the kitchen – then everyone take your places. Ask Ruby if you need anything.' The older woman wiped her hands on her smock and picked up Darren's bag before marching towards the kitchen and deliberately hanging it onto a hook. Darren followed without commenting and Ruby nodded, distracted. Something was nagging at her. What had she missed? It was to do with something April had said... She'd have to check her emails and call Anna again later. Had she forgotten something important, missed a task she'd promised to complete?

Lila started out with introductions and a quick chat about fire exits, pottery etiquette, and a brief outline of what everyone could expect. Ned and Patricia watched in animated awe, while Darren sat on his seat staring at his bitten-down nails. Then Lila sat at her wheel and did a brief demonstration, crafting a perfect bowl while offering simple instructions and tips. Ruby noticed that Gryffyn was unfocused throughout. He barely watched Lila, but his attention was fixed on the block of clay on the table in front of him. He cocked his head, staring at it as if he were trying to figure something out. Then he bunched his hands into fists before stretching his fingers out, like a musician limbering up before a performance.

'Right,' Lila said, walking into the middle of the studio where she could see all four students. 'If you can get into position behind your wheel like I showed you, and dampen its surface like in the demonstration.' She waited while the students mounted their stools. Gryffyn scooped up a handful of water without waiting and swiped it across his wheel, getting it started. Lila's eyebrows met. 'That's perfect,' she murmured. 'You're obviously a natural...' There was no sarcasm in her grandmother's tone, but Ruby could detect an air of interest before she turned to the trio on the other side of the studio. 'Dampen the wheel. Not too shiny! Be sparing with the water.' She waited as Ned and Patricia did as they were told while Darren used far too much liquid. Ruby suspected it was deliberate because of his smirk. 'Oops,' Lila sang. 'Wipe some off, yes, that's right. Now, mould the piece of clay into a small grapefruit and put it in the centre of the wheel. As I mentioned in the demonstration, that's the perfect shape to start with if you want to make a smallish bowl. Yes, Gryffyn, that's exactly right.' Lila's lips pursed. 'You're way ahead of me again. Yes, and you wet it just like that. Goodness, you could have been doing this for years...' She waited while the others caught up. Their movements were clumsy, but they got the positioning right in the end. Darren cursed a couple of times, but Ruby spotted the triumphant grin when he got his piece in the correct spot before it was quickly extinguished.

'What do we do now?' Darren moaned. 'This is taking too long.'

'Now you have fun!' Lila said.

'Lessons aren't fun,' the teen snarked.

'Now that's where you're wrong,' Lila trilled. 'Because we have three rules in this studio and they're easy to follow: keep your clay wet; once the wheel is on, keep it spinning; and most importantly, enjoy yourself!' She clapped her hands and Ruby grinned. She couldn't help it. There was an energy in the room, an energy which shone from her Nanou like sunbeams; even Gryffyn and Darren were no longer frowning. Lila put a record on her player, and switched it on. A song by the Beatles with a hard, rocky beat filled the room. 'Hold on to the edges like I showed you earlier, centre it, now squeeze and make a cone.' Lila continued to pace the studio, wriggling occasionally in time to the music before she sharpened her gaze on each of the students in turn. It was obvious Gryffyn knew what he was doing. So why had he pretended he hadn't?

Gryffyn was concentrating hard and Ruby watched hypnotised as his fingers worked on the clay, moulding it into a perfect shaped bowl. She doubted even Lila would be capable of producing something so perfect in such a short time. He swiped on an intricate pattern with a couple of the tools they'd left out for a future lesson. Lila's forehead squished as she studied the design before she turned back to Ned, Darren and Patricia. Ned was struggling as his clay bowl began to wobble.

'Don't worry!' Lila said. 'Push down and then forward, drive it to the middle. This is your first go on the wheel. I want you to have a try and then I want you to push your clay, flatten out the bottom, squeeze and play with the pressure. Get to know how it feels. This is all about exploring.' Patricia began to laugh as the sides of her bowl suddenly flopped inwards and the whole thing collapsed. Ned joined in, chuckling loudly when his bowl buckled, spraying the uneven sides to the far edges of the wheel. Darren's splatted to the side and he tried to reconstruct it, looking frustrated until Lila shook her head. Then she waved her arms in the air and cheered. 'That's exactly what I was looking for, team! You build your walls until you wreck them. The goal of this session was for you to learn and play until you crashed.'

'I don't like getting things wrong,' Darren said, his words clipped.

'To be an artist you have to learn what failure feels like,' Lila said as her eyes shot to Gryffyn. 'Unless you're very fortunate and get everything right first time, but seriously, failure is the sign of a true potter. Knock your work down and build it up – it's how you learn. It's all about getting a feel for the clay and finding out what you can do.'

'Or can't.' Gryffyn glowered at his creation.

Ned stopped spinning his wheel and snorted loudly. 'I definitely know what failure feels like now.' He frowned at the mess and shook his head. 'This pottery lark is harder than it looks.' His eyes flicked across the room to the perfectly crafted bowl Gryffyn had finished.

The older man saw him and scowled at his creation again. He stared at it critically, looking disappointed, then used the side of a fist to smash the bowl to mush. 'Yep. That's what failure feels like,' he said quietly. 'Sometimes, it's better to fail. You don't learn anything if your life's too perfect. Except how hard it is if it all gets taken away.'

'Is everything okay?' Patricia asked, her voice kind.

'Sure,' Gryffyn said, showing far too many teeth for his smile to be genuine.

Lila cleared her throat. 'The good thing about clay is there's always more to work with. Always an opportunity to dust off your wheel and have another spin.' Gryffyn didn't look convinced, but he nodded. The room remained silent as the moment stretched, until Lila clapped her hands again, breaking the odd mood. 'Good work, everyone. I'm impressed. You're showing signs of being a very talented bunch. Best I've had this year!' She flashed a smile, whirling around to change the record on the player, this time going for something by Queen – earning another groan from Darren.

'You got anything by the Arctic Monkeys?' he asked.

'There are no monkeys in my studio, lovey, only cats. Now, use the wire I left out to cut through the walls of your pot – if you haven't completely obliterated them.' She directed her comment to Gryffyn. 'It's good to check the thickness, to see how even it looks – that way you'll discover how you could improve on it next time. Darren, that was a great first attempt.' She turned her attention back to the young boy as he clumsily tried to slice a section out of the clay and a wave of colour rose up his neck. 'It'll get easier,' Lila commiserated, patting his shoulder.

'Mine's all over the place,' Patricia lamented.

'It's all part of the learning process. I wouldn't expect anything else. That was your first ever attempt. Take pride in it! Now, if you can all slide the clay off the wheel, like I showed you in my demonstration. Put it to one side and Ruby will collect the remnants. She'll also help if you get stuck.' Her expression was assessing as she watched Gryffyn expertly lift the clay from the wheel and plop it onto the side before cleaning his hands on his apron. 'Why don't you take a moment to stretch your legs, get some more tea or coffee. When you return, scrape the wheel and clean it like I showed you – remember, you don't wash it.' She waved a finger again. 'But you want to make sure it stays damp. In a few minutes, you'll be trying that whole thing again. This time you'll probably be surprised at how much you've improved!'

'There's a long way to go,' Ned muttered, shaking his head before heading towards the kitchen following a despondent-looking Darren. Lila turned her attention to Gryffyn as he stood and stretched. He glanced across the room at Lila but didn't hold her eyes. Then he followed Ned into the kitchen.

'Well, he's a mystery,' Lila whispered to Ruby, as she began to collect up the pieces of used clay. 'If that man's a beginner at pottery, I'm a fairy princess from the planet Zog. He knows what he's doing all right. I wonder why he's here and why he lied on the questionnaire.' She tapped a clay-smeared fingertip on her chin. 'I swear I've met him somewhere, but I don't recognise the name. I expect it'll come to me.'

'Perhaps he's been on one of your courses before?' Ruby suggested.

'I think I'd remember… In the meantime, it's nice to have an attractive man to flirt with. It's been a while.' Lila fluttered her eyelashes. 'I do love a man of mystery – especially one with a dark temper. Imagine all that untapped passion bubbling under the surface. Picture what he could do on a pottery wheel with the right incentive.' She winked suggestively.

'Nanou!' Ruby flushed.

'Pet, you really need to open yourself up… loosen a few of those invisible buttons and have a little fun.' Lila patted her hand and chuckled as she made her way towards the kitchen to join the others. Ruby watched, wishing she could be more like her grandmother. A little freer with her feelings, more open to life.

But she'd spent far too many years being let down and hurt by her father. She'd never open herself up to that world of pain again.

6

Ruby sat in her bedroom and briefly scanned the emails on her laptop to see if she'd received a response from her dad. She'd messaged again the evening before, requesting a timeline for when he planned to return Lila's money. But aside from a couple of client enquiries which she quickly answered and some junk which she immediately deleted, she'd heard nothing. It was hardly a surprise, but she was still disappointed. No matter how many times she tried to quash the tiny piece of hope that her father would finally measure up, it kept rising to the surface, a nugget of childish optimism she was determined to crush. She typed him another firmer email before slamming the lid of her laptop shut.

Still irritated, she pulled out her mobile and texted Anna. She'd tried to call again yesterday, but her friend hadn't picked up. *Hello, lovely. Is everything okay – are you feeling all right, how's the flat hunt progressing? I've got the strangest feeling I've forgotten something.* She waited to see if Anna would text back, guessed her friend might be feeding or bathing Maisy – or was still reluctant to talk – so grabbed a cardigan from her bed and headed out of her Nanou's house into the drive. She'd call again later.

Gabe had finished his session with Lila ten minutes earlier, and Ruby had left them to pack up on her grandmother's insistence, so she could change clothes ready for their evening patrol of the beach. He was standing by the side of a black Volvo waiting for her, stroking Walnut, one of Lila's less skittish cats. When he straightened up to greet her, she spotted the scratch that ran across the side of the passenger door, which he'd mentioned at The Marples meeting. It was deeper than she'd expected and implied something more sinister than a mere teenage prank. Gabe swung the door open as she approached. 'Your chariot awaits. Your grandmother said to go ahead – she's knee-deep in the kiln and doesn't want us to miss the best of the evening light.' Ruby climbed inside, pausing when she saw that the dark leather seats in the front had been badly gnawed along the edges.

'Courtesy of Sammie,' Gabe explained, pulling his seatbelt on and pointing to the set of bars that separated the back seats from the large boot. 'I naively thought I'd be able to leave the dogs in the car for two minutes while I paid for some petrol, and he managed to get through.' He rolled his eyes, grinning, and the dimple in his left cheek winked. 'I honestly didn't know whether to reprimand him or audition him for a show in Vegas.' Ruby chuckled as he pulled out of the drive and turned right. Handsome and funny, Gabe Roskilly was a tempting combination. The type of man she could let herself admire, perhaps even like in another life. She respected his cool parenting of the naughty dog. A lesser man might have used the bad behaviour as an excuse to dump Sammie at the closest rescue centre.

'I need to pop to the brewery to pick up the dogs for our walk. I avoid bringing them to the pottery anymore.' Gabe lowered his voice. 'After the incident with your grandmother's cats.'

'What happened?' Ruby smiled, glancing out of the window at the tall banks of grass peppered with pink wildflowers that lined the road. The sun was high and it was still hot. It had been an unseasonably warm summer; uncomfortable when you worked in an office in London poring over people's accounts, but a lot nicer in a pottery barn in Cornwall. She rarely made it out in the evenings at home, and was looking forward to the fresh air and to stretching her legs.

'We try not to talk about it. Suffice to say, I brought a suitcase filled with cat treats to the Pottery Project the next time I visited,' Gabe said gravely, his eyes twinkling as they drove into the harbour, then followed the busy seafront back up the hill and past the railway station.

'You've known my Nanou long?' Ruby asked, sitting back in her seat and staring at Gabe's profile. He had full lips, high cheekbones and the beginnings of stubble running across his jaw, which she found inexplicably sexy.

'Feels like all my life,' Gabe said, his voice filled with affection. 'This is the first time I've done a stint in the studio, though. I'm not sure I'm cut out for a pottery career. Not enough patience. You must be good if you've got Lila's genes?'

'I tend to leave the creativity to her,' Ruby said, looking out of the window. The car fell silent and she sank into her seat, expecting Gabe to ask more, knowing she didn't want to talk about the reasons why she'd given up pottery. Sometimes, she could hardly understand them herself.

He was silent for a beat and she held her breath, anticipating his next question. 'I've decided if I ever have to give up the brewery, I'm destined for a career as a dog trainer. Although I'm guessing I'll starve.' He glanced at the particularly large hole in Ruby's headrest and rolled his eyes. She laughed, relieved and reluctantly charmed. 'What would you do if you could be anything?' He turned back to the road.

Potter. The word invaded Ruby's brain before she could

stop it. 'I love numbers, I wouldn't change a thing,' she murmured.

'Pretty and smart.' Gabe nodded, sounding genuinely impressed. 'I wish I shared your fondness for sums, but on balance I'm probably better at dog training. The brewery's located about a mile from here,' he said, still smiling. 'Lila said you've not been before? Weren't you born in Cornwall?'

'Yes, but I moved away with my mother when I was six weeks old,' Ruby said.

'Did your dad not go too?' The probing question was perceptive, and she forced her lips closed. 'Sorry, that's personal. I've been spending too much time talking to the dogs. I've forgotten how to hold a civilised conversation.' His cheeks flushed.

'It's okay, it's not a secret,' Ruby soothed. 'My dad went to pick up some nappies from a supermarket in the high street when I was five weeks old, and didn't come back.'

'Wow,' Gabe said. 'That's...'

'Oh, he left a note,' Ruby added.

'What did it say?' Gabe asked, taking a right turn.

'He wasn't ready to be a parent. Thirty-plus years on and he's still not.' Her voice barely betrayed the hurt and anger she still felt when she thought about him. It's why she felt honour-bound to track Maisy's father down. 'I'm sorry,' Ruby said, suddenly embarrassed. 'Being in Cornwall tends to bring things back.' And somehow, despite her desire to change the subject earlier, she was spilling her secrets to a man she barely knew.

'Don't apologise,' Gabe said gently. 'Can I ask what happened?'

Ruby sighed. 'Mum gathered what she could of her dignity and moved to Buckinghamshire to stay with her best friend, who's the mother of my closest friend now, Anna. Mum got a job and a flat. We kept in touch with Lila and holidayed in Indigo Cove most years.'

Gabe grunted. 'I think I met your dad once – Ross Penhaligon?' he asked, and she nodded. 'He was visiting the Pottery Project but didn't stay long.'

'He travels around. He's in Spain now, but I've no idea what his future plans are,' Ruby admitted.

'Don't you see him?' Gabe took a left into a narrow country road surrounded by fields. To their right, Ruby could see hints of sea glittering next to the horizon. Her eyes skimmed the pretty scenery before catching on Gabe's hands as they gripped the steering wheel. They were tanned and muscular with a row of jagged cuts across the knuckles. Those hands told of hard work and commitment, the kind her father had never had. She looked back out of the window, trying to focus on his question.

'When I was younger, he used to turn up every few months. Wanted to have a relationship.' She put the word in air quotes. 'I told him I didn't want to see him after my mother died. So, our paths have barely crossed for the last ten years.'

'It's hard to lose a parent,' Gabe said quietly. 'Must be harder when the parent's still alive...'

She shrugged. 'It took me a long time to see Ross Penhaligon for what he was, and I have no feelings for him.' She swallowed as something caught in her throat. 'My mother never gave up on their marriage, or on believing he'd come back for good when he made the fortune he kept promising us. She had a cardiac arrest when she was forty-three. I think in the end he literally broke her heart.'

'That's tough,' Gabe said quietly.

'I'm sorry, that was a lot to lay on you. I'm not sure where it all came from.' It was that pressure inside, the need to relieve it. And in some ways talking with Gabe had helped.

He shrugged. 'How about you ask me something to even things up? I promise to be just as candid. I don't have many secrets, but I could make something up.'

Ruby laughed and mulled the offer, realising she did want

to know more about him. 'Okay, tell me about your parents. The truth is fine.'

'My mum died about five years ago; my dad never really got over it.' Gabe gave her a sweet smile. 'They had a good marriage, the kind we all dream of.'

Ruby nodded. Her dreams didn't involve marriage at all, but Gabe took it as a sign to continue.

'My father passed almost two years ago after a short illness – but he was the best. He handed the brewery to me and my brother just before he went. All I've ever wanted was to make him proud... and to ensure the brewery flourishes as a legacy to him.' His forehead pinched; it was almost imperceptible, but Ruby noticed.

'That's... admirable,' she said, her voice warm. Loyalty to family was an appealing quality – one she admired. Especially because it had been so lacking from her dad.

They lapsed into a companionable silence until Gabe took a right into a large gravel car park. The brewery was a huge building with a facade crafted from wood that had been painted a deep charcoal black. A white-and-red hand-painted sign announced they'd arrived at the Roskilly Brewery, home of the award-winning Deep Water Ale. There was a set of concrete steps leading up to the entrance, which on closer inspection were splattered with small mounds of what looked like mud. A rare gust of wind blew in through the car window, and it was immediately obvious from the smell that it was something else.

'What the—' Gabe gasped, pulling the car to a sudden stop in the middle of the car park and hopping out. Striding up to check the steps, he held his arm up to his nose as he studied the mess. 'Someone's just dumped this.' The scent was pungent, and worsened by the heat from the evening sun, which was focused on the front of the building. Ruby pushed her cardigan into her face as she got out of the car and walked up to join him.

The car park was empty, aside from a beaten-up orange Nissan Qashqai parked in the corner.

'Could the culprit still be around?' Ruby pointed to the car, but Gabe shook his head.

'That belongs to my head brewer, Jago. This wasn't here when I left.' He eased his way past the first pile of dung and carefully moved up a step.

'Do you want me to call the police?' Ruby pulled her mobile from her pocket as the doors at the entrance to the building opened and a man strode out, followed by Gabe's two beagles who scampered down the steps, yapping excitedly.

'Stop!' Gabe yelled, as manure went flying under the force of their paws. 'Rex!' he shouted. One of the dogs halted and sat perfectly still, but the other ignored him, charging down two more steps before leaping at Gabe who scooped him under an arm. 'Sammie,' he groaned.

'What the hell!' The man in the dark overalls jerked to a stop at the top of the steps, his eyes widening as he took in the scene. 'Where did that come from?' He scrubbed a hand through his hair, glaring at the dogs. 'I only turned my back for two minutes.'

'I don't think even Sammie is capable of doing this.' Gabe put the beagle on the ground, shoving his hands into the pockets of his jeans as he spun around to scour the car park.

'We've had no visitors for half an hour. The last couple bought two kegs of Deep Water, which I helped carry to the car. This mess wasn't here then.' Jago glowered at the manure. 'There's been no one in the brewery since. As far as I know, the car park stayed empty. I've been working out back – I didn't hear movement on the gravel, but it's noisy in there.'

'Can we check the security cameras?' Gabe asked.

Jago shook his head. 'They're still playing up. I asked Aaron to look into it last week but...' He raised his hands and dropped them. 'I tried to book an engineer today, but there's no one free until the end of next month.' He sighed. 'I meant to put the barrier over the entrance, but I knew you'd be coming back for the dogs and I...' Jago studied the steps again, his lips twisting. 'Sorry.'

'It's not your fault,' Gabe soothed. 'Ruby and I were going to patrol Smuggler's Rest looking for vandals, but it seems they decided to hit closer to home. Perhaps it's too hot to stray far from the village today.'

Gabe's joke fell flat and Jago frowned. 'This is the third time they've targeted you or the brewery in the past week. You need to speak to the police.'

Gabe shook his head. 'This is happening everywhere. Ella at The Beach Cafe has a long list of incidents, I've just been unlucky.' He glanced around. 'We're miles from anywhere – it's an easy place to target without being seen. I wish I understood what this is about. It's very organised for bored teenagers. They'd have to get this stuff here, for a start.' He frowned at the steps and then across the car park at the Qashqai. 'Do you still keep a spade in your boot in case of emergencies?'

Jago nodded.

Gabe let out a long breath and turned to Ruby. 'I'm sorry. I don't think we can do our patrol, after all. Do you mind if I drop you back at the Pottery Project?' He frowned at the steps. 'I've a feeling I'm going to be here for a while.'

'I'll call the police while you're gone,' Jago said, pulling out his mobile. 'We ought to report this before tidying it up.' He nodded at Ruby. 'Nice to meet you. Lila talks about you all the time. Sorry if this has ruined your evening.'

'It's fine,' Ruby murmured, staring at the steps, wondering exactly what was going on.

It didn't take long to drive back to the harbour. The traffic was light, but they still had to wait at the far end of the high street when a bus stopped to let passengers off.

Ruby stared out of the window as Gabe drew the car up next a shop that had once sold records – she'd been there once with her mother, poring over their favourite artists until they'd settled on an album by Janice Joplin. The store had obviously changed hands since because now it traded in ice creams. A huge mural had been painted on the wall of the building, which faced a selection of metal chairs and tables where a few customers lounged in the evening sun eating vanilla, chocolate chip and raspberry cones.

'That's pretty.' Ruby leaned out of the window to get a closer look. The mural featured colourful mermaids who were flapping their fins as they were spun on a carnival wheel while a crowd of holidaymakers surrounded by seals, dolphins and seagulls waved at them from the ground.

'It's fairly new,' Gabe said.

'It's very unique, I swear I've seen it somewhere...' Ruby searched her mind. 'I've no idea how.'

'It was painted for the launch of the Spring Carnival last year. The local council commissioned an artist,' Gabe explained, easing the car forward as the bus set off. 'Perhaps Lila sent you a picture?'

'I swear I saw it on social media, and my grandmother's not a fan.' Ruby cast her mind back. 'It must have been on Instagram because it's the only network I use. Nanou definitely doesn't have an account.' She pulled out her mobile, wondering why the mural had made her think of Anna. So many things were bothering her. It was as if a hive of bees had taken up residence in her brain and were buzzing back and forth, telling her she'd missed something important. Her mobile had barely any signal, so she put it back in her bag.

'It was decorated last year, so it's been up around...' Gabe paused, screwing up his nose. 'Fifteen months.'

'Ohhhhhh,' Ruby said, as things began to click into place like pieces of a puzzle finding their perfect spot. Fifteen months ago, she'd visited Lila with Anna; she had been poorly with the awful bout of food poisoning. Anna had been out most evenings, enjoying the carnival. Some nights she hadn't returned to the Pottery Project until the early hours. April Brown's baby was six months old exactly and so was Maisy, which meant they'd likely got pregnant at the same time. *So could someone at the Spring Carnival, maybe even a man who lives in Indigo Cove, be responsible?* She huffed out a breath. Why hadn't Anna told her? Why wasn't she in contact with the father? Surely it wasn't all about keeping Simon happy? Her friend needed money and support. Maisy needed her father – surely it was worth Anna swallowing her pride for that? As soon as Gabe pulled up on the gravel driveway outside the Pottery Project, Ruby shoved the door open and leaped out. 'I'm sorry, I've got to... check my phone.' Gabe looked surprised. 'Good luck with the shovelling.'

'Perhaps we can try our evening patrol again in a few days?' he suggested.

'I'd like that. Maybe see you here tomorrow,' Ruby said, and he nodded before backing the car out of the driveway. Then she turned and dashed into The Little Cornish House.

'Nanou!' Ruby called out, but her grandmother didn't respond – she was probably still working in the Pottery Project. She ran into her bedroom and shoved her bag and cardigan onto the bed so she could check her Instagram account, breathing out slowly when the Wi-Fi kicked in. She searched for Anna's profile and began to scroll through the multiple photos of Maisy – including the one Anna had posted announcing her six-month birthday. Her heart was beating wildly. She had to track down Maisy's father. She was determined to hold him accountable, to make sure he didn't abandon Anna and her friend's child like her father had abandoned her and her mother. 'Come on!' she snapped, flicking through old photos of Simon and Anna, back through pictures of daffodils, a Christmas tree, Halloween when a pregnant Anna had dressed up as a pumpkin, before she finally got to the photos that had been posted last spring. Then she slowed, recognising Lila and the Pottery Project, a picture of herself when she'd started to recover from the food poisoning. There was one of the four cats basking in sunshine, a small crowd of people sitting outside the Lobster Pot Inn in the high street – faces she recognised, some she did not.

Then she stopped scrolling as the breath left her chest. There was a photo of Anna and a man with his arm thrown around her shoulder, cuddling her into his side. They were sitting next to the mural and she recognised the man immediately, felt her blood run cold. She lifted the phone closer; there was no mistake. She quickly checked the other shots, and found a dozen more of them both. In one they were kissing; in another Anna sat on his lap. Ruby blinked back tears, feeling ridiculously hurt and disappointed. Because the man in the pictures with Anna was Gabe.

7

'We need to talk,' Ruby said early the next morning, as soon as Anna picked up her mobile.

Ruby heard Maisy gurgle in the background, then hurl something against a wooden surface. 'It's 5.30 a.m. I thought everyone in the civilised world was still asleep,' Anna joked, sounding exhausted. 'We're on breakfast number two and Maisy's whacking a wooden spoon onto the table in our hotel room, if you're wondering what that noise is. It's her new favourite game – if she carries on much longer, she'll have muscles to rival a lumberjack's.' Maisy chortled and gave the table another good smack. 'I went to see a studio flat yesterday afternoon,' Anna continued. 'The accommodation is small, but it'll be the first step to me getting on my feet... I'm looking forward to having my independence back.' Something was off about Anna's voice, and Ruby was immediately flooded with sympathy.

'I know who Maisy's father is,' she blurted, desperate to help. 'And I know you met last year, here in Indigo Cove.'

'What!' Anna shrilled.

'But I don't understand why you've kept it a secret.' The

muscles across Ruby's back bunched and stiffened, and she fought the wave of hurt that pinched bone-deep.

'There's no way you've found him, Ruby. *I* don't even know who he is!' Anna exclaimed, obviously flustered.

'What does that mean?' Ruby bristled, ready for an argument. Her friend might be prepared to walk away from Gabe, but she wasn't going to let him evade his responsibilities. Ruby's mother had struggled for years to raise her alone, and her father had missed all her formative years – all those milestones and important moments. Both Anna and Maisy deserved better, and Ruby was going to make sure they got it.

'I called the father when I got back to London and found out I was pregnant. But he fobbed me off, then when I called again, the number had been cut off,' Anna explained.

'Cut off?' Ruby repeated, frowning.

'Yep. He must have changed it,' Anna admitted.

Ruby swallowed as ice settled into the pit of her stomach. She'd liked Gabe. Was her judgement that off? 'Did you search for him online?'

'I did. He told me his name was Alfie Smith, but when I looked up the name, I found two people in Indigo Cove called that – one was eighty-six and the other was five. We were either alone or in a love bubble that whole long weekend, so I didn't hear another person call him by name. The address he gave me was false too. He lied to me, Ruby.' Anna puffed out a breath. 'What we had was supposed to be a fling, so I guess I can't blame him. What happens in Indigo Cove stays in Indigo Cove – you know the kind of thing?'

Ruby grunted. 'I don't understand why you're not angry.'

'I was at first, but I got over it. Besides, that had been a joke between us the whole weekend we were together, how it was all just a one-time thing. It's why I didn't mention him while I was there. You were sick and, well, it was all part of the crazy interlude when I was supposed to be getting over Simon...'

'But?' Ruby asked, getting up to pace her bedroom as a fizz of annoyance rose to the surface of her throat. All these lies – why had Gabe told them? It didn't fit with the man she'd met. Then again, hadn't she learned that lesson from her own father? How many times had he lied to her? It had taken her years to see through him.

Anna let out a breath. 'I thought he liked me. I was surprised by how much I thought about him when I got home. Then I learned I was pregnant, tried to call and... it was obvious Alfie – or whoever he was, had lied.'

'You didn't say,' Ruby said, her voice hurt. She turned to look out of the window at the view. The sun had begun to move up from the horizon, announcing it was morning, and the light glittered on the sea, creating a triangular pathway across the bumpy surface of the waves.

The baby grumbled and it took Anna a while to respond. Ruby guessed she was giving Maisy something more to eat. 'I was embarrassed and worried about how you'd react. You've got... very strong ideas about how parents should behave, about fathers being around and measuring up. I'd decided to confess all and just before I did, Simon turned up on my doorstep and asked if we could give our relationship another shot. I told him about the pregnancy – he was surprised, then he said we could tell everyone the baby was his, but I had to go along with it. He wasn't keen on people knowing. Even you. You know how jealous he gets, and he said it would complicate things, mean he couldn't take Maisy on as his own when he was ready. Turns out that day never came.'

Lemon wandered into the room and hopped onto the bed, purring loudly. Ruby went to join the cat on the duvet. 'I suppose I can understand why you didn't tell me.' She stroked a hand across his yellow fur, feeling instantly soothed.

'I'm embarrassed now that things are over with Simon, and

I'm sorry. I obviously have the worst taste in men.' Anna fell silent.

'This is not your fault,' Ruby grumbled. Too many of her evenings had been spent listening to her mother lamenting the same. Taking all her father's commitment issues onto her own shoulders.

'You said you know who the real father is?' Anna asked suddenly, obviously remembering the reason Ruby had called. 'How?'

'Since you told me Simon wasn't Maisy's dad, I've been trying to work out who is. She's six months old now, which means you got pregnant fifteen months ago.' Ruby outlined her theory on Lemon's belly as she explained. 'A pregnancy lasts for nine months, and since you dated no one but Simon that I know of—'

'None!' Anna interjected.

Ruby nodded. 'I worked out you must have fallen pregnant when you were in Indigo Cove last spring.'

'You're a regular Nancy Drew,' Anna said dryly. 'No surprise it was the numbers that caught me in the end.'

'It took me long enough, but once it clicked, I found pictures on your Instagram account of you at the carnival,' Ruby said. 'There's this same guy in a few – and in one you were kissing. His face was very clear.'

'Right. I remember now.' Anna sighed. 'I forgot all about posting those. Once I realised Alfie had lied to me, I guess I blocked out everything about him. I suppose I should delete them...'

'The thing is,' Ruby said, getting up to walk back to the window, 'I've met him.' Her blood pumped faster as she thought about Gabe and she fought the surge of disappointment, wanting to kick herself. She should have expected this, should never have let her guard down.

'You have?' Anna squeaked.

'His name's Gabe Roskilly. He part-owns the brewery in Indigo Cove and he's, well, a... nice man.' At least she'd thought so. Clearly, she was just as deluded as her mum, desperate to believe in a goodness that simply wasn't there. She shook her head. No wonder she didn't want to emulate either of her parents. But she'd almost let herself get sucked in. 'I'm going to tell Gabe about Maisy – and you,' she said firmly. 'See if he has a reasonable explanation for what happened. He should be involved in your lives, Anna, even if it's just financially. It's not okay for him to walk away. He should take responsibility, give you some help.' Ruby glanced at the photo beside her bed again.

'I know how you feel about what Ross did, Ruby,' Anna said slowly. 'I've watched you struggle with it, watched it turn your mother inside out. I know how hard you've worked to block him from your world because he never measured up. You have to know, I don't need this Alfie, Gabe – or whoever he is – in my life and neither does Maisy. Same as I don't need Simon. I'm happy and she's fine. She's loved and I take good care of her. This Gabe is no different from your dad. He doesn't want to be here, and I'm not going to force that.' Anna paused. 'I know I've got things to sort out and I'm in a mess financially, but I'd rather wait for a man to come along who *wants* to be part of our family. I'm not looking to force a stranger into taking an interest. I don't want you to track him down.'

'I...' Ruby let out a long sigh. 'I'm sorry, Anna, but he should know he's got a daughter,' she said quietly. She didn't tell her friend she'd liked Gabe, had felt she could trust him. Which was odd. 'At least let me talk to him.' She checked her watch; it was almost 6 a.m. She wanted to get to the brewery before any customers arrived so she could have a private conversation with the man himself. 'I'm going to head out to see him now. I'll call later, tell you how it went.'

'Ruby, listen. I know you think you're helping, and I appreciate it, but I don't want that—' The baby began to howl. 'I'm sorry, I've got to go.' Anna hung up and Ruby stared at the mobile, feeling torn. She didn't want to upset her friend, but she had to learn the truth. To hold Gabe accountable. Anna would understand, perhaps even thank her, in time.

The sun was still low when Ruby slowly drove up the track that would lead her to the Roskilly Brewery. Lila had loaned her the Beetle when she'd said she felt like an early walk along the cliffs, and had told her to take as long as she needed – but Ruby wanted to be back at the Pottery Project before lessons began. She hadn't confided in her Nanou about what she'd learned – she wasn't sure how Lila would take the news about Gabe, or whether she'd encourage Ruby to leave well alone. In many ways she and her grandmother were similar, but in their attitudes to relationships and commitment they were miles apart. Her Nanou had always been too forgiving, too laissez-faire about life. But there were rules to follow, things that had to be done right.

The car park was empty when Ruby drove in, aside from the orange Qashqai and Gabe's wounded car. She hopped out of the Beetle, holding her arms by her sides as she marched up to the main doors. The steps were clean now and someone had obviously hosed them down because the whole area smelled sweet – reminding her of the wildflowers on the hedgerows that she'd passed on the drive here. Ruby's temper heated as she got closer to the entrance, and by the time she'd walked through, it was bubbling hot.

How could Gabe have lied to Anna like that? There was no reasonable explanation, she'd tried to think of one all night. The facts added up to a man who only thought about himself. So much for her well-honed bullshit detector, it was obviously faulty. Which meant everything she thought she knew about the man had probably been wrong. She shook her head. Why hadn't she seen it coming? What was it about him? She'd never been taken in by a handsome face before.

Ruby paused just inside the shop and took in a breath, smelling an earthy combination of hops and ale. To her right and left, small booths displayed a series of taps and racks of tiny glasses where customers could sample the different brews before committing to one. She puffed out a breath as she spotted Gabe lounging behind the long counter at the end of the room. She recognised him immediately from his height, the angle of his nose and the naturally sun-bleached highlights in his sandy hair. He looked up as she approached, but his expression remained blank. Pain stabbed her solar plexus. Why wasn't he smiling? Had he somehow guessed why she'd come?

'Good morning, darlin',' Gabe said smoothly. 'Can I help?' His eyes flicked up and down Ruby's body, and she had to fight the urge to leap across the counter and slap his face. What was he playing at? She opened her mouth as he interrupted. 'Stupid question, you're in a brewery. Sorry, it's a bit early for me. I'm guessing you're not just here to see me. Did you want to buy some beer?' He flashed his charming smile, his expression on the edge of lascivious. She was angry, but her body still warmed and her legs seemed to liquify. 'It's early, only just past seven – are you heading to a party? If you are, can I come? I've been here an hour already and I'm bored out of my mind.' He laughed heartily.

'Look—' Ruby said, confused.

'I get it,' Gabe interrupted again, rooting around underneath the counter and pulling out two tall beer glasses, winking as he held them up. 'You want to sample the merchandise before you decide? How about we forgo the Scrooge measures and hop straight to pints?'

'I need to talk to you in private,' Ruby hissed, then she took a deep breath, aiming to leash her irritation. She didn't want to scare Gabe off. She had to approach this rationally, couldn't let personal feelings get in the way. She was aiming for a win-win, trying to ensure Maisy got the chance to meet her father. That Anna got the support she so desperately needed and deserved.

Gabe's eyes sparkled and Ruby had to stop herself from reacting. 'Now that's an offer I can't refuse.' For the first time, Ruby began to realise she didn't know Gabe at all. He'd obviously kept this whole side of himself hidden until now. It was likely he had form – how many women had he seduced and lied to? He really was just like her dad; how had she missed it? He glanced towards the solid oak door at the back of the shop and waggled his eyebrows, making Ruby swallow a wave of revulsion. 'There's an empty office out back. Shall I bring the drinks?' He waved the glasses.

Ruby yelped in disgust and put her hands on the counter, leaning forward to glare into his face. 'You really are incorrigible.'

He winked. 'So I've been told. But you like that about me, right?' He still had the shadow of hair across his jawline and his green eyes sparkled. Last night his expression might have set off a firework in her belly, but now Ruby just wanted to thump him. 'If you're not keen on beer, we've got something stronger in the office – if I lock the door, we won't be interrupted.' He waved the glasses again, making Ruby's stomach churn.

'We don't need privacy and I'd rather have this conversation sober – we've a lot to sort out,' she snapped.

'Oh?' For the first time Gabe looked confused, then the cheeky smile returned. 'Like who gets undressed first?' He was flirting with her, oblivious to the waves of anger and revulsion. They'd spent time together, talked. Didn't he know her at all? She obviously didn't know him, hadn't seen even the slightest hint that he was this kind of lowlife. Ruby swallowed disappointment – in herself and him.

'I'm here to talk about Anna Lovejoy.' Something flashed across Gabe's eyes and Ruby knew in that moment that he recognised her friend's name. Any vague hope she'd had that she'd somehow got this wrong evaporated. 'You met her last year at the Spring Carnival – you gave her a false name. She called but you ditched your mobile.'

'I don't know what you're talking about,' Gabe said, his voice hardening as the sparkle disappeared from his expression, rendering him barely recognisable from the man Ruby had thought she knew. 'And I don't know an Anna Lovejoy.' His eyes darted left and right, and she wondered if he planned to leap over the counter and make a break for it. He wouldn't get far, of that she was certain. 'Plus, I wasn't in Indigo Cove much last year.'

'You need to stop lying,' Ruby bit back, leaning further forward. 'You've got a daughter, Maisy, and she needs her father. However... misguided he might be. Don't you want to meet her?'

'No!' Gabe's eyes widened and he took a step away from the counter, thumped the glasses down as if they'd burned his fingers. Ruby might have laughed if it hadn't been so tragic. 'I'm not anyone's dad,' he snapped. 'I never plan to be.'

'It's a little late to decide that now. I've got pictures,' Ruby promised. 'Maisy looks like you.' Now she was studying Gabe's face she could see the similarities – they had the same shape nose, the same colour eyes. Why hadn't she seen it before?

He shook his head vehemently. 'You've got me mixed up with someone else. I'm barely in the area and...' His eyes darted around the shop as if he were searching for an escape. 'Seriously, you need to talk to my brother.'

Ruby shook her head; the man was even more of a louse than she'd thought. 'Blaming someone else for your mistakes is lower than I expected you to stoop,' she managed. She could be speaking to her father – it made her hate Gabe even more.

'You need to listen,' Gabe said, his face contorting with a mixture of annoyance and fear.

'This isn't a discussion,' Ruby snapped. 'It's important you drop this act so we can sort things out.'

'What's going on?' a familiar voice rang out from behind them – and when Ruby turned to check who was speaking, her jaw dropped.

8

Ruby's eyes widened and her whole body seemed to slump. For a moment, Gabe thought she was going to pass out, but then her eyes cleared and darted to Aaron before they rested back on him.

'Everything okay?' he asked softly. Had Aaron upset her? His brother was normally good with women – way better than him. That fact had been annoying once, but he'd learned to get over it. He hadn't had the time to hone the same skills, and after what Aaron had been through with his illness, it only seemed fair.

'No, it's not okay,' Ruby ground out, her attention skidding back to Aaron again as she stared at him. 'You're the brother.' The way she said it suggested Ruby wasn't impressed. Gabe frowned; something was happening here and it wasn't good. His instinct was to protect Aaron, but there was another deeper part of him that wanted to understand what had got Ruby so upset. Obviously bored, Sammie bounded up to sniff her shoes, pawing at her pretty loose trousers. Instead of knocking him away, Ruby bent and stroked his ears, shaking her head. 'No one told me you were twins,' she muttered, looking up, her expression accusing.

'Sorry,' Gabe said. In truth, it hadn't occurred to him. Or perhaps he'd just wanted to enjoy her company without bringing his sibling into it?

'Yup,' Aaron said, nodding and grinning, his whole body loosening as he relaxed. Ruby rose again to face him. 'Aaron Roskilly.' He held out a palm, but she didn't take it. His brother dropped his hand and a crease marred his forehead. 'I'm sorry for the confusion earlier. I guessed you knew my brother but couldn't resist teasing you. It's not every day a beautiful woman walks into the brewery in the early hours.'

Ruby stared and shook her head, her attention darting back and forth between them. 'You're identical.' Her voice was filled with shock. 'Even if I studied you for days I couldn't tell you apart. I thought that only happened in the movies...' She drew in a breath and Gabe frowned. He wasn't normally jealous of Aaron, but he wasn't comfortable sharing Ruby's attention. Which made little sense.

'It's rare,' Gabe admitted. 'Our parents could tell the difference. When people get to know us better, they usually can.'

'It's true – I'm the handsome one, his eyes have always been too close together,' Aaron flirted, flashing Ruby another broad grin, but it dropped when her eyes narrowed.

'As I was saying, I think you got my best friend pregnant last year, Aaron. She has a daughter, Maisy – she's just turned six months,' Ruby said softly.

The shock stole Gabe's breath as he took a moment to digest her words. His eyes shot to his brother, who was shaking his head. As if sensing their agitation, one of the dogs started to yap. 'I'm sure that's not possible, Ruby. I mean, if Aaron had done that, if it were true, your friend would have told him before this, right?' He grasped at straws, striding the last couple of steps to the counter before turning to her. Sammie tried to jump up, hooking his paws into Gabe's trousers.

'She tried to tell him,' Ruby said patiently, her voice cold. 'But the man took her call and then changed his number. He gave her a false name too.' She speared Aaron with another searching look. 'Are you really not going to fess up?'

'Oh... well,' Gabe murmured as his chest tightened – caught in between wanting to protect his brother and not wanting to upset the woman he liked so much. 'I'm sure this is a simple mistake. The Aaron I know wouldn't do something like that.' His eyes shifted from hers and met his brother's. 'Would you?' He could hear the uncertainty in his voice and wanted to kick himself. He was supposed to be protecting Aaron – it was what his father had wanted. He wasn't supposed to let his feelings for a woman get between them. It's why he'd finished with Camilla, dismissed the stories she'd told him about Aaron. He had to put his brother first – why couldn't he bring himself to do the same now?

'Never,' Aaron said tightly, his green eyes wide as he gazed back. They were the exact shape and shade of green as his own, but in this moment Gabe couldn't read them. He had no idea if Aaron was lying, which was odd. 'This is an awful misunderstanding. Like Gabe says, a mistake. Sounds like your friend met someone all right, but it wasn't either of us.'

'There's a photo of Aaron with Anna on her social media account. It was taken at the Spring Carnival last year and that's about the time she got pregnant.' Ruby folded her arms.

'That doesn't mean anything. Strangers get photographed together all the time,' Aaron said, sounding defensive.

'You're kissing.' Ruby looked at his brother like a bug she wanted to squash. 'In one Anna is sitting on your lap – you do that with a lot of strangers?'

Aaron flushed as he glanced at Gabe. 'Photos are easy to misinterpret. These kinds of shots aren't always accurate – the man could be someone else. Let's face it, I look like my brother – you couldn't tell us apart. It could even be him?' He flashed Gabe a cheeky grin.

'I don't make a habit of sleeping with women I barely know,' Gabe muttered. He knew his brother was joking, but it wasn't appropriate; he had to take this seriously. 'My brother wouldn't do something so callous.' Gabe gazed at Ruby, taking in the strain around her eyes. This was harder on her than she was making out. He knew her history, knew how she felt about her father – perhaps this was a simple case of transference? 'I'm sorry, but I think this might be a misunderstanding. Perhaps your friend – or you – have got it wrong?'

'I have evidence,' Ruby seethed, digging into her bag and pulling out her mobile. 'On Instagram, there are the pictures on Anna's account.' Gabe watched as she flicked through a series of pictures, her mouth tightening as she searched. 'Hang on,' she murmured as she continued to scroll, her eyes growing wide. 'They're gone. Everything from before October has been erased.' She gulped and looked up into his face. 'Anna must have deleted them.' Her eyes skidded to Aaron. 'She doesn't want me to find you, but I was hoping...' She swallowed. 'I thought you'd want to meet your baby.'

Gabe's heart sank as he watched Ruby check her mobile again, shaking her head. Then her expression softened as she scanned through some other photos and shoved the screen under Aaron's nose. 'This is my friend and her baby. She's got purple hair, which makes her easy to remember.' Gabe watched his brother carefully for signs he recognised her. 'Maisy's eyes are the same green as yours,' she added, sounding desperate.

Aaron gazed at it for a few seconds, his expression one of cool disinterest, then he pursed his lips and shook his head. 'She doesn't jog any memories – the kid's cute and yes, her eyes are green, but it's not an uncommon colour.' His attention shot to Gabe. 'We both have the same shade. I'm sure whoever the dad is will be delighted to hear about her once you track him down. What about you – do you recognise her?' He looked at Gabe, and Ruby reluctantly flipped the phone around so he could see. He took his time studying the woman. She was pretty, and the bright hair colour would make her difficult to forget. The baby had huge eyes – and yes, the shape and colour were familiar. But that didn't prove anything.

Gabe cleared his throat, glancing at Ruby when she dropped her hand. 'I'm sorry – I don't recognise her. Thousands of people come to Indigo Cove for the Spring Carnival, so I guess that's not necessarily a surprise. I know I spent most of it in the brewery last year, so I'd have been unlikely to bump into her.' He blew out a breath, eager to help. 'How about I give you my number so you can send me a copy of the picture. I could show it around, see if anyone remembers anything. Perhaps we could share it with The Marples at our next meeting?' He shrugged. 'Between them, we might be able to find something. To see if anyone recognises her. A lot of the locals will have photos from last year – we could get people to check and see what they can find.' He was keen to assist, both to convince Ruby it couldn't be Aaron and also because he wanted to. He hated seeing her so upset.

He watched her consider the offer and was pleased when she nodded. 'Okay. Sharing it with The Marples is a good idea. I'll print out some copies of the photo, see what we can learn.' She speared Aaron with a hostile glare. 'I'll also speak to Anna, see if she'll give me those missing pictures.'

Aaron cleared his throat noisily as something crashed in the back of the brewery and Rex and Sammie began to bark, scampering towards the door. 'That sounds bad. Why don't I see if Jago needs help. I hope you find the man you're looking for... I'll, um. Leave you two to catch up.' He didn't wait for a response; instead, he bounded over to the doorway and disappeared through it, taking both of the dogs.

When the door slammed behind him, Gabe turned back to Ruby. 'I'm sure if we investigate more, we'll track down the father,' he said softly, fighting the urge to reach out and rub her shoulder. So many emotions were at war in her face that he couldn't read them, but he could see confusion, definitely worry and hurt.

Ruby stared at him, considering. The moment reminded Gabe so much of Camilla, when she'd worked herself up to telling him that Aaron had made a pass at her. His brother had denied it of course, and that had spelled the end of the relationship. It had hurt, but he'd known then he had to put Aaron first. So why wasn't he turning his back on Ruby now?

'I know we need to investigate further, but I saw the photo and it was Aaron,' she muttered, shoving the phone back into her handbag. 'I just want you to know.'

Gabe took in a long breath. 'Aaron isn't always reliable, but he'd never lie about something like this,' he said, knowing he sounded desperate. 'I don't want to offend you, or tell you that you're mistaken. I believe there were photos.' His eyes moved to Ruby's handbag where she'd stashed the mobile. 'But I also know how easy it can be to get the wrong end of the stick. My twin is a friendly guy.' He shoved his hands in his pockets and leaned back on his heels. 'He's popular with women. At his worst I'd call him an incurable flirt. But he wouldn't do this.' He held her eyes and felt that frisson of heat again, tried to ignore it. 'If he had, if he thought he'd got a woman pregnant, I'll tell you now he'd say it was him.' His voice had deepened, filled with emotion. He badly wanted Ruby to believe him. He didn't want Aaron to get between them. 'I'll help you look,' he offered. 'My dad always taught us about taking responsibility for our actions, about doing the right thing. If the father of your friend's child is in Indigo Cove, I promise we'll find him.' His eyes drifted to the door that led to the office. 'And Aaron will help.'

Ruby bit her lip, staring at him. For a minute, he wondered

what she was going to say. If she'd refuse, bat away his offer, walk out and never come back. It was disconcerting how much lighter he felt when she nodded.

'Okay,' she said softly, and he felt his body relax. He wondered what had got into him – and whether spending more time with Ruby was the right thing to do. He knew he already had feelings for her; should he risk letting them grow? Especially considering her thoughts on Aaron... Then again, if he really wanted to protect his brother, surely the best idea would be to keep her close.

9

'Painting.' Gryffyn scratched his salt and pepper beard as he frowned at the four pots Lila had set up on his worktable. 'I thought this was supposed to be a pottery course?' He picked up his mug of black coffee and sipped slowly, glaring at the perfectly sculpted pieces that Lila had pre-prepared for the class.

'I prefer drawing with charcoals,' Darren challenged, swiping a shiny black curl of hair from his neck. 'Painting pottery's boring.'

'How would you know until you try it?' Gryffyn muttered, his eyebrows meeting as he studied the boy, who held his eyes for a beat before jerking them away.

'I love painting!' Patricia declared, clapping her hands as Ned, who was standing beside her, grimaced. 'I used to do loads of stuff in watercolours and oils with our kids when they were your age.' She nodded at Darren, who looked surprised. 'They're both travelling around Australia at the moment. I miss them... It's why this course is such a lifeline,' she continued. 'I've been missing the company, especially of younger ones.' Her mouth pinched.

'I'm glad coming here is helping,' Lila said, her expression kind. 'I think doing something creative could solve a lot of the world's problems. It's always helped me.'

'I prefer numbers,' Ruby interjected, wishing she hadn't when her Nanou's eyes clouded.

'I'm all for numbers, sweetie, but sometimes a little unpredictability is necessary for us to thrive,' Lila said quietly. 'Where would we be if we all knew exactly what to expect?'

'Bored,' Darren muttered, and Lila gave him an approving nod.

'I don't know about any of that, but I redecorated our bathroom last week and it definitely helped me to think. I'm not sure that's the kind of painting you mean, though,' Ned joked, reaching out to squeeze his wife's shoulder as she gave him a wistful smile.

Lila swept her cat Ginger off her teaching table before plucking a small paintbrush from her hair and waving it at the class. 'So it's day three of our course, and I thought after the last two when we were focusing on using the wheel and creating shapes, it might be a good idea for you to learn how to decorate your pieces. Then we can look at painting your own work later in the week.' She picked up a pot from her table and dabbed the dry brush over it. 'It's all about taking your time. As you'll discover throughout today, there are a lot of different finishes and looks you can achieve. Knowing what's possible may influence what you decide to make in the classes in future, which is why we're focusing on this today.' She raised an eyebrow at Gryffyn, who continued to sip from his mug. 'We're going to start simple. These bowls are all fired and ready to jazz up – I'll show you how to glaze them after you paint and I re-fire them tonight.' She put the container down and walked around the studio. 'What I love about this stage of the process is that you rarely know exactly what your work will look like when it comes out of the kiln.' She clapped her hands, her cheeks ruddy with excitement. Lila loved pottery; it seemed to glow from her every pore. Ruby even found her insides twitching with excitement as her Nanou continued to talk. 'Every time I get the pottery out of the kiln, it's like unwrapping a present from Father Christmas!'

'You mean you sometimes end up with a lump of coal?' Gryffyn asked dryly.

Lila chuckled and shook her head. 'Not in my class – at least, not unless you misbehave.' She winked. 'I've given you all a selection of underglazes to work with; there's a guide too, so you can see how the colours are likely to look once they've been fired. There's a selection of sketch pads along the back counter if you want to prepare your designs in advance. Perhaps you'd like to paint a set, or a random collection. You'll get to keep whatever you make and decorate, so consider what will work in your home. Ruby and I are on hand if you have any questions or need advice.'

Gryffyn gulped the rest of his coffee and clunked the mug noisily onto one of the shelves before shoving on his glasses and picking up one of the bowls, rotating it in his fingers as he studied it, almost dropping the thing in the process. 'Pedestrian shape, but at least there are no cracks,' he grumbled.

Lila patted a hand against her chest and beamed. 'Be still, my heart. Gryffyn Brown – was that a compliment?'

Darren chortled, Ned snorted, and Ruby fought a smile as the old man's cheeks flamed. He flipped off the glasses and slapped the bowl on his worktable. Lila had been teasing Gryffyn mercilessly over the last two days, trying to get him to relax. She'd always had a way with people, a knack for cutting through barriers and getting them on side – Darren was definitely starting to engage more, even if his comments were still a little petulant, and Ruby wondered if her Nanou's talents would eventually work on the older man too. So far he was showing no sign of thawing. He picked up one of the brushes and studied it critically.

'I think I'm going to paint the kids' names on my bowls; that way they can use them when they come back from their trip,' Patricia said, picking up her brush.

Beside her, Ned let out a long sigh. 'I've no idea what I'm doing.' He grabbed one of the larger brushes and randomly shoved it into one of the paint pots.

'Slow down,' Gryffyn barked from the other side of the room. 'Think about what you're trying to achieve. What it's saying to you. Pick it up, see if it speaks.'

'Seriously?' Ned's mouth twitched, but he picked up the small bowl and held it in the warm morning sunlight, which was now streaming into the studio from the skylights above. 'Did it just say "paint me"?' He grinned, Patricia barked out a laugh, and Darren snorted into his hand.

'Yes, lad,' Gryffyn said to Ned before Lila could respond. 'If you can hear that, it means you're on the right lines.'

'I don't understand.' Ned looked confused.

Gryffyn gazed skywards before nodding. 'Okay, let's try this. What's your favourite colour?'

'Blue,' Ned said slowly.

'So start with that. Think of patterns, the line of the clay, the way the bowl shape is formed. There's a rhythm to it, like it was meant to be that way – do you want to paint something in the centre? Concentrate.' Gryffyn held up his pottery, swirling one of his long fingers around the inside to illustrate.

'I like fishing,' Ned said, as his imagination caught and his face illuminated. 'I could add something, a picture – water, maybe even a trout?' He wriggled excitedly, waving his brush.

'A goldfish might be better?' Lila pointed to the bowls in front of him on the table. 'If you use that orange, it will really pop against the blue.'

'A pond!' Ned declared, bouncing on his heels. 'We had one in our old garden with three koi carp, but the frost got to them last winter and we knew we were moving so I didn't get more.'

Patricia nodded. 'They were beautiful fish, we were devastated. It took Ned months to get over losing them.'

'I miss my fish. We're going to put a pond in at the new house in the autumn.' Ned sighed as a notch appeared in his forehead. 'But I could paint my fish in the meantime – put Mathis, Kaleb and Jerry in each of the bowls so they get their own.' Ned put the piece of pottery down before rushing over to the counter along the back wall and opening one of the sketch pads. He picked up a pencil and began to draw, suddenly oblivious to everyone in the room. Ruby gazed after him as a memory prickled at the back of her mind, of her father painting with her in this exact spot. She took in a long breath and breathed out, expelling the memory, the feelings it evoked. She would not allow her father to sneak into her head; there was no space for him in her life.

'What about you, boy?' Gryffyn asked as Darren stared at his piece.

'I can't see anything, this is stupid,' he muttered, scraping a finger along the bowl.

'You sure?' Gryffyn asked quietly, staring at him as the room fell silent. 'Look harder,' he growled. 'Clear your mind.'

Darren's lips pursed as he stared, then his face cleared. 'I might see something,' he said, his lips twitching. He put the bowl down, giving Gryffyn an odd look. Then he moved to join Ned beside the sketch pads. Seconds later, he was drawing.

'Bravo.' Lila's attention slid back to Gryffyn, her grey eyes sparking. 'If I hadn't read your questionnaire, I'd have sworn you'd done this before.'

The older man frowned. 'Teaching is hardly rocket science.'

'There you go again with those compliments.' Lila giggled, her cheeks flushing pink as she watched Gryffyn carefully cradle his bowl. 'My head's going to get so big I won't be able to fit it through the entrance soon...' She turned her back to speak to Patricia, and Ruby studied Gryffyn as he looked up and watched her Nanou intently for a moment before gazing back at his bowl. He stared at the shape before he glanced around again. Then his attention caught on a shelf on the other side of the studio where an array of pottery was on display. Ruby had noticed Gryffyn studying the same objects a few days before and watched him stride over to take another look.

She wandered up to join him. 'Looking for inspiration?'

'I've got some ideas, I'm just letting them settle.' He shrugged. 'This work isn't bad.' He pointed to a delicate teacup and saucer with lifelike feathers painted across the curves. Ruby had heard it described by some of Lila's previous students as a masterpiece. 'I like the lines on that one.'

'My father painted it.' Ruby didn't elaborate and Gryffyn didn't ask.

Instead, he looked more closely at a globe-shaped vase, then picked it up carefully, sliding his glasses back onto his nose. 'That pattern would be hard to get right, especially on porcelain. That's complicated and very well done.' His lips thinned.

'My grandmother made it,' Ruby said quietly. 'She's very talented. You'll learn a lot from her on this course.'

'Perhaps... or maybe I've learned everything I need to know.' Gryffyn glanced across the room at Lila. 'So you're a family of potters?'

'I'm an accountant.' Lila must have heard because she left Patricia who was now dabbing paint onto the base of her bowl and strode over to join them.

'My granddaughter has a unique creative flair, but...' Lila shrugged. 'Unfortunately, she gave it all up for a life of numbers.' She smiled, taking any bite out of the words.

'You can't have both?' Gryffyn asked, his eyebrows drawing together as he seemed to see Ruby properly for the first time.

'Keeps life simple if I focus on one thing at a time,' Ruby said lightly. 'Besides, I was only ever passable at pottery, but I'm a genius with a spreadsheet. At least, that's what I've been told. And I make a decent living at it, so I focus all my energy on that. This is just a holiday,' she added when his eyes skirted the room. 'I'm here to help my grandmother while her assistant's away.'

'This was also an excellent opportunity for my granddaughter to take a break.' Lila winked at Gryffyn, making Ruby wonder if she'd somehow been duped into coming. Had this been more about her Nanou getting her here and less about her needing help? She couldn't really blame her; she'd avoided coming for too long.

Before Ruby could ask, the older man nodded. 'Being the best at something is hard to give up, but sometimes you have no choice in the matter. Make sure you have an idea of what you'll do with your life if for any reason you have to give up accountancy.' With that, he abruptly turned and walked back to his workstation.

'Intriguing,' Lila said, watching as Gryffyn picked up his pot. 'I know why you gave all this up, pet,' she said quietly. 'But shutting down a whole part of yourself is a mistake. You might just find it popping out in other parts of your life. Places you might not expect.' With that, she strode back to her teaching station to watch the other students as they painted. Ruby ignored the overwhelming need to join in, and dug her hands into the pockets of her shorts. She could feel that tautness across her chest, the odd tension, and fought to suppress it. She wanted to get her hands on some pottery, wanted to pick up one of the brushes. But if she did, she was afraid she wouldn't be able to stop. And if she let pottery back into her life, allowed her heart to unfurl even a little, how long would it be before she let other, more dangerous things into her world too?

She shook her head, looking around the studio. Gryffyn was still staring at his pot. Suddenly, he picked it up and dabbed on a wisp of dark blue underglaze before switching to red and then yellow. His strokes were tidy, intricate and exact – although every now and then Ruby noticed his hand shake. A tiny jerk of the wrist later and an almost imperceptible blur marred the pattern, but Ruby wasn't sure if the older man saw it. Gryffyn continued to flick his brush, taking his time, his body stiff with concentration as he slowly added to the colours, creating a beautiful multicoloured pattern that spread across the piece. Then he added a bird in the centre of the bowl with delicate wings that looked lifelike. When he'd finished, Ruby moved closer to study it in detail.

'That's going to be beautiful – a masterpiece!' Lila cleared her throat, approaching Gryffyn as he added a few finishing touches before placing the bowl carefully on the work surface.

He slid his glasses onto his nose again to examine it. He nodded and almost smiled, then twisted the piece slowly clockwise until he spotted the mistake. 'No, it's not,' he groaned. He sighed, picked up the pot and walked over to one of the bins at the edge of the studio before throwing it in. The smash as it hit the bottom was loud, and it was obvious the bowl hadn't survived. Then Gryffyn marched into the kitchen and the room fell silent as Ned, Darren and Patricia studied the pottery they were working on.

'Do you think we should hide these before Gryffyn chucks them out too?' Ned joked, clearing his throat. 'Because I've got to say, my work isn't a patch on his. Although, Darren, you'll give him a run for his money. That is stunning.' The younger man flushed and the edge of his mouth jerked up. He'd painted a series of monkeys and cats across the side of the pot. The effect was beautiful.

'Just proving cats and monkeys can work,' he joked, flushing.

Lila chuckled. 'You're right, love. It's brilliant, your paintings are all brilliant. No one on this course is here to judge –

you're all uniquely talented and...' She trailed off as Gryffyn returned with a mug filled with black coffee. He stomped back to his worktable and picked up the next bowl, glaring at it and muttering under his breath. 'I think we need music – one incense stick wasn't enough to cleanse this negativity!' Lila declared, opening her record player and flicking through her vinyl before selecting a record and putting it on. Seconds later, 'Feeling Good' by Nina Simone filled the studio. Ruby knew this was her Nanou's go-to track when she wanted to pacify the students – or encourage her tomato plants to bear more fruit. 'That'll get your creative juices flowing!'

'Don't you have anything from this century?' Darren moaned.

'Listen to the words, let them flow through you,' Lila soothed, and the teen frowned before tipping up his ear. Then the door flew open, and Gabe strode into the studio.

'Good morning!' he said, his eyes instantly finding Ruby. She swallowed as awareness skittered through her. What was it about this man? She'd hoped after what had happened this morning that the attraction would fizzle out. It would be better all round, considering what she believed about Aaron and how determined Gabe was to protect him.

'You made it!' Lila turned the music down and gave Gabe a quick peck on the cheek. 'The latest batch of tankards have turned out really well. You're getting better. Class, this is Gabe, he and his brother run the Roskilly Brewery.'

'Do you make Deep Water Ale?' Ned asked.

'Some of my mates drink that, they think it's ace,' Darren muttered in a rare moment of openness.

'It's our signature brew.' Gabe nodded.

'I tried some in the Lobster Pot Inn and it was—' Ned mimed kissing his fingers. Beside him Patricia nodded enthusiastically.

Gabe grinned. 'We aim to please.'

'Why are you making tankards?' Patricia asked, as she swiped a few finishing touches onto one of her bowls. On the other side of the room, Gryffyn continued to stare blankly at his second. Ruby watched him pinch one of his hands with the other before straightening it out. There was definitely something wrong, but what?

'The tankards are to go with a special edition brew we're creating at the moment. We're going to give them away with larger barrels of our new ale to celebrate the brewery centenary. The idea is that each tankard has been made and hand-painted by the owners themselves.' Gabe waggled his fingers. 'I've got an hour and a half's break before I have to run a brewery tour, so I thought I could get a few painted before then. Time's running out to finish.' He nodded at Lila. 'We've been working on this together for a couple of months now and I've made ninety-eight tankards. The goal is to get to a hundred, so I'm almost done.'

'How many have you painted?' Gryffyn asked gruffly, glancing up from his undecorated bowl.

Gabe pulled a face. 'This will be my first. They all need finishing before the end of July. It's why I've decided to start coming here in the daytime.'

'The tankards are in the back room if you want to grab one. Ruby will show you.' Lila pointed to the empty table beside Patricia. 'We're going to be here all day, so you can dip in and out if you like. Did you decide on the colours?'

Gabe nodded. 'I finally pinned Aaron down.' His eyes flicked to Ruby. 'We're going for black and white with a red trim, to match our logo.'

Lila nodded. 'Ruby can help you pick the correct shades – you might want to spend a minute with her to make sure you get the best match. Think of her as your teacher-stroke-assistant for the next couple of weeks. If you're doing the painting alone, you're going to want some help. Do you have a copy of the logo with you?'

Gabe nodded and Ruby swept her arm towards the back, guiding him into their small storeroom. She could feel a buzz across her back, a reaction to him being close. She grabbed one of the colour charts and held it up as the pressure in her chest increased. 'Do you want to see which colours are the best match?' Her voice sounded a little off key, but Gabe didn't seem to notice.

He swiped his wallet from his pocket, slid out a business card and held it next to the chart. 'I think those two.'

'They'll work,' Ruby said, studying him. 'I'll get them ready.' She turned her back to pour some of the underglaze into smaller bowls to make them easier for Gabe to work with. He leaned on the counter beside her. She could feel his eyes on her and her stomach knotted.

'I showed the photo you sent me to everyone who works in the brewery before I came,' he said quietly. 'No luck, I'm afraid, but I'll keep asking. We need to show it to The Marples at our meeting tomorrow. If we're lucky, the father will be local and we'll track him down.'

'Thank you.' Ruby turned to look at him. 'I appreciate the help. Even if I'm not sure why you are helping.' She frowned. 'You know I still think it's Aaron?'

Gabe shrugged. 'Maybe I just want to prove to you he's not.' He shoved his hands into his pockets. 'My brother has been accused of a lot of things. He's not a saint, but... he's not all bad either.' His voice had deepened and suddenly the room felt smaller.

'Time will tell.' Ruby jerked her head. She cleared her throat, battling her growing feelings for him. 'I have to get on,' she muttered, as she grabbed the pots of paint and marched out of the room. She already admired and liked Gabe more than she wanted. Added to that, she knew Aaron was Maisy's father and intended to do everything she could to prove it.

Which meant allowing this attraction to grow would be a

disaster. But for the first time in a very long time, Ruby wondered if she was strong enough to control it.

10

Dear Rue,

It was SO brilliant to hear from you. I almost dropped my beer when I opened the email. I'm still in Spain, but now I know you're in Indigo Cove, I'll book a flight and make sure I visit before you leave. It's been a long time. Too long. I tried to call a few times, but I think you've changed your number? Or maybe you've blocked me, ha, ha. I'm hoping your email means you're ready to put everything behind us. You're obviously worried about Nanou, but don't be. I've got this investment in the pipeline and it's a sure thing. I know I've said that a hundred times before, but this time I mean it. I know people here, important people, and this is going to be huge. I can't say anything else because I don't want to jinx it, but I guarantee everything's going to come good. We're talking LOTS and LOTS of money, all the things I promised you and your mum. You wouldn't believe how much people are making. I'll pay every penny back to Nanou with interest. It's just going to take time. Can't wait to see you.

Saludos,

Dad x

Ruby slammed the lid of the laptop and shut her eyes. She'd always hated her dad's nickname for her – Rue. It implied a level of intimacy they simply didn't have. She wasn't worried he'd follow through on his intention to visit, though – after all the birthdays, school plays and exhibitions he'd assured her he'd be there for and then missed, she was certain he wouldn't get around to it. Something would catch the interest of his butterfly brain and he'd forget. Leopards didn't change their spots – it's why she didn't believe in giving people second chances.

Her Nanou could kiss goodbye to her savings, though – if her dad had already invested them, they were gone. He'd taken money from her mother whenever he'd visited and stuck it into whatever crackpot scheme he had on the go – and every one of those had failed too. Or even if they hadn't, she and her mother had never seen a penny of the promised goldmine.

She headed into the hall to open the door of the office. It looked awful and smelled worse than it had when she'd arrived four days before. Tomorrow she'd rip up the carpet and throw it away, see if she could contain the damage. It might not be as bad as her Nanou thought. She stepped further into the room and grabbed a handful of colour photos from the printer. There were ten in total – most were recent shots of Anna and Maisy, but she'd printed some of Anna separately just in case. She tucked them into her handbag as Lila called out.

'Ruby, are you ready to go to The Marples? Gabe's just finished painting his tenth tankard and it's drying, so he's already left for home to pick up the dogs. Apparently, Aaron was supposed to watch them this evening, but something important came up.'

Ruby shook her head, irritated on Gabe's behalf. Of course

his brother had let him down. What would Gabe do once Aaron was finally exposed as Maisy's father? The idea of upsetting him made her uncomfortable. He was obviously a good man, unwilling to see the truth about his brother. It was one of the reasons she liked him so much. How many years had it taken her to finally see through her dad? In some ways they were kindred spirits. 'I'm ready.' Ruby dashed back into her bedroom to check her make-up and scrape a brush through her hair, studying herself critically before swiping on more lipstick.

Lila was waiting for her in the hall when she walked out, looking bewildered. 'I've forgotten something, I know I have.' She glanced around the hallway, then looked down before patting herself on the head, dislodging a stray paintbrush which had somehow got lost in her bun. 'Of course. I'm still wearing my apron, my hair's full of pottery tools, and my bag's in the bedroom.' She barked out a laugh. 'I blame Gryffyn Brown – the man's got me all aflutter. He's a mystery. He's definitely done pottery before, but there's something odd going on and I'm determined to find out what. Go and get yourself strapped into Beatrix, I won't be long.' She charged down the hallway towards her bedroom. Ruby stepped onto the driveway, almost tripping over one of the cats, who immediately shot between her legs and disappeared into The Little Cornish House. She climbed into the passenger seat of the Beetle and leaned her head back, fighting the waves of despair she always felt after any contact with her dad. She didn't know why he still got to her, had never managed to entirely tune him out.

Lila emerged a few minutes later and hopped into the car, clicking on her seatbelt and firing the engine. 'Did you secure the doors, Nanou?' Ruby asked, turning just in time to see that the entrance to the Pottery Project had been propped open and the front door of the house wasn't shut. 'You've left everything unlocked again!' She squeaked, holding on tight to the handle of the passenger door as Lila shot out of the drive and squealed left, joining the empty road. The roof of the car was down and the wind whistled through Ruby's hair, giving her a welcome break from the humidity.

'It's hot. We need air in the place. It'll be fine,' Lila shouted. 'I rarely lock up. Whose going to bother breaking in – there's nothing to steal aside from a slice of my coffee and walnut cake.' She grinned. 'And everyone's welcome to help themselves to that.'

'You're too trusting. I've never understood it...' Ruby shook her head, glancing in the wing mirror as Beatrix gathered pace, hurtling around a corner.

'There's good in everyone, love. You just need to know where to look,' Lila yelled, but Ruby didn't respond. They'd had similar conversations in the past and hadn't been able to agree then. Her Nanou's blind faith in the human race was a testament to her kind heart and good nature. Ruby was never sure whether to pity or admire her. Mostly it just made her exasperated.

They reached the high street in what felt like minutes. It wasn't busy and Lila screeched into the same spot she'd parked in a few evenings before. Gabe's 4x4 was parked up already, and Ruby watched him hop out and grab both dogs from the boot. He secured them to their leads, but Sammie immediately began to strain in the direction of the beach, so Gabe scooped the dog into his arms before wandering up to join them.

'He managed to get in from the back again and chomped another hunk out of the car,' Gabe said, frowning at the dog who was now trying to grab a mouthful of his green T-shirt. 'You'd think I starved him. Although Aaron was in charge of feeding them today...' He trailed off. 'I didn't check they'd eaten before I left because it was past dinnertime and my brother was already out. He had an important meeting apparently.' He scratched Sammie's head. 'Sometimes, I wish you guys could talk.'

Sammie barked and Gabe chuckled. 'Not what I meant.'

'Ella will have something in the cafe. She's started baking dog biscuits and sometimes babysits for a neighbour's poodle. I'm sure we'll be able to rustle up a meal,' Lila told him, as they crossed the road and followed the pavement that hugged the beach. 'Dog biscuits are another thing Claude's been teasing Ella about. Hopefully, he won't do it today – it's way too hot for fireworks.'

Gabe grinned. 'Claude's crazy about Ella, but he's a braver man than me. She took an instant dislike to him when he moved to Indigo Cove, and every time he teases her, it just gets worse.'

'After what happened with her husband, I suppose it makes sense,' Ruby murmured, earning herself a curious look from Gabe.

'You don't think she should give him the benefit of the doubt?' he asked. 'Claude isn't to blame for someone else's mistakes.'

Ruby shrugged. 'Once bitten, twice shy. She's just protecting herself.' Gabe gazed at her for a moment, his green eyes thoughtful, making her stomach flip.

'These things have a way of working themselves out,' Lila said sagely. 'They always do. Any news from the estate agent?' she asked, dodging a large family who were just leaving the beach, carrying bags filled with colourful towels and tubes of sun cream. Lila had mentioned over breakfast this morning that Gabe was in the process of selling a field next to the brewery.

'An estate agent from Talwynn came to see it earlier this week, but I've heard nothing since.' Gabe frowned. 'Aaron told me the man seemed keen, but I've messaged and called and heard nothing.' He scratched his head. 'I thought the market was supposed to be hot – he was excited when I first talked to him about it.'

'I'm sure he'll be in touch – summer's probably their busiest time of year,' Lila said.

'I wish I didn't have to sell at all,' Gabe confessed. 'I promised Dad we'd expand the brewery. It was his dream.' He smiled at Ruby and she found herself smiling back. Gabe was everything she admired. Loyal even to his father's ghost. He just kept chipping away at her carefully constructed walls, getting further under her skin.

'Darlings, you came!' Lila shouted, suddenly making Ruby look away. Her Nanou was waving at Ned and Patricia, who were standing outside the front of The Beach Cafe. 'I'm so happy to see you!' Lila said, sweeping them up and herding them through the cafe entrance before they could say hello. Ruby waited while Gabe put Sammie on the ground, and both dogs dashed to a water bowl that had been left out. Everyone was already seated when they finally made it inside. Claude had claimed one of the spaces on the table closest to Ella, who was ignoring him. There was the same array of cakes and hot drinks laid out, and two empty chairs side by side at the end. Gabe tied Sammie and Rex to a table leg and pulled out a seat for Ruby.

She slid into it, then cried out when Sammie immediately scrambled into her lap.

'I'm sorry,' Gabe groaned, reaching for him.

'It's okay,' Ruby said, as the small dog stretched, then closed his eyes.

'I've never seen him behave like that. He might be lulling you into trusting him before he makes his move.' He shot worried eyes at the food on the table. 'Remember, he's not to be trusted.' Strange how blind Gabe was to Aaron when he could so clearly see the tiny beagle's faults. Why was that?

'Ella already put out some of the dog biscuits she made,' Lila said, passing a handful to Gabe who was staring at Sammie, still as a statue.

'Maybe you're a good influence?' he murmured to Ruby. 'I never thought I'd see him behave. Months of training didn't produce these results. Perhaps old dogs can change?' Ruby pursed her lips but didn't respond. Gabe fed a handful of biscuits to both dogs, who gulped them down.

'Dog biscuits?' Claude asked, watching Sammie and Rex. Everyone at the table seemed to draw in a collective breath as the silence stretched.

'Why not? Are they too basic for a Michelin-starred chef?' Ella's tone was acidic.

Ruby saw the chef swallow before he shook his head. 'I was going to ask for the recipe,' he said, as Gabe pulled up a chair and began to help serve the cake and hot drinks. Ruby hadn't eaten before the meeting, so she tucked into a scone.

'I'm sure they won't be good enough for your fancy restaurant,' Ella countered, but her cheeks flushed with obvious pleasure as she looked away.

Lila stood up. 'Now that's settled, I've got good news. The Marples are expanding again! I want to introduce you all to Patricia and Ned who've just moved here from Dorset. They're doing my pottery course and wanted to meet some new people, so I thought this would be the perfect opportunity, plus we could do with the extra help.' The group waved. 'Ned is an ex-security guard, and I'm sure he's going to have lots of useful ideas about catching our vandals,' Lila continued. 'I gave them both an overview of the incidents, so they know what's going on.'

'It's shocking,' Patricia murmured, her eyes widening as Ned picked up a slice of chocolate cake and bit into it. 'We'd like to help you get to the bottom of what's happening in the village.'

'We could definitely use more people patrolling.' Clemo shook hands with them both. 'We've formed teams and have been walking around, keeping an eye out.'

'I'm sorry.' Gabe cleared his throat. 'Ruby and I got waylaid by an... incident at the brewery. So we've not managed to do our bit – but we could find a day soon?' He lifted an eyebrow in Ruby's direction.

'Ruby's free most evenings,' Lila offered before Ruby could respond. 'Come and paint more tankards one afternoon and perhaps you could head off after that?' Ruby shut her eyes when Gabe nodded. The last thing she needed was a wily Cupid trying to fix her up. What was her Nanou playing at – was this all part of her grandmother's quest to encourage her to have more fun?

Ella flicked her pad to a fresh page. 'I heard about the manure on the steps of the brewery and made a note. Nothing similar has happened in the village. Someone made off with the traffic cone next to the bus stop, but it's been surprisingly uneventful.' There were murmurs of agreement from the group.

'The fact that it's quiet is good news,' Lila said. 'Perhaps our patrols are acting as a deterrent? I suggest we continue. Patricia and Ned – if you coordinate with Ella and Claude, maybe you could do alternating evenings?'

They all nodded.

'Before I forget, I can't host our next meeting here,' Ella said suddenly. 'I've hired a crew to deep-clean the cafe on Sunday evenings for the next three weeks. Unfortunately, that means we'll have nowhere to sit.'

'We can all go to my restaurant,' Claude offered. 'I'm closed on Sunday evenings. I'll make sure there's food.' His eyes strayed to Ella. 'It will be an opportunity for me to cook for you.' He checked his watch. 'We have many bookings this evening, I told my team I wouldn't be long.' He rose from the chair and spared the crowd a quick glance. 'I'll see you on Sunday.' With that, he turned and left the cafe. Ella gazed after him with her lips pursed, then turned back to her coffee when the door shut.

'I've got something I wanted you all to see.' Judging that this was a good time to introduce a new subject, Ruby carefully reached into her bag without disturbing Sammie. She pulled out the pictures of Anna and Maisy and placed them face up on the table. 'It's a long shot, but my best friend got pregnant in Indigo Cove at some point during the Spring Carnival last year.' She'd told Lila the story earlier over a lunch of carrot cake, so the revelation wouldn't be a shock. 'The father...' She paused, trying to find the right words, aware Gabe was sitting next to her. 'May not wish to be identified. He gave my friend a false name and disconnected his phone when she tried to contact him.'

'Or Anna might have got confused?' Lila interjected, her smile bright. 'It happens. We should give the man the benefit of the doubt until we find him.' Her Nanou picked up the pictures from the table and handed them around.

'Maisy's just turned six months. I included a photo of her just in case anyone wants to see it. I'm keen to find anyone who recognises Anna. She's easy to remember because of her purple hair. They might recall where they saw her and who she was with. They may even have pictures from the carnival.'

Ned gazed at the image. 'I wasn't in Indigo Cove then, but even if I was, that's a long time ago...'

'I have an excellent memory for faces and hair,' Ella piped up. 'If I'd seen your friend, I would remember. So it wouldn't be impossible.' She frowned. 'Unfortunately, I wasn't in Indigo Cove last spring either, and Claude moved here in the autumn.' She glanced at Ned and Patricia. 'A lot of us weren't in the area at the time, but I don't mind asking my customers if you want to leave a picture here. What do you want to know exactly?'

Ruby took a breath. 'If they recognise Anna, would they be happy to speak to me? I want to track down the man she spent time with. He might want to know he's got a daughter.'

'I know I would,' Gabe said quietly, making Ruby's heart stutter. 'I've shown all of my staff and a few customers already, but I'll take a picture to put up in the brewery shop.' He grabbed one, folded it and slid it into his pocket.

'Thank you,' Ruby said.

'What about the photography exhibition in Talwynn?' Clemo ran a hand through his beard. Talwynn was a large town about a twenty-minute drive from the coast which housed their local hospital, main library and town hall. Ruby hadn't been for years.

'I thought all the pictures in that exhibition were of buildings?' Ella asked.

Clemo shook his head. 'I heard the photographer did some collages using shots from events in the local area. Word is she included some from the Indigo Cove Spring Carnival last year. I know because I'm supposed to be in one. I've been meaning to go. It might be worth checking out?'

'I could take you,' Gabe offered, turning to Ruby. 'I need to go to Talwynn anyway; I want to speak to the estate agent and find out why he's been ignoring my calls. They have offices on the main high street.'

'Tomorrow would be a good day,' Lila jumped in. 'Because we only do a half-day on a Friday.'

'Sounds good,' Gabe agreed, before Ruby could think of an excuse. She nodded, already fully aware that spending more time with the man was probably a bad idea. The more she knew of Gabe, the more she couldn't help liking him – and opening herself up to people had only led to disappointment in the past.

11

Aggravated, Ruby paced at the front of The Little Cornish House and checked her watch for the fifteenth time as all four of her Nanou's cats wound themselves around her feet, almost tripping her over.

'You not left yet?' Lila popped her head out of the entrance to the Pottery Project, where she'd been putting the plates Gryffyn, Ned, Darren and Patricia had made that morning into the drying room. All four cats dashed over to greet her, and Lila grabbed a handful of grapes from her pocket and began to peel them, feeding the skinless fruit to each of the cats. Lila had insisted Ruby get ready for her 'date' with Gabe and had pushed Ruby out of the studio half an hour earlier, much to her irritation. She hadn't been able to stop herself from putting on her favourite shorts, or the pink top her Nanou had said suited her, though.

'He's almost an hour late,' Ruby sighed, checking her watch again as acid gurgled unhappily in her stomach. She didn't know why she was still waiting. She'd been pacing the house, unable to settle, and had no idea why she was still here. 'He's probably not coming,' she grumbled, as memories of her father rose to the surface and she pushed them away. This was why she avoided spending time with people. This was why she kept her life free from attachments. Then again, hadn't this been what she'd wanted all along? A reason to dislike the man she'd been finding herself increasingly drawn to? She should be relieved, but she wasn't.

'Gabe will arrive,' Lila soothed, offering Ruby a grape, which she refused. They both turned towards the entrance of the drive as an engine misfired in the distance. 'Don't base all your expectations on your dad, love.' Lila frowned. 'I know Ross is my son, but not everyone's cut from the same cloth. He's a lot like his father. I loved the man, but he was full of wild dreams and hot air.' She shrugged. 'As I told your mum years ago, it's best not to expect too much. I wish she'd moved on, stopped hoping he'd change.'

'She never did,' Ruby said sadly.

'But that doesn't mean everyone's like your dad,' Lila promised. 'I've known Gabe all his life and he's as reliable as they come. He's got a solid head on those shoulders – sometimes, I think he carries way too much, he could do with lightening the load.'

Gabe's 4x4 suddenly rounded the corner and pulled up on the driveway as the cats scattered into the studio. Ruby pursed her lips as he climbed out looking harried and weary. 'I'm sorry,' he said as he tracked up to join them. 'I know I'm really late. Sammie made off with my car keys and wallet when I was showering.' He grimaced. 'He's got a habit of burying things in the garden – I had to dig around for over an hour before I found them. I dug up a pair of sunglasses and my favourite sunhat while I was looking.' He sighed as the dog barked from the back of the car. 'I meant to call but... I couldn't find my mobile either.' He glared back the Volvo. 'I think the reprobate buried that too.'

'You're here now,' Ruby said, trying hard to shake the

annoyance. 'Bye, Nanou!' She walked to the car as her temper simmered. She knew it wasn't Gabe's fault, but her father had always been full of excuses too. *My car broke down; the plane was late; I lost my passport; there's this investment that's just too good to miss; I can't deal with this crap at the moment.* Meanwhile, her mother had picked up the pieces. She opened the passenger door and climbed in. The dogs were in the back and as soon as they saw her, they began to bark.

'Simmer down. We've got company,' Gabe murmured, firing up the car and turning right out of the drive, in the opposite direction to the harbour. Ruby opened her window and stared out at the lush hedgerows. The weather was hot again and the breeze was welcome. After about ten minutes of silence, Gabe pulled up in a layby beside a field of pink and blue wildflowers. 'I'm really sorry.' He touched Ruby's arm, sending a shiver of awareness skidding across her skin. She turned to face him; he looked genuinely upset. 'You've told me enough about your father for me to get I've cocked up. I understand about being let down.' The edge of his full mouth rose. 'It's not a good excuse, but I've got a lot on my plate at the moment... I know that doesn't mean being late was okay. I can only apologise and tell you it won't happen again.' He looked into the back of the car again and fixed Sammie with a stare. 'Will it, Sammie?'

Ruby looked at her hands, touched by the apology which had felt so genuine. 'I'm sorry too. I have a few... triggers. People not turning up and not calling if they're going to be late are two of them.'

'I get it,' Gabe said softly. 'It makes you feel like you don't matter.' He let out a breath and gazed out of the front of the car. 'But I promise that's not true.' The tips of his cheekbones flushed and he didn't look at her. Ruby's heart skipped a beat and her whole body broke out in goosebumps. 'Being reliable, on time, and never breaking my word. All those things were ingrained into me my whole life by my parents. So much so that

I've been accused of being dull... But being dependable matters. Some people jump out of parachutes, but reliable and boring is my thing.' He glanced in the interior mirror at the reflection of the dogs. 'At least, it was...' He grimaced. 'Now, we'd better change the subject before I send you to sleep.'

'I don't think you're boring,' Ruby said, her voice husky.

'I appreciate that. You might want to reserve judgement until you've spent a full day in my company,' Gabe murmured. 'I've got smelling salts somewhere just in case you drift off.' He tapped his pocket and offered her a shy smile.

She reached over and brushed her fingertips on his arm, ignoring his look of surprise and the tingles that spread across her skin before turning to face the front. The moment felt intimate, as though they'd connected on a level she didn't understand, wasn't sure she wanted to. 'We'd better get going if we're going to see this exhibition,' she said.

Gabe fired the engine and pulled out without saying a word, leaving Ruby thinking that every time she tried to draw away from Gabe, he managed to break through her defences a little more.

The photography exhibition was in the Talwynn town hall, a large Victorian building with marble pillars that framed the entrance at the top of a run of wide steps. When they were halfway up, Gabe stopped and cursed.

'Dammit, I didn't think about the dogs.' He frowned, looking down at Sammie and Rex. 'I won't be able to take them inside, and I can't leave them here on their own – they'll probably start a riot or worse.' He swiped a hand across his forehead. 'That was stupid.'

'It's fine,' Ruby said. 'I didn't think about it either. If you can wait, I won't be long. I'll check the collages and take pictures if they'll let me. As long as you're happy for me to go in alone?'

Would Gabe trust whatever she found? If there was a picture of Aaron and Anna together, would he be angry, or try to convince her she was mistaken?

'So long as you promise to come back,' Gabe said, glancing around. 'There's somewhere at the top of the steps in the shade. I know someone in the town hall leaves water bowls out, so we can wait there.' He trotted up the steps just ahead of Ruby, and she observed him for a moment – saw how he waited patiently for the dogs, how women turned and watched as he passed. She felt a twinge of jealousy and pushed it away before making her way up the steps too and wandering inside the building. The town hall ceiling was vaulted and the marble theme continued. She asked a curator for directions and made her way into a room on her right where a selection of pictures were displayed. The area was empty and she was able to study the photos alone. She recognised the first picture as Indigo Cove harbour. It must have been taken in the evening because dozens of boats were moored and the beach was empty – aside from a flock of seagulls. The photographer had caught the sunset and played with the light, giving it an unreal pinkish hue. There were ten more prints of locations and buildings Ruby guessed were from villages further down the Cornish coast. She took time studying each one, hoping if she looked carefully, she'd spot Anna and Aaron like characters in a *Where's Wally?* picture book.

She continued to move along the wall studying each photograph in turn, aware Gabe was waiting with the dogs, wondering if he'd still be alone when she got outside or if some smart woman would have set her sights on him. 'You're being ridiculous,' Ruby muttered, and moved to the next picture. The collages Clemo had mentioned were at the end of the wall and there were three in total, all framed in gilt like the rest. She studied the first, staring at the people behind the glass. It took her a while to adjust her vision to the mass of eyes and noses, trying to see if she recognised anyone in the sea of faces. She worked her way from the top left down, scanning vertically as if she were studying a tricky set of accounts. Ruby was used to detailed work, used to searching for clues, numbers that didn't fit. She grinned and let out a small squeak of delight when she spotted Clemo eating a Cornish pasty, convinced now that she was going to find something to prove Aaron had been with Anna – but there were no more familiar faces. The second picture featured an array of buildings, and in the centre Ruby spotted a huge carnival wheel similar to the one Indigo Cove hosted during the Spring Carnival. She looked closer, wishing she had a way of making the pictures bigger.

'Of course!' she groaned, pulling out her mobile and glancing behind to make sure no one was watching. She took a picture so she could blow it up on her computer later, study it more closely just in case she'd missed a face. She did the same with the next picture, checking her watch. She'd been inside for twenty minutes now – a long time for a man and two dogs to wait. Would Gabe grow impatient? Would he still be there? Her insides knotted and she took a few more shots, scanning to see if anything caught her eye. She'd known this was a long shot, but that didn't soften her disappointment. The thought of Maisy growing up without knowing who her father was twisted her insides. She knew Anna wasn't keen on her searching, but her friend had a good relationship with her dad. She had no idea about the pain of being abandoned. No sense of how Maisy would feel in years to come, how lonely she might feel.

She turned back to the final photo. It showed fewer people and the colours were muted, giving the collage a retro feel. Ruby stared at the bottom right, skimming upwards until she let out a small gasp. 'Anna!' Her friend was standing next to a candyfloss stall, grinning. Her shining eyes were fixed on someone to her right – and when Ruby leaned closer, she could see an arm resting on her shoulders. But the person's face had been obscured. 'Dammit.' She traced a fingertip over the picture, wishing she could peel the glass up and look below.

'No touching!' She jerked around. A curator stood at the entrance, glaring. 'You'll leave fingerprints,' he complained, marching over and pulling a cloth from his pocket to polish the glass until it shone.

'I'm sorry, it's just... I'm trying to find someone. That's my friend.' Ruby pointed to Anna. 'I want to know who she was with, but the person is hidden. It's important I find them.'

'You'll have to contact the photographer,' the man snapped. 'There are business cards by the entrance. If you call, they might be able to help. If not, whoever's in that photo with your friend is going to have to remain a mystery.'

'Okay, I'll get in touch,' Ruby said, leaning closer to the photo. Just a few more inches and she'd have all the evidence she needed to prove to Gabe that his brother had been lying. 'Could you show me where the cards are, please?'

The curator nodded and marched back towards the exit. Ruby kept an eye on him and pulled her mobile from her pocket again to snap a quick shot of the section that included Anna so she'd remember where it was, before following him out.

12

Jones & Jones Estate Agents was heaving when Gabe walked inside the large open office. There were four desks, all busy with clients, so he decided to wait. He could see Ruby from the large window at the front of the shop and found himself hovering so he could watch her. Sammie and Rex were sitting on their haunches as she chatted to them in that low, sexy voice, stroking each of them in turn. Even Sammie was behaving, his eyes round with adoration as he watched her. He felt something pitch in his chest and turned away, determined to ignore it. That would be a terrible idea, in a year when he could do without any more of them. She was Lila's granddaughter and she was leaving Indigo Cove in a couple of weeks – added to that, she was convinced Aaron was the father of her friend's child. He'd spent years protecting his brother, had lost one girlfriend because of it. He wasn't about to let Aaron down now... But it didn't stop the connection he could feel building between them, the frisson of awareness he was finding it harder and harder to ignore.

A couple passed him on the way out of the shop, and a

woman wearing a dark blue suit immediately stood and strolled out from behind her desk. 'Can I help?' she beamed.

'I hope so.' Gabe reached into his pocket and pulled out the slip of paper he'd noted the information about the field on. 'I was dealing with Mr Jones – I'm selling some land and he came to see it on Monday, but I've been having trouble getting hold of him since. I wondered if he was sick?'

The woman's eyebrows rose. 'That's odd. He's my husband and he's been at work all week. Can you tell me a little more?' She guided him towards her desk and sat, perching her glasses on her nose before studying the computer. 'Your name?'

The moment Gabe told her, the temperature in the room seemed to drop. 'Ahhh, Mr Roskilly – I remember, you're the one trying to sell the field beside the brewery in Indigo Cove?' Her voice was clipped.

'That's right.' Gabe leaned back in his chair, feeling uncomfortable. 'Is something wrong?'

The woman folded her arms. 'I'm sorry, but we're not able to represent you at this time. My husband should have explained. Our books are completely full, and we don't have the manpower to manage your sale. Fortunately, there are plenty of other estate agents in Talwynn you could speak to.' For the first time since she'd stepped out from behind her desk, she avoided Gabe's eyes.

'I'm confused,' he said gruffly. 'Did we do something wrong? Your husband was keen when we spoke on the phone. He didn't mention you were too busy. He drove out to visit...'

'I really can't help,' the woman said abruptly, standing and staring until Gabe was forced to rise too. 'I wish you luck.' She herded him towards the exit until he was standing back on the high street, staring at the door she'd just closed in his face.

'What the hell?' Gabe took in a long breath. What exactly had happened? This made no sense.

'Everything okay?' Ruby called from the other side of the road. He crossed and slumped beside her on the bench.

'I'm not sure.' He frowned. Sammie jumped up to put his paws on Gabe's knees. 'What happened with the photographer?' he asked, keen to change the subject.

Ruby frowned. 'She's away. Family emergency. She said she can't get access to the photos until she's in the country.'

'When will she be back?' he asked.

Ruby's pretty eyes narrowed. 'She's not sure. Could be a week, might be two. She promised to call as soon as she knows.'

Gabe nodded. 'Hopefully, some other clues about the father's identity will come up in the meantime. Once The Marples get their hands on a mystery, not much gets in their way.'

Ruby stared at him. 'What's wrong? I can see something is by that look on your face. What happened with the estate agent?'

Gabe wasn't used to sharing his problems with anyone. Mostly because there was no one to share them with aside from Jago – and he didn't want to worry someone who relied on the brewery for their pay cheque. It would be a relief to unload, even if he knew he shouldn't, but Ruby was hard to say no to. 'The woman told me they can't sell the field because they can't handle any more work. I've never heard of an estate agent being too busy, have you?'

Ruby frowned. 'That's odd. What did the company say when you first contacted them?' She leaned down to stroke Rex, and he nuzzled her hand.

'The man I spoke to, Mr Jones, was excited.' Gabe could remember the conversation clearly. 'He immediately made an appointment to view the field.'

'What did he say when you met?' Ruby studied his face.

'I didn't exactly...' Gabe paused. 'I had to head back to the brewery to run a tour and Mr Jones was late – Aaron offered to show him the field.' Ruby remained silent and Gabe rushed to fill the space. 'My brother told me everything went well, that the estate agent was really interested... I can't understand what happened.'

'How does Aaron feel about selling?' Ruby asked gently.

'It's not going to be anything he's done,' Gabe snapped, immediately regretting it. 'I'm sorry. In truth, he isn't keen, but he wants the brewery to succeed as much as I do – and we need the money. He won't have done anything to jeopardise the sale...' He trailed off, wondering who he was trying to convince. Why did looking at his brother through Ruby's eyes make him suspicious?

Ruby held up her hands. 'Do you want to try another estate agent while we're here? There are two more on this road I can see.' She pointed along the high street. 'I'll watch the dogs.'

Gabe pulled the piece of paper from his pocket. He had all the information he needed. If he was going to make this happen, he had to get on with it.

It was still hot when Gabe arrived home hours later, after dropping Ruby back at the Pottery Project. Aaron was dozing in the garden on a lounger with three empty beer bottles lined up on the table beside him. Gabe checked his watch, wondering who was closing the brewery this evening. Jago again? He hadn't asked Aaron to shut up shop, so this was on him. He sighed – he'd water the dogs, shower, and head over once he'd caught up with his brother. His head brewer could do with a break.

He strode in through the front door, which was wide open, with both dogs trotting at his heels. The cottage was ancient, with low ceilings that Gabe regularly bashed his head on when he forgot to duck. But the building had been in the family for generations and living here meant he got to feel close to the people he no longer had in his life. History mattered, seemed like it mattered more as he aged. The house had a pretty – if temperamental – thatched roof, and four bedrooms with the master situated in the loft conversion his dad had added years before. It had been their parents' room and when their father died, Aaron had claimed it. The arrangement suited them both. Aaron had his own bathroom and plenty of privacy; Gabe got the whole of the second floor, including the family bathroom and his own ensuite. Even better, he didn't have to live with all the memories of better times when they'd regularly raced each other upstairs to wake their parents.

Downstairs consisted of a large kitchen diner with the rustic units his mother had designed and his father had built, a sitting room and small conservatory at the back that boasted exquisite views of his mother's cottage garden, which Gabe did his best to keep up with when he could. Which wasn't often these days. Behind that stretched fields and fields, which were either used for farming, grazing sheep, or as a nirvana for bees and butterflies. Gabe had moved out of his rented flat and lived here since his father passed. After claiming the top bedroom, Aaron had gone back to Ibiza straight after the funeral for a few months, because 'being in Indigo Cove is hard to deal with' – although in his less charitable moments Gabe had wondered if his brother had just wanted to avoid the paperwork. Death spawned a lot of paperwork. Which wasn't his brother's strong suit. Then again, his recent dedication to the design course proved Aaron might finally be ready to take on some responsibility.

Gabe left the dogs in the kitchen with a bowl of fresh water so he could shower. When he returned, both had disappeared, but he could hear Aaron talking to them in the garden. He grabbed drinks and strode out to join in. His brother's face was drawn and he was drumming his fingers on the table, looking distracted.

'You okay?' Gabe asked, handing Aaron a glass of cold water.

'Any beer?' His brother frowned as he stopped drumming, took the drink and swallowed the lot.

'Plenty – we own a brewery, remember.' Gabe perched on the deckchair opposite the lounger and pushed his bare feet into the grass, relishing its coolness. 'I went to the estate agent today,' he said carefully.

Aaron's lips pinched. 'Problem? Because you sound just like Dad did whenever I borrowed the car without asking.' He leaned back, perching on his elbows.

'I don't know. They said they were too busy to take on the sale of the field.' Gabe paused and sat back in his seat, scrutinising his brother. It was always odd looking into your own face, but it meant Gabe was familiar with the full range of his brother's expressions. He could usually read each tick and jerk of the mouth as if they were his. Which is how he knew Aaron wasn't surprised at the news. He sipped some of the cold water, feeling a wave of disappointment wash over him, and fought to contain it. There could be a simple explanation – he'd have to wait for it. Since his illness, Aaron wasn't keen on opening up.

'That's strange. He was very enthusiastic when I talked to him.' His brother glanced down at Rex and grabbed the ball out of the dog's mouth before throwing it across the garden into their mother's best rose bush, crushing one of the flowers – all the while, avoiding Gabe's eyes. 'Perhaps we should park the idea of selling the field. Maybe the estate agent knows something we don't? Didn't Mum always say we should listen to signs?' He wiggled his fingers and stood, stretching. Aaron had lost weight; the belt on his trousers had moved down a notch. When had that happened? Was his brother not eating? Gabe stopped himself from asking, knowing Aaron would accuse him of trying to parent him – at thirty-one he was way past needing that, he knew. But he couldn't help feeling protective. Too many years of stepping up had conditioned him to put Aaron first, to make allowances and bend to ensure his brother was safe and content. For the first time, Gabe wondered if that was normal – if instead of protecting his brother, he was enabling him. He sighed, pushing the errant thought away.

'Mum also believed in grabbing opportunities when they presented themselves. I don't want to park it, we need the money. I went to see a couple more estate agents while I was in Talwynn.' Gabe watched his brother turn towards the house. Had his steps faltered a little? Were all these doubts brought on by stress or were Ruby's suspicions rubbing off? He knew he shouldn't let her get to him, but he respected her loyalty, her need to do the right thing. It was a shame she'd be leaving in a couple of weeks, as she was the first woman he'd met in a long while that he'd wanted to spend time with. The first one he'd dreamed about in the dark hours of the night.

Aaron cleared his throat. 'Great,' he said quietly. 'Fancy a beer? Or I might get out the Jack Daniel's, I feel like something stronger.' He didn't turn around before he headed into the house. Gabe slumped back in the deckchair and ran a hand over his forehead, wondering if he could feel the effects of stress etched across his skin. He knew his brother was hiding something... Was he sick again?

Even after all this time, Gabe couldn't help feeling responsible. He'd been the healthy twin, the one who'd been able to go to school and leave Indigo Cove – go to university – while Aaron had missed much of his education due to his illness and struggled after he got better, before giving up. Girls had fancied Gabe first too – few had been willing to take on the burden of a sick boyfriend. Although Aaron had made up for that in spades since the treatment that had reset his life. Was Aaron somehow angry with him?

For the first time, Gabe considered the likelihood that Aaron might be the father of Anna's child. He stared at the house where his brother was now before shaking his head. If he believed that, even considered the possibility, it would be like he was giving up, finally accepting that the man who shared his DNA was nothing like him at all. Indecision tangled his mind, making him waver. The need to be fair and do right by himself, even Ruby and the brewery, warred with his need to protect his brother. If only Aaron would talk to him, if only he could see into his brother's brain; understand what he was thinking, how he really felt. His mind drifted to all the things that had been happening in the brewery, to the times his brother had disappeared without explanation, and he pursed his lips, thinking of Ruby again.

Then he shook his head. He had to trust Aaron, had to have faith. Because if he didn't, his brother could be lost to him forever, his whole family would be gone – and worse, he'd have let his father down.

13

Dear Rue

I've got amazing news! I'm booked onto a flight at the end of the week and I'll arrive in Indigo Cove on Sunday evening. I was lucky because all the flights back to Cornwall were full, but I pulled in a favour. Please don't tell Nanou, I want it to be a surprise. I wanted to give you some warning, though. I know it's been a long time and you may have mixed feelings about seeing me, but I hope you'll give me a chance this time. A chance to prove I've changed.

It's been so long since I saw you, so much is different. I know you're eager for news on the investment, but unfortunately there's not much I can share at the moment. I can say things are looking really good, and I'm confident I'll be able to return all Nanou's money and a lot more by the end of the month. I know I've said that before, but have faith. I've got a lot to make up for – I'm not going to let you down again.

Can't wait to see you.

Saludos,

Dad x

It was hot, and Ruby tied her hair back and took a deep breath before opening the door to her Nanou's office. She'd just returned from driving Gryffyn, Patricia and Ned to The Beach Cafe for lunch. Darren had gone for a walk in the garden with a slice of Lila's best chocolate cake, citing a desire to be alone and avoid 'the olds'. Ruby had an hour until she had to gather everyone to finish their lesson. Plenty of time to tackle Lila's office while working off the ribbons of stress pulling tight across her neck and back. Or what she liked to call her 'Ross-ache'.

'I think it would just be best if we left it as it is.' Her Nanou stood in the hallway of her bungalow with her hands in the pockets of her vibrant yellow smock, which clashed with today's orange Doc Martens. 'Your dad told me he's going to pay me back everything he owes – and when he does, I'll organise a builder and they'll do all this.' She swept a curl of silver-grey hair away from her face. 'I made a ginger cake last night – I thought we could sit outside on the patio and enjoy the sea view.' She looked longingly down the hall in the direction of the front door.

'We can't keep ignoring this, Nanou – and you know you can't rely on Dad.' Ruby swiped a hand over her forehead and sighed, feeling frustrated. Why couldn't her grandmother see? 'He's never come through before, and the damage in the house is going to get worse. We need to see how bad it is so we can work out a plan.'

'I don't need you to rescue me, love. You spent your life looking out for your mum; I don't expect you to do the same for me. You should be concentrating on enjoying life. It's one of the reasons why I wanted you to visit. I probably could have managed without Morweena, but it's time you had a little fun.'

Lila frowned and shook her head. 'Remember, if we leave things long enough, they'll work themselves out.'

'Alternatively, everything will start to rot,' Ruby grumbled, taking in a deep breath and holding it before striding into the office and opening the window wide. 'It looks and smells worse than yesterday in here.' She coughed as she took in a breath, moving to push the large oak filing cabinet in the centre of the carpet over to the far corner of the room. She yelped as a grey mouse dashed from underneath and disappeared into the hallway. 'You've got four cats!' Ruby squeaked, shuddering. 'I thought catching mice was in their job description?'

Lila chuckled. 'I'll make sure I mention it at their next performance review.' She watched Ruby move another piece of furniture. 'I'm sure if you wait, Gabe will help with that. He's coming later to paint more tankards.' Lila took another step into the room and screwed up her nose.

Ruby shook her head. While she'd spent time with Gabe and had liked what she'd seen, what she knew about him was only skin-deep. She'd spent the weekend considering her fascination with him and had convinced herself she was bound to learn something nasty at some point. Just look at his brother – they shared the same face; what else would she find they shared if she let herself get any closer to him? 'I'll have to take the carpet out in pieces.' She pulled her hair back from her face and slid a scalpel from her pocket, kneeling to slice off the worst. The wool had rotted so badly in the corner that the blade went through it like butter. She stood and threw the small segment out of the window, frowning at the dark stain which had spread across the solid oak floor. 'That looks bad.' She gently tapped a heel on the wood and heard a crack. 'You didn't mention we'd need to replace the floor.' She spun round to Lila, who was now standing in the hallway trying not to look.

'I have a quote for the work somewhere... I'm not really sure what it included,' her grandmother said vaguely, scratching her head and dislodging a pottery tool which she caught before it fell. 'It doesn't matter now. I've not got the money to pay for the repairs, it's why we're waiting on your dad.'

Ruby closed her eyes, wondering whether it would help if she counted to ten. 'How many clients have you got booked in over the summer? Are there deposits we can draw on?'

Lila frowned. 'Not really – I told you it's been quiet.' She winced. 'Things are bound to get better in time. Would you like a cup of tea?' She used her sing-song voice again, and Ruby wondered if her Nanou was going to put her fingers in her ears and hum a tune. Perhaps she had the right idea?

'Sure.' Ruby shook her head when Lila disappeared. The damage to the floor and wall was worse than she'd expected. She'd have to work out how to save her Nanou's house and the Pottery Project. She scratched her chin and frowned, wondering if one of the members of The Marples might know of a decent builder. Once she'd spoken to them, she'd scour her grandmother's books again, perhaps see if they could remortgage or figure out some other way of raising the money. She wasn't going to let her Nanou lose everything like her mum. She wasn't going to let her dad destroy another life. She remembered the email she'd received from him this morning, wondering if for the first time in living memory, her father was going to visit as he'd promised. Then she shook her head. When had Ross Penhaligon ever followed through? How many flights had he mysteriously missed or never actually booked? There was little chance he'd make it to Indigo Cove. Leopards didn't change their spots – no matter how many times they vowed they would.

'So where exactly did Clemo say someone saw the graffiti?' Ruby shouted as Lila jerked Beatrix around another sharp bend, startling a couple of basking seagulls who immediately took off and whizzed above their heads, squawking. Clemo had called at the end of the day's pottery lesson, and her Nanou had insisted on a short road trip to check things out.

'Just at the edge of Sunbeam Moor,' Lila yelled, squinting before taking a hand off the steering wheel and pointing ahead, making Ruby's heart thud. 'I know it well. It's a pretty place to visit, I should have brought a picnic or some cocktails. We're almost at the car park – it'll just be a quick hop, skip and jump from there.' Ruby gripped her seatbelt as they sped up and found herself smiling. Her Nanou was so full of life – she almost envied the older woman's ability to open herself up so thoroughly to every experience. Then Lila took a sudden hard right and squealed into a dusty square layby before coming to a stop. 'We're here!' she sang, hopping out of the car before Ruby could respond. The older woman headed right and charged down a track so fast Ruby had to run to catch up. 'There,' Lila said proudly, aiming a finger towards a small hill framed by a set of gigantic grey granite rocks that were flanked by a series of smaller flat stones. As they approached, Ruby could see something had been painted across the sides of each of the formations.

'Are those flowers?' She joined her grandmother, who'd stopped to take in the artwork. The rocks featured delicate drawings of long green stems with pink, blue and purple flowers along their tops. They were finely detailed and lifelike.

'They're really good,' her Nanou gasped, walking closer before pulling out her mobile to take a few shots. 'We can share these with The Marples, they might be a clue.' She wetted a thumb and scraped it across one of the painted stems, leaving a gap. 'Doesn't look like the paint is permanent. I'm guessing it'll all wash off at the first sight of rain. The artist has talent.' She shook her head. 'Shame this is how they choose to use it. Although I once did something similar on a tent at a music festival when I was in my twenties.' Her eyes sparkled. 'It got me thrown out at the time – but I heard they kept my painting for a while because so many people commented on it.' Her expression turned nostalgic.

Ruby could imagine that – her Nanou leaving a lively reminder, adding a splash of colour and fun wherever she went. What had she left behind in her short time on this planet aside from pottery and people? Dismissing the uncomfortable thought, Ruby wandered further into the clearing and glanced around. On the ground beside the giant rocks, she spotted a handful of sweet wrappers and bent to pick them up, shoving the litter into her pocket. 'Whoever did this obviously has a sweet tooth,' she observed.

'The best people always do,' Lila said wisely and winked, moving along the rocks to study the work more closely. 'I wonder if they've ever tried their hand at pottery, I've an inkling they'd be good. Perhaps I could offer a discount. I suppose that would be one way of getting my class numbers up?'

Ruby shook her head but couldn't stop the chuckle. 'Not a strategy I'd recommend. I'm not sure you want a load of graffiti artists at the Pottery Project. Besides, we'd have to find them first.'

Lila shrugged. 'They'll turn up in the end. Remember, life has a way of working itself out.' With that, she beamed and set off back towards where the car was parked, leaving Ruby following in her wake, wishing, not for the first time, that her grandmother was right.

14

Gabe parked the car and hopped out, popping the boot open and letting Sammie and Rex scamper into the car park before clipping on their leads. 'We made it, finally.' He grinned at Ruby, pointing to a small gate to the right of them which led to a path. 'If we take that track, it'll lead us up to the cliffs – there's a steep incline about half a mile along. If we follow it down, we'll get to Smuggler's Rest. Very few people know it's there – at least they didn't, but I've heard a lot of talk of kids and someone in the brewery mentioned they saw a fire burning by the cliffs yesterday. I wondered if we should check it out, just in case it's our vandals again?'

'Sounds good,' Ruby said. 'Perhaps we'll catch them at it today.' She was looking forward to another walk, to working off some stress. It had been a long afternoon in the Pottery Project. Gryffyn had been particularly cantankerous, Darren had been sarcastic, while Ned had needed a lot of additional help with the cup and saucer they'd been making. Despite four attempts it had still turned out wonky, and she'd had to fight the almost overwhelming desire to get her own hands on some clay. 'I've not heard of that beach,' she said, following Gabe as he led the dogs through the metal gate and waited for her to catch up. She'd changed into shorts, then had almost put on long trousers when she'd noticed how pale her legs were. But Gabe had come searching for her and she hadn't had a chance to throw on a different outfit. Gabe, of course, looked flawless in a dark blue T-shirt and jeans which moulded themselves to his legs, emphasising their length and shape. He had a light tan on his forearms – probably from walking the dogs – and looked healthy and gorgeous, if a little harassed. 'Any luck with the new estate agents?'

He nodded, pulling Sammie back when he tried to chase a seagull to the edge of the cliff. 'They both popped over this morning and were really enthusiastic. I'm waiting for an official valuation, but they seemed confident the field would sell quickly. I didn't mention Jones & Jones; I suppose they could have been telling the truth about being too busy...' He scratched a hand through his hair, mussing a few strands.

Had Aaron been at the meeting with the new estate agents? Ruby wondered if Gabe would drop another clue her way. She was all about building a picture, getting a full understanding of the brother he was so determined to protect. It would be interesting to see if one of the new estate agents suddenly developed cold feet. She was concerned Gabe's brother had something to do with the last one backing off. If he'd lied about having a relationship with Anna, she could only imagine what else he might be lying about. 'Are you worried about something?' she asked, as a new crease marred Gabe's forehead. She was getting used to his face, had already learned some of his tells.

'Maybe, I don't know.' He shrugged. 'I just hope the new estate agents are right about getting a quick sale. We've had a problem with water pressure at the brewery today.'

'Is that bad?' Ruby asked. 'I mean, I know it's a problem if you're having a shower...' The joke was weak, but for some reason she wanted to make Gabe smile.

'I wish it were that simple. Ninety per cent of what we do is cleaning, the other ten per cent is brewing, so a problem like that has a big impact.' The crease in Gabe's forehead deepened. 'It set us back hours, which means less time for all the important stuff – it's like the whole place has decided to implode.' He pointed to an opening on their left. 'We go this way. I'll let the dogs off so they can run ahead – after here it's almost impossible for them to go another way because of the undergrowth.' He stopped to unhook their leads and both dogs shot off, barking excitedly. 'I put beer and wine in my backpack, thought we could sit on the beach later, take in the view if that's okay with you? I've not been down this way for at least two years and I used to come all the time.'

'Sounds good. I'm sorry about all the trouble you're having.' Gabe waited for her at the top of the walk, watching the dogs as they disappeared down the steep incline. Ruby stood and stared at the zig-zag track; it was narrow, but there were plenty of lush shrubs between them and the sharp fall, so she set off at a brisk pace.

'Thanks.' Gabe let out a long breath. 'At least one good thing is going on in the brewery at moment.' When she nodded at him to continue, his expression softened. 'Aaron is loving his design course. I'm pleased – he really seems to be enjoying himself. He's never been that interested in the business, but he designed the new packaging for our centenary ale, redesigned our emails and offered to do some flyers today. I feel like we're really turning a corner, getting on track.' His chest puffed like a proud parent, and Ruby had to bank the wave of concern. What was Aaron's angle?

The beach looked empty as they rounded the last curve, which would take them down another narrow path until they reached their final destination. Even from here, Ruby could tell the sand became much smoother towards the sea and coarser as it got closer to the cliffs. The whole area was littered with pretty white shells that sparkled as the evening sun hit them. She took in a long breath of salty air, gazing at the view. The sea was a gorgeous indigo hue, and Ruby could see a shallow area where waves washed back and forth – it would be the perfect spot to paddle in. A couple of metres further and the colour of the water deepened to a dark greenish-blue, suggesting there was a sudden drop. 'Is it safe to swim here?' Ruby asked, wiping a bead of sweat from her forehead. It was hot and she was glad now she'd worn shorts, but her body still felt sticky and uncomfortable.

'Very safe, I used to come with Aaron and my dad a lot – at least, before Aaron got sick.' Gabe stepped over a large jagged stone before waiting to offer Ruby his hand.

'I'm okay.' She shook her head and balanced carefully as she climbed over. They walked in silence, and she processed what he'd just said. 'Your brother was ill?'

Gabe nodded. 'Rex!' he yelled, when the little beagle decided to stop and sniff a rock on the far edge of the cliff before scampering ahead of them. 'He got sick when we were in our early teens. It took a while, but they diagnosed leukaemia, which was a shock.'

'That's awful.' Ruby didn't trust Aaron, but she could still feel sympathy for the teen who'd been through so much. 'Is he cured now?'

'He's in remission – has been for years.' Gabe's full lips thinned. 'But it took a big toll on him – he missed out on school, became withdrawn. I don't think he ever fully got over it... I'm guessing you never do.'

Was that why Gabe was so determined to believe the best of his brother no matter what the evidence pointed to? In a strange way Ruby could understand it, perhaps even sympathise. 'That must have been difficult to watch.'

He stopped and turned to study her face. A shadow skipped across his – nothing Ruby could read, though. Or perhaps she just didn't trust herself to see the truth when it came to Gabe Roskilly. 'It was,' he said simply. 'It's difficult watching someone you care for going through that and not being able to help. I felt like the bad guy because I wasn't sick – and the more I tried to connect, the more Aaron shut me out. In the end, all I could do was try to be there for him when he needed me.' He pursed his lips and turned again, following the dogs.

'I can relate to that,' Ruby whispered, too quietly for Gabe to hear. She'd watched her mother emotionally waste away for a man who didn't deserve her but who she loved anyway. Any protests Ruby had made had fallen on deaf ears, and in the end she'd had to stay silent. She'd never met anyone before who would relate to the push and pull of that relationship, how difficult it had been to navigate. How useless she'd felt. How many more things was she going to discover about Gabe Roskilly? How many more ways was he going to break down the barriers she'd spent a lifetime building – and how could she stop it?

They completed the rest of the walk in silence as they both brooded on their conversation, but Ruby started to feel better as she looked up again and took in more of the view. It had been months since she'd spent time outside and being here felt good. She could leave everything behind here, pretend it didn't exist for an hour or two. Her grandmother, the Pottery Project, Aaron, her father, Maisy and Anna, even her feelings for Gabe – none of it seemed to matter when she was enjoying the sunshine, surrounded by a beauty with the power to steal her breath.

As soon as they reached the beach, the dogs charged left towards a patch of flat grey rocks located close to the cliffs. 'Sammie!' Gabe cried out, but the dog ignored him and Rex scampered after his brother. 'Looks like we'll be checking the beach for signs of our vandals now.' Gabe mouthed an apology as they padded along the shingly, glittery sand until they reached the patch of rocks. Ahead of them, Sammie barked and scooted up onto a low boulder discoloured by seaweed before diving into what looked like a black hole. 'Stop!' Gabe yelled as Rex looked on, then hurtled in too, disappearing from view. 'Where the hell are you both headed?' Gabe broke into a run and Ruby followed, feeling her heart kick up a notch. Were the dogs hurt? Where had they gone?

When they got to the place where Sammie and Rex had jumped, she let out a long sigh when she saw a small, sandy clearing nestled between four overhanging sides of rock. The two dogs were running fast rings on the sand, yapping excitedly. There were a couple of chairs surrounding a wide patch of burnt wood and the remnants of a fire. 'This is almost impossible to see from the beach – it would make a great hidey hole if you didn't want to be seen.' Empty pop bottles and beer cans were strewn at the sides of the clearing and Gabe shook his head. Both dogs suddenly ran up to sniff the two chairs and Sammie cocked his leg. 'No!' Gabe yelled, hurling himself down to chase the beagle away, then kneel beside the chair. 'I think these are Ella's.' He picked one up to examine it, dusting sand off the legs. 'They are.'

'How did they get here?' Ruby asked, looking around. The beach was empty and the only access was via the track they'd just walked down; a difficult enough journey without the added burden of furniture.

'You can walk around from the harbour if the tide's out, or come by boat,' Gabe murmured, picking up the other chair and dusting it off too before placing it on the smooth rock they'd just been walking on. 'They look okay, they're just dirty and a little scratched. I can take them back to the car when we leave, they'll fit on the back seat. I'm sure Ella will be happy to be reunited.'

'That's decent of you.' Ruby shoved her hands in her pockets, wondering if Gabe would ever do anything to disappoint her. 'We should clear up this litter,' she suggested.

'I've got a bag in my backpack.' Gabe knelt on the sand

before scooping up a few cans. Ruby joined him and cleared a handful of sweet wrappers that had been tucked under a rock. They were the same brand as the ones she'd found the day before. There were also a couple of bus tickets from Indigo Cove, suggesting the culprits might be local.

'This looks like teenagers,' she said. 'I'm guessing the same ones responsible for the graffiti at Sunbeam Moor. Do you think we should take photos for The Marples?'

Gabe tugged his mobile from his pocket before snapping a couple of pictures, then gathered the final few pieces of litter until the bag was full and tucked it into his backpack. 'Not sure what they'll learn from them, but it's good to have a record,' he said. 'I guess now we know where our vandals are meeting. Strange they bothered to come all the way to the brewery to puncture my tyres and dump manure. It's a long way from here, it makes no sense... Perhaps Jago refused to sell them beer and they got upset?' He scratched his chin, rising as both Sammie and Rex scampered around them, sniffing rocks. 'I think we should move before Sammie gets ideas.' As he spoke, the dog whined, then scrambled onto the rocks again. His ears twitched as he spotted the sea in the distance, then suddenly he broke into a run. Rex took one look at Gabe and his ears twitched too, then he hopped onto the boulder and followed his brother. Gabe groaned. 'I need to go after them.' He frowned at the chairs.

'We could leave them here,' Ruby suggested. 'Come back after the dogs have burned off some energy. It's a good spot for those drinks you mentioned.'

Gabe nodded and stepped up onto the boulder before helping Ruby up too. They watched the dogs zig-zag along the beach, heading straight for the water. 'I should catch up.' Gabe slid off his shoes and socks and, clutching them in one hand, began to jog towards the sea, leaving Ruby to bring up the rear.

She wasn't in a hurry, so took her time slipping off her

sandals and pushing her toes into the sand. It felt good, and she watched Sammie and Rex reach the waves and dive into the water, saw Gabe catch up and drop his footwear, roll up the bottoms of his jeans and step in after them. When Ruby caught up, the dogs were swimming further out in water that was so clear she could see a school of tiny grey fish darting back and forth under them. Gabe was paddling in deeper too, staying away from the sharp drop, keeping a careful eye on the dogs.

'I didn't bring any trunks, but now we're here I'm thinking of going in,' he said without turning.

'Won't someone see?' Ruby asked.

'I was thinking I might risk it.' He pressed his hand to his forehead and gazed back at the path they'd followed. It was empty and there was no one around. 'You might not believe this, but in my younger days I was quite the exhibitionist.' He grinned. 'Far less boring than I am now.'

'I told you, you're not boring,' Ruby muttered, glancing back at Gabe. He was smiling, but there was something about his face that made her wonder if he was serious. 'Even if you are, is that so awful?' *You knew where you were with boring... there was nothing lurking in the shadows waiting to let you down.*

'Aaron thinks so,' Gabe responded. 'He says I've turned into a dull old man. Sometimes, I wonder if he's right.' He rolled his shoulders before glancing at Ruby, his cheeks flushing. 'Ignore me – it's been a long day and this beach is far too pretty for you to listen to me droning on. You should have told me to stop.'

'I can appreciate a good drone when it's earned. I'm guessing yours is—' Ruby let out a gasp as she dipped a toe into the water. 'That's cold! If I don't go in, will that make *me* boring?' Sammie swam back towards the beach, trotted onto dry land and seemed to grin at them both, then shook himself vigorously, spraying water all over Ruby's shorts and top, completely soaking them. 'Seriously?' she shrieked, half laughing as frigid water dribbled down her face and neck. The change in temperature was a welcome contrast to the humidity.

'I'm so sorry. What's wrong with you?' Gabe asked, wagging a finger at the dog who was now heading back into the water to join Rex – job done. 'If you put your clothes on one of those, they'll dry quickly.' He pointed to a formation of large jagged rocks close by. 'They won't get submerged until much later this evening. In answer to your question: *yes*, if you don't go in, I will definitely think you're boring.' He grinned.

Ruby frowned at the beach. It was surprisingly tempting. There was no one around and she'd pulled a bikini on under her clothes – despite the fact that she had no intention of going into the water – so she wouldn't have to completely strip off.

'I promise not to peek,' Gabe said, putting his hands over his eyes before sliding a finger down to create a gap.

'I knew you couldn't be trusted,' Ruby muttered, knowing on some level she did trust him, which was disconcerting. She tugged off her T-shirt and shorts, feeling self-conscious as she tracked back to the rock and laid them in the sun. Gabe had turned to face the sea again and she was relieved he hadn't watched her undress. She hurried back to the water and – ignoring the cold – dived in, shucking in a breath as the icy liquid shrank her skin, covering it in a layer of goosebumps. 'Wow,' she spluttered as she came up for air. Gabe was standing at the edge of the water watching her. 'What happened to you?' she shouted.

'Appreciating the view.' He grimaced, crinkling his nose. 'That was corny, sorry. I'm out of practice. In truth, I didn't think you'd go in.'

'Neither did I.' She dived again, watching the fish dart back and forth as they swam around her. Gabe was standing closer to the edge of the waves when she surfaced. 'I think I've discovered my inner mermaid.' Or perhaps she was finally losing her mind? Ruby felt lightheaded and more carefree than she had in years... but she liked it, liked this feeling, wanted to let herself explore it.

'That's it.' Gabe pulled his T-shirt over his head, chuckling. 'I'm coming in!'

Ruby was glad she was in the water because her mouth suddenly went dry and her whole body heated despite the Arctic temperature. Gabe's chest was honey brown, muscular and ironing-board flat. She moistened her lips, unable to tear her eyes away as he unselfconsciously shrugged off his jeans too, leaving his clothes next to his shoes. He wore black boxers that were moulded to his legs and bum, skimming the base of his stomach where an arrow of dark hair dipped low and disappeared. He pushed his fingers into his underwear and began to draw it down; Ruby sucked in another breath as her pulse went wild, then deliberately ducked her head under the water. What had got into her? She was doing exactly what she'd expected Gabe to do to her – ogling him as if he was some kind of sex object. All sense and reason had evaporated from her brain when he'd started to remove his clothes. Which made no sense – it hadn't been *that* long since she'd seen a man naked.

When she came up for air again, Gabe was swimming towards her, looking stunned. 'It's so cold I can't feel my body.' He stopped to paddle beside her as the dogs swam around them like part of an unconventional synchronised routine. 'Hang on, I have to check my feet are still attached to my legs.' He dipped his head and bobbed up again, swiping water from his grinning face. 'Panic over, they're just numb. This is amazing. I can't believe I've not been in the sea for so long.'

'Why haven't you?' Ruby asked, turning to watch. They were facing each other now, treading water. She just managed to stop herself from looking down and checking if he'd stripped or had just been teasing. But a part of her knew she might still do it.

'I don't know. There's always so much to do,' Gabe said,

looking surprised. 'I never thought I'd end up being the sensible brother – I used to be fun, some might say exciting. But I suppose life takes us on different paths. Paths we might not have chosen had we had the opportunity to plan our lives better.' He tipped his head back and gazed at the sky, lifting his legs so his toes poked out of the dark cloak of water, and Ruby saw the outline of his boxers and bit back a surprising flutter of disappointment. Caught up in his obvious enthusiasm, she moved so she was on her back too. There were hardly any clouds and the sky was an almost unreal shade of blue. They could be anywhere, floating silently away from the world. Then a seagull swooped overhead, making for the horizon, and Ruby followed it with her eyes.

'What path would you choose now if you had the chance?' she asked, straightening up.

Gabe moved too until they were facing each other again. He frowned as he considered the question. 'It wouldn't be so different. I love the brewery and my part in it. It's challenging, if a little frustrating at times – but it's mine and Aaron's to do with as we wish and that's something to take pride in. Sometimes, I'd like to have more time to myself – and a bit less to worry about. I don't enjoy feeling like I'm responsible for the whole world.' His eyes crinkled as Rex swam closer and flicked water into his face with a brush of his tail – but rather than being cross, Gabe chuckled as the dog swam off. He watched him for a moment before turning back to Ruby. 'Dogs are like kids: they understand that whole living-in-the-moment thing. I've got out of the habit of just enjoying what I do and where I live. I used to do more – date, have fun, be reckless. And I used to be a lot closer to Aaron. I miss that.' He looked up and his nose wrinkled. 'I'm droning on again. You were supposed to tell me to stop.'

She smiled, charmed, and flapped her arms slowly in the water, feeling weightless. Even her head felt light, and that permanent heaviness across her shoulders, the pressure in her chest, had lifted a little. Was her Nanou right; did she need to relax more too? 'Why would I, when I want to hear it? Tell me more. If you could do anything right this minute, what would you choose?' Ruby wasn't used to men opening up so thoroughly. The moment felt intimate. She wasn't sure if she could entirely trust Gabe's words, but in this moment, she found she wanted to, found her eyes tracing his lips – they were full and smooth and didn't look like they were capable of deceit. What would they feel like against hers? The thought flew into her mind from nowhere and she let it stay, chewed it over like a sinful snack as the desire to set herself free from the constraints she imposed on herself almost consumed her. What would happen if she gave up the fight and let something happen between them? Would it change anything? Was it really such a risk when she was leaving soon?

Gabe swam closer, his expression thoughtful. 'Anything?' he asked, reaching out a hand to swipe a drip from her cheek and setting off a wave of tingles across her skin.

She nodded, then waited while he considered the question.

'I've always wanted to kiss a mermaid,' he said seriously. 'It was a childhood fantasy. You can't live in Indigo Cove without believing in such things.'

'You believe in mermaids?' she asked.

'Not for a long time,' he said quietly, staring at her with eyes as green as the water they were swimming in. 'But I'm beginning to come around to the idea.' His meaning was clear and Ruby felt a heaviness low in the pit of her stomach.

Was it lust? Longing? Definitely madness. But a madness she had the power to turn away from. She knew she was still in control. She could stop this if she wanted to. 'If I'm a mermaid, what does that make you?' she asked eventually, finding herself paddling a little closer as her voice grew husky.

'I don't know.' The edge of his mouth jerked up. 'Still boring, perhaps a little less now I'm in the sea...'

'Ahhh, the power of Mother Nature. I get it – I might even appreciate it,' she said, moving closer still until their legs brushed, wondering how it would feel to kiss him. 'Something strange is definitely happening to me...' Just an hour ago, she wouldn't have entertained the idea of being here, but there was something about the sea, something about being half-naked, that was opening her up to all kinds of possibilities. She wasn't sure if she wanted to fight it because it felt so good. So long as she stayed in control it would be okay. *Do it!* a voice in her head which sounded a lot like Lila sang. *Let go...*

Then Gabe's mouth was on hers, gentle at first, definitely warm. His tongue grazed the seam across her lips as if he were requesting permission to proceed. It took Ruby a moment to decide. But it was just a kiss, one she'd been imagining anyway – and what was a kiss between a mermaid and a mere mortal? So she opened her mouth, swung an arm around Gabe's shoulder and pressed her body into his, waving her other arm in the water to stay afloat. His chest was warm and smooth and she wanted to wrap herself around him as she tightened her grip. She could do this, stay in control, just enjoy the feel of his mouth, the touch of his skin, and the way the blood in her veins was thundering in her ears.

Still in control, she thought again – a little desperately now – as she wrapped her legs around his hips, almost ducking them both under the water as her hormones drove her with a powerful need. Sammie barked, but they both ignored him, even as the dog swam up to get a better look, flicking them with his tail as he turned and paddled off towards the shore with Rex when he decided they were boring.

But there was nothing boring here. This kiss was everything *except* boring.

Gabe's hands crept from Ruby's waist downwards until his fingertips threaded under her bikini and rested on the soft skin of her bottom. It was sensitive there and even the cold from the sea couldn't stop her insides from melting, couldn't stop her from squirming against him. But she knew Gabe was affected too, could feel his hardness pressing against her through her bikini. He pulled back a little, peppering kisses down her cheeks onto her collarbone. 'I'm thinking we should move to shallower waters,' he spluttered, after going under and swallowing a mouthful of seawater. 'You might be a mermaid, but I'm going to drown in a minute and that's the last thing I want to do. I've got plans; drowning would definitely spoil them.' While he was talking, he'd started to paddle to the shore, taking Ruby with him. She didn't unwrap both legs, but she used her left to paddle too, and swam with her right arm still secured to Gabe because she knew if she let go, the spell would be broken, and she wasn't ready for that to happen yet.

Still in control, but only just, when they reached the spot where Gabe could put his feet on the ground and stand. The tide must have started to come in because now, instead of being up to his knees, the sea reached the bottom of his collarbone – convenient, because most of their bodies were hidden from view. Not that they had much of an audience, unless you counted the dogs and three seagulls perched on rocks – the rest of the beach was blissfully empty. Ruby wrapped her arms around Gabe's neck as he kissed her again, then pressed her centre against him harder this time, eliciting a groan. What had got into her? This wasn't careful Ruby who held herself back. These were her father's genes breaking through. All those wayward cells encouraging her to ignore any consequences, telling her she could walk away. She knew she shouldn't, but she couldn't stop herself from reaching one arm behind herself and undoing the top of her bikini. She pushed it round so the string stayed tied at her neck and the rest of it floated on top of the waves as her whole body lit up. The freedom of throwing rules, inhibitions and caution to the wind and doing what you wanted was thrilling. She swallowed as their skin met, soft against hard muscle, and gulped as another, stronger flood of lust engulfed her. The water was lapping against them, egging them on. Heat was building inside her, making Gabe even more impossible to resist.

Not in control now, Ruby thought, as his clever fingers dipped beneath her bikini bottoms again and swirled inside, making her gasp. Her nipples pebbled and a powerful want pumped through her, a desire she'd never let herself feel before now.

Was it the sea, being so far from home, or Mother Nature calling, making her do things she'd never conceived of until this moment? This was reckless and wrong. But she couldn't seem to stop. All that wayward DNA she'd spent the last ten years crushing was exploding out.

'We should probably stop,' Gabe ground out, breathless as he tried to pull back, but Ruby held on. She squeezed her eyes shut, almost half-mad with lust, and shook her head.

'I don't want to.' She kissed him then, ignoring the rational voice in her head which was even now adding up all the ways this was a mistake, creating a stark column labelled 'The biggest blunder of your life' and highlighting it in crimson red. *Oh God*, it was flashing in her mind now, desperately trying to get her attention.

But the kiss was slow and deep, and as Gabe's arms tightened around her back and pressed her closer, Ruby decided to let madness rule, to let that piece of herself she kept locked away come out to play – at least for a while. She could seal the lid on it again later. She undid the string on the right side of her bikini bottoms and eased back to let it drop, pressing her centre to him.

'I... this...' Gabe gasped and stopped talking when Ruby swirled her tongue on his neck, tasting salt, then kissed her way to the smooth dip at the base of his throat. 'This is probably...' he tried again, sucking in another breath. 'I don't...'

'I'm on the pill,' she said. 'I've never done anything like this, but *oh* I want to. Don't ask me why, even I don't understand it,' she whispered. 'Call it madness. I'm going to...'

She pushed at the waistband of Gabe's boxers and waited to see what he'd do. She needed him to know she was walking in with her eyes wide open, even if she was totally out of control.

He tipped her head up until their eyes met and stared into them. He looked confused, more than a little mussed – but his pupils were huge and his other hand was gripping her so tightly she wondered if he'd leave a permanent mark. 'Tell me you want this,' he said, searching her face. 'Tell me you're not going to regret it in an hour. We've only just met, we're on a beach...' He whistled and looked away, clearly trying to find some semblance of control. But she could feel the heat pulsing from his body, the intense need, and knew he was having as much trouble reining himself in as she was.

'Stop talking yourself out of this,' Ruby said breathlessly, taking his chin in her hand and turning his face back to hers. 'You wanted reckless and wild, and I'm here to deliver. I'm promising no regrets, I'm telling you I want this too. Please decide... before we both drown.' Before the doubts began to creep in and stop her. Before she lost her nerve and forced her reckless self back inside.

Gabe stared at her for a beat and then nodded – it was an almost undetectable movement, but she rejoiced in it, and immediately helped ease his boxers over his thighs, freeing him. There was no control now, not even pretence, because with one quick thrust, he was inside her and she let out a low moan as they began to move. Ruby dug her heels into Gabe's bare bottom and kissed her way along his shoulder, tasting salt again until he fixed his mouth on hers. The kiss was deep and hot, matching the pace they were setting with their bodies. She heard the whisper of waves swirling around them, as if Mother Nature herself were goading them. She gripped Gabe tighter as she felt her muscles start to tense, felt the liquid heat inside go up in flames. Then she let out a long gasp and lifted her eyes to the sky as Gabe thundered his own release in her ear. She rested her head on his shoulder, felt his hand stroke her softly down her back. She closed her eyes, fighting the trickle of guilt. But she'd told Gabe she wouldn't regret it – she'd promised herself the same. Now she had to follow through.

'Are you okay?' Gabe asked, as Ruby slowly unhooked her legs and caught the strings of her bikini, which were dangling from her left thigh. She tried to stand on the seabed, but the water was too high and she almost went under, would have if Gabe hadn't caught her arm and held her up.

'I'm fine,' she said, nodding. 'I don't regret that. It was what I wanted. You don't need to worry.' She pulled away, swam a little closer to the beach, so she could get her feet onto the ground and retie the bikini strings, while Gabe pulled up his boxers and came to join her. She felt awkward but turned to face him anyway. He was looking at her with a quiet intensity, but she couldn't read his expression. 'Are *you* okay?' she asked.

He dipped his head. 'I'm baffled, surprised, but definitely okay. I'm...' His forehead creased. 'I don't make a habit of this kind of thing...' He circled a hand above the water as it lapped at his chest. 'I don't do one-night stands – at least, I haven't in years.'

She cleared her throat. 'Neither do I,' she said softly. 'Ever. I'm sensible Ruby. I don't tend to let out my wild side, but I think I just went a little crazy.' She swiped a hand through her wet hair. 'Normal service will be resumed shortly. I might get...' She pointed to their clothes and Gabe nodded as she started to wade towards the beach. The dogs were standing at the edge of the waves as they approached. Gabe kept pace with her, and turned his back as Ruby pulled her shorts and top over her wet bikini, which she appreciated. It was an odd gesture considering what had just happened, but thoughtful. He was so considerate, twisting every assumption she'd ever made about the opposite sex and proving it wrong. He shrugged on his jeans and T-shirt too, then picked up the backpack from the sand, ignoring Sammie who'd begun to sniff at the zip.

'I know we did this the wrong way around, but can I offer you that glass of wine?' He smiled, looking unsure.

Ruby nodded, then let him take her hand to guide her back the way they'd come. She tried not to think too much about how good his touch felt. She wasn't going to regret what had just happened. It had been wild, sensual and amazing. She felt different now, freer, that incessant pressure in her chest had eased – and for the first time in forever, Ruby didn't have a plan for what happened next.

15

'I've got to make a quick phone call to the vet. Walnut's limping and I want to get him checked out,' Lila murmured to Ruby as she ran her eyes around the Pottery Project the following morning. Gryffyn was glowering at the fruit bowl he'd been crafting, and Patricia and Ned were hard at work trying to make the pottery wheel behave. Darren was working quietly and for the first time since the course began, he appeared to be enjoying himself. Patricia's bowl was shaping up nicely, but Ned's had begun to invert around the edges. 'Could you keep an eye on the students for me, please?' her Nanou asked, frowning when Ned cursed and Patricia admonished him for swearing. 'I won't be long. Maybe put some music on... the tomato plants are looking a bit fed up, not to mention the students.'

'Sure.' Ruby nodded as Lila swept out of the studio, pausing beside Gryffyn to raise an eyebrow at his creation.

'Are you sure you haven't done this before?' she asked, earning herself a dark scowl. The older man's bowl was an almost perfect oval with high sides and a fancy rim. Ruby would have been hard-pressed to make anything as good in the half hour he'd been given.

'Beginner's luck?' he muttered. What was it with the man; why was he lying?

'Dammit!' Ned yelled, sweeping his hand across his forehead as his clay collapsed on the pottery wheel in a squidgy heap. He shoved his stool back and stood, glaring at the mess. 'I don't know why I'm here. I get worse each time I put my hands on the stupid clay.' He got up and paced the studio, his expression thunderous as he stalked over to where Gryffyn was working. 'How do you do it? Make something so *sodding* perfect every time?'

'That's not perfect,' Gryffyn growled, standing to examine the bowl on his wheel before dabbing a bowed finger at a slight dip on the edge. 'Not even close.' He used his fist to squash the bowl, eliciting a yelp from Patricia. 'Which is why I'm not keeping it.' He shook his head. 'This is a waste of time.'

Next to Ned, Darren stopped his wheel to inspect his creation, which even from where Ruby was standing looked good. Gryffyn bent to check it and raised a bushy eyebrow. 'You've a talent, boy,' he said gruffly.

'What, this old thing?' Darren grunted, and Ruby saw the corner of his mouth twitch. 'It's all right, I suppose.'

'I can help you set up if you want to make another,' Ruby offered, striding up to join the men. 'Let's clear the clay off your wheels. I'll get you more and we can start again – but slowly this time, and I'll talk you through it. Maybe we'll put on some relaxing music?'

'Please noooooo,' Darren moaned, shoving his hands over his ears and staining them with clay.

Gryffyn chuckled. 'I'll show him – without the racket in the background.' He turned to Ned. 'Throwing a bowl is easy, but you've got to get your head into the right space. Stop telling yourself it's sodding impossible.' He mimed air quotes around the last two words and rolled his blue eyes. 'Start insisting you *can* do it. I can hear your brain whirring from across the studio.

Negative self-talk does *not* feed creativity. You've got a good head on your shoulders, and as far as I can tell, you're able-bodied.' He clenched his hands into fists and uncurled them. 'So there's no reason why *you* can't make a decent bowl.'

Ned's eyes widened. 'Okay, sure...' he said, tentatively following as Gryffyn stalked across the room, then perched on Ned's stool. The older man's eyes shot to Ruby and he flicked a finger at the wheel. She nodded, then went into the storeroom to pick up some fresh clay. When she returned, Gryffyn had already cleaned the wheel, so they were ready to work. He quickly moulded a perfect globe, then darted a finger at Ned. 'Get a chair, boy, and watch closely. Don't take your eyes off what I'm doing. I'm going to demonstrate, then you're going to copy what I do. Lila showed you how to throw a perfectly acceptable bowl earlier, so I'm not sure why you couldn't manage to do it the first time.'

There was a bark of delight from the studio entrance, and when Ruby looked up, her Nanou was watching. 'Another compliment!' she sang, grinning as Gryffyn began to rise. 'Oh no, be my guest.' She wandered further in and was joined by Patricia and Darren. They all stood circling Gryffyn while he glowered up at them. 'I'd love to see what you can do. It's not every day I see a *beginner* lead a pottery class.' She winked and smiled. 'Go on.'

The older man stiffened and carefully straightened the collar of his blue shirt, then puffed out a long breath and nodded, pressing his foot onto the foot pedal, making the wheel spin. 'I haven't been watched like this for a while.' He scooped a little water over the clay and looked up at Ned. 'Pay attention, boy,' he muttered, pressing his fingertips into the firm ball and slowly squashing it out. Ruby watched transfixed as Gryffyn murmured clear instructions, looking up every few beats to make sure Ned was watching. Darren shuffled closer for a better view. He watched intently, all his dry sarcasm and disinterest forgotten. They stood mesmerised as Gryffyn worked. He was a master with clay; Ruby didn't think she'd ever seen anyone with so much innate skill, not even her grandmother. It was as if he was communicating what he wanted via the power of touch, transforming simple raw materials into something breathtaking and unreal. Within ten minutes, Gryffyn had created a perfect bowl with thin, smooth, even sides. The result was so exquisite she wanted to touch it.

Ruby linked her fingers together, effectively imprisoning them as she fought an overpowering urge to sprint to one of her Nanou's pottery wheels and press her fingers into the clay. She loved her job as an accountant – loved the certainty of the numbers, the fact that she could trust whatever she found – but nothing had ever made her heart sing the way crafting clay had. The simple release had always relaxed her. This was the first time since she was twenty that she'd allowed herself to acknowledge how much she missed it. But she didn't want to engage with anything that reminded her of her father, or could draw him into her life. It was as if the mere act of being at a wheel would somehow connect them, and she didn't want to risk it. She'd lost her head, deviated from her path, enough recently.

Gryffyn used a wire to cut his bowl from the wheel and carefully placed it on the counter beside him. He dug his fingers into his palm and winced before claiming another chunk of clay and putting it back on the wheel.

'Now it's your turn.' He pointed to the stool he'd just vacated. When Ned sat, Gryffyn wiped his fingers on his apron, then patted the younger man's shoulder. 'You can do this. Pottery is as much about mindset as it is about experience. It's all about letting go.'

'You've done this before?' Patricia asked, sounding surprised. 'You can't possibly be a beginner like us.'

Darren stepped into the circle. 'Pottery's boring,' he huffed. 'But that.' He pointed to Gryffyn's bowl. 'It's like art.'

'Yep.' Patricia stared at Gryffyn's work and sighed. 'If I could make something that amazing, I'd never stop doing pottery.'

The older man's expression dimmed. 'Depends on what the world expects. If you've only produced perfection, people won't be sympathetic when you're no longer as good.'

'And if you're only ever used to producing perfection, you're probably not that sympathetic to yourself,' Lila said softly, cocking her head as she studied Gryffyn's face. 'There's something familiar about you, but I still don't know why.'

She continued to stare at the older man with canny eyes until he looked away. 'I've no idea what you're talking about,' he said softly before glaring at Ned. 'Now you try – I'll talk you through the process as you go. This time, trust in yourself!' His voice was menacing and Ned pulled a face. But when he put his hands on the clay and started the wheel, Ruby could see he was fully focused on his task and far more determined to get it right this time. She saw Lila tip her head in Gryffyn's direction, watched him frown when she winked, wondering exactly who he was and how long it would take her Nanou to find out.

Ruby pulled Beatrix into the driveway after dropping Gryffyn and Darren at the harbour for lunch. Ned and Patricia had taken their own car so they could have a quick walk along the cliffs. Lila popped her head out of the house as Ruby hopped up from the car. 'Come here,' she whispered dramatically, looking furtively towards the Pottery Project as if she suspected someone might be spying on them. 'I need you to see something.' She didn't wait for Ruby; instead, she marched into the studio, heading for the back room where pieces of discarded clay had been laid out on the counter. As Ruby drew closer, she recognised the bowl Gryffyn had squashed earlier. Lila carefully held up the piece and inverted it, pointing to a couple of initials that had been etched across the base. 'Gryffyn must have scratched these on his bowl by mistake,' she said theatrically. 'I *knew* I recognised him.'

Ruby edged closer, reading the signature. 'G. L. Who's that?' Lila grabbed her hand and tugged her out of the studio towards the house. 'Where are we going?'

'You'll see!' her Nanou sang, marching through the front door and taking a right into the sitting room before drawing Ruby to the huge sideboard where her most important pieces of pottery were displayed. She picked up a vase and held it aloft triumphantly. 'Gryffyn Lowe. I knew I recognised his work.'

Ruby had a vague recollection of the name from when she'd been studying for her degree. He was a potter, well known for using mixed media in his designs. 'Are you sure?' Ruby took the piece from her Nanou's hands and turned it round. The workmanship was exquisite and she knew it was worth a fortune. 'I thought Gryffyn's surname was Brown?'

'Seems he's here incognito. I suppose that's why he lied on his questionnaire.' Lila took the vase from her hands and placed it reverently back on the sideboard. 'But I don't know why. I googled him while you were out,' she whispered. 'He dropped out of the public eye about three years ago, but no one knows what happened. He shut his studio, stopped making pottery.' She shook her head, her eyes shining. 'It's a mystery... no one seems to know where he went.'

'Until he popped up here,' Ruby said. 'But what's he doing on a beginner's pottery course – and why didn't he tell us who he was?'

Lila tapped her nose. 'That's what we're going to find out.' She grinned.

16

Ruby wiped the counters in the studio and packed the small dishwasher in the kitchen as Ned, Patricia and Darren said their goodbyes. Ned stopped at the exit and dipped his head towards Gryffyn. 'Thanks, mate. I had no idea I was capable of making something so... presentable. You should consider teaching.' His cheeks pinked as he waggled his fingers at Lila. 'Not that you're not brilliant, of course, it's just...' He pulled a face. 'I think I needed someone who wasn't so nice today.'

'I'll remember that next time I ask you to take out the bins,' Patricia joked, as she grabbed Ned's arm and tugged him outside. 'See you tomorrow, folks, have a good evening.'

'Thanks,' Darren added, dragging his feet as he made his way towards the exit. He glanced back at the older man, looking conflicted.

'You should take up pottery, boy,' Gryffyn said quietly. 'I know talent when I see it and you've got it in spades.'

The teen swiped a hand across his mouth. 'My dad wants me to be a solicitor like him.' He sighed, looking at the ground. 'He thinks art's a waste of time.'

'What do you think?'

Darren screwed up his nose. The gesture was so childlike Ruby fought a smile.

'Then I suppose it's time for you to decide,' Gryffyn said bluntly. Darren stared at him for a moment, then nodded and walked slowly outside.

Ruby checked her watch. Gabe was due to arrive any minute to paint his tankards and she still hadn't decided if she was going to avoid him or not. She had no idea what she was going to do. She'd spent her life avoiding strong feelings, staying safe in her career and relationships – but with him she lost all control.

Gryffyn tugged off his apron and hung it on one of the coat hooks before turning towards the door, but Lila intercepted before he could leave. A couple of the cats scampered into the room and wound themselves around the older man's heels, trapping him. 'I know who you are,' Lila said quietly, fixing him with serious eyes. 'It's been bothering me since you joined the course. I own one of your vases – it's been in my sitting room this whole time.' She shook her head, her eyes shining with admiration. 'You're Gryffyn Lowe – you told me your surname was Brown.'

He stared at the floor before glancing back up. 'I didn't say anything. You heard April's surname and assumed.'

'Why didn't you tell me?' Lila probed.

He shrugged. 'I'm not here to draw attention to myself. It seemed easier to let you believe what you wanted.' He grimaced, glancing around the studio.

'What are you doing taking a beginner's course?' She waved her palms. 'You could be teaching me. In fact, would you? There's plenty of clay out back.' She smiled up at him, her face open and warm.

'I'm done with that side of my life,' he ground out. 'At least I was, until I got that stupid Christmas present from April and came here.'

'But why? You're a genius.' Lila's forehead creased in confusion. 'People write about you.'

'*Wrote*. I'm not so brilliant now. Now I'm as good as useless,' he said gruffly, trying to step around her. But she reached out a hand and rested it on his arm.

'What I saw on that wheel today was dazzling. The work you've been doing here...' She shook her head. 'I've been teaching for over forty-two years, and I've never had a more talented person in my studio. I'm in awe.'

He stared down at her, his face tired. 'I'm not what I was,' he said softly, locking his hands together in front of him as if the mere act of doing so would somehow illustrate his point. 'The magic's gone.'

'What do you mean?' Lila stepped forward and Ruby took a step back. Watching the intimate exchange made her feel like a voyeur and she didn't want to crowd them – but she didn't want to leave either. Why would a man with so much talent walk away from something he loved? The irony wasn't lost on her, but Ruby knew why she'd walked away from pottery and her reasons were sound.

'What I create isn't perfect and I need it to be. It always was before,' he said faintly.

'What happened?' Lila asked gently.

It took Gryffyn a moment to respond. At first he looked angry, then his face slackened. 'If you must know, I had a stroke. It took everything at first. My voice, my whole right side. I've regained most of what I was, but...' He held out his hands, straightening his fingers; one of them was twisted inwards. It was almost undetectable, only visible if you studied them closely. 'Not these.' Then he tapped the same finger against his temple. 'And not this. I've lost something and according to the doctors – and the fact that it's been three years – I'm unlikely to get it back. What I throw on the wheel now is good, but not good enough. I make mistakes, there are flaws, and I'm not a man who'd be content with half measures.'

'So your solution is to give up?' Lila gaped, putting her hands on her hips. 'Walk away from a talent most people only dream of because you're no longer capable of "perfection"?'

Gryffyn frowned, clearly not used to dealing with someone so forthright. 'That's right. What of it?'

'Then you're an old dope,' she said, shaking her head. 'Brilliant – but a dope. You brought Ned out of his shell today, taught him something I've been trying to do for over a week. But he heard it when you said it, he listened. Darren hangs on your every word. I saw you speaking to the child just now – you could be the reason he takes up pottery, decides to take his art seriously. He could even become the next you... Surely that's worth something?'

'It's hardly bringing the magic in your head to life,' Gryffyn bit back.

'Ah, so this is because you're no longer being adored and complimented?' Lila said, moving closer, somehow managing to avoid stepping on a cat. 'Is your ego really so huge?'

Gryffyn's expression darkened as he frowned down at her. Ruby took a step away too, bumping into one of the worktables. She'd rarely seen her Nanou like this. Usually the older woman was laid-back, determined to solve life's problems with a cup of tea and slice of cake. Or to wait for everything to somehow mysteriously fix itself. But there was something about this man and his refusal to embrace his talents and what he could give that clearly got to her. Something she was prepared to fight for. 'I'm...' He stumbled back another step as Lila pressed herself closer. 'I like you better when you're being agreeable,' he growled.

Her Nanou's eyebrows shot up. 'Not used to people calling out your nonsense then?' Her lips made a thin line. 'Perhaps it's time they did. I'll warrant your granddaughter April has been saying the same things. Why did she book you onto this course, after all?'

His shoulders dipped. 'I've no idea. Perhaps she just enjoys interfering. Or maybe she wanted to get me out from under her feet.'

'But you came,' Lila said. 'And you kept on coming – that tells me a lot. Maybe you're not so done with pottery, after all?'

'Or could be I made a mistake.' Gryffyn fixed Lila with a sour stare. 'April will be here to pick me up soon.' The instant he said the words, Ruby heard a car pulling up on the gravel driveway. 'As I said, probably best if I go.'

'Before you do.' Lila reached up and gently cupped Gryffyn's face. The gesture was so unexpected he balked, but didn't pull away. 'Think about how you feel when your fingers are in the clay. Because I've seen the way your face lights up, the way your body comes alive. It's almost spiritual. I know that feeling... and I know I couldn't live without it.'

Ruby swallowed, pushing the visual of her own hands steeped in clay from her mind as her Nanou continued. But the warmth, the need, flooded her veins.

'So what if you can't make what you could? If you love what you do, surely just the act of doing it is enough? Perhaps you can find some other way of using your talents. You'd make a good teacher.' Lila's grey eyes bore into his. 'You could share your love of pottery with others. I've spent my life doing just that. If that's not worth something, I don't know what is.' With that, she turned and stomped out of the exit with the cats following at her heels, leaving a baffled Gryffyn staring after her.

. . .

'Sorry I'm late.' Gabe looked tired, but his handsome face still had the power to stop Ruby's breath. She nodded as he breezed into the studio, wearing scuffed jeans which hung loosely on his rangy frame and a dark blue T-shirt that hugged the hard planes of his chest. Lila had popped into the village to visit Ella and burn off some of her frustration about Gryffyn, and Ruby had spent the time alone tidying up after the pottery lesson and putting everyone's work into the drying room. The act of clearing away had given her time to focus and think, allowed her brain to mull over her predicament. If she were in her office at the accountancy firm, she'd create a complex spreadsheet in Excel with two columns. In the 'against' column she'd list all the reasons why spending more time with Gabe was a terrible idea – and there would be plenty of those. She already knew the 'for' list would be mostly empty – but as Gabe swept in from outside with Sammie and Rex harnessed to their leads, her heart still jumped and her body began to heat from the outside in.

'I had to bring the dogs,' he said apologetically, glancing at the beagles who gazed up at him with innocent brown eyes. 'Aaron wasn't home and Jago couldn't stay in the brewery to watch them because his wife is going out and he had to mind the kids. I didn't want to leave them by themselves. Not without risking Armageddon.' He turned around, scouring the immediate area. 'Are Lila's cats here, or can I shut the door and let the dogs off their leads? I promise they'll behave, won't you, Sammie?' His voice was harsh, but the beagle just widened his mouth and grinned.

'No cats,' Ruby confirmed, swallowing the urge to reach out and touch Gabe. Instead, she wandered to the entrance door and pulled it shut, willing the bubble of rebellion in her chest to quiet. 'I need to...' As she turned, she found him standing in front of her, staring down. 'Oh...' Breath rushed from her lips as she lost the words she'd had in her mind. The blood pumping around her body seemed to thicken and slow.

'I haven't said hello properly. You look pretty today,' Gabe said softly, brushing a strand of hair from Ruby's face before leaning down to stroke his lips across hers. He nodded as he pulled back. 'Yep, you taste as good as I remember too.'

'Um,' Ruby mumbled and dipped her head before sidestepping him. Her heart was beating wildly now, filling her head with a rush of noise. She'd never been overwhelmed by a man, never felt like this. Even her skin was tingling, begging her to turn and lean in for another kiss. Only this time she wanted it deeper – and she wanted it to last. 'I'll get the tankards,' she croaked, scurrying into the back room where shelves of fired, unpainted pottery were stored. She grabbed two and headed back breathing deeply, trying to get a firm grip of herself. She was a level-headed woman fully in control of her emotions, not prone to rushes of affection or going off at the deep end. She'd spent years perfecting her ability to protect her heart. It was iron-clad, safe and locked down. She wasn't in the habit of losing her head; she could walk away anytime.

Gabe was standing by the table he usually worked at. He'd already gathered brushes and a black apron which he'd knotted around his front. He looked up and smiled, his eyes twinkling as Ruby approached. 'Can I do anything to help?' he asked, his voice deep. *Oh boy.* She shook her head and turned away to grab some underglaze from the back room before returning.

'About yesterday...' Gabe picked up a brush and dipped it into the red paint pot.

'I still don't regret it,' she said quietly. 'What happened was a little confusing. It's a side of myself I've tried not to become too familiar with.'

He nodded and cocked his head. 'Would you like to get to know her better? Because I would.' He tangled a hand in his hair, suggesting he wasn't as relaxed as he looked. 'I'm not just talking about the sex, although...' He flashed a small smile. 'It was mind-blowing. But I've not met anyone for a long while I wanted to spend time with. Up until now, if I had, I'd probably have made a lot of excuses, convinced myself it was a bad idea because I don't have time for a relationship. After yesterday I've realised I need to change something before my whole life disappears into a myriad of work, responsibilities and meetings. I was wondering if you felt the same?' The look on Gabe's face was oddly vulnerable. For a moment, Ruby wished she had the power to reach into his head and see exactly what he was thinking. It would make it so much easier to decide.

'I'm going back to London in a couple of weeks,' she said.

Gabe nodded and distractedly dabbed paint onto one of the tankards. Ruby's stomach sank. If he was that easy to put off, perhaps this wasn't meant to happen, which would be easier all around. 'I know,' he said quietly. 'If I were being sensible, I'd say that means we should let this go, but...' His eyes met hers and liquid heat pooled in her belly. How did he do that – was it chemistry or some kind of mind control? 'I'm bored of being the sensible, responsible brother. I'd like to go a little wild again... my gut says you might feel the same?' Ruby stared at him, then rubbed a hand against the back of her neck, mulling the question. 'Or maybe that feeling in my gut is the pizza I ate for lunch.' He didn't smile; instead, he waited while she continued to consider the invitation, rolling it around her mind. She wanted to say no. The accountant part of her, who had already summed up the risks and found them too huge to contemplate, was screaming at her to *run*. What if she couldn't keep this as just fun? What if her heart got involved and Gabe hurt her? What if she started to want or expect something from him and he let her down? But the other side of her, the one that had been nudging its way out since she'd arrived in Cornwall, the bit which was even now staring at Gabe's mouth, was pushing up like a hidden spring desperate to find daylight. Should she do this? There were a million reasons why not... Aaron was only part of it.

'We'll need firm ground rules,' Ruby said, clenching her fists. 'It's important we both understand where this is going – or *not* going, to be more precise – and what we do or don't want.'

'Will there be a contract?' Gabe quirked an eyebrow as his whole body relaxed. 'Because I won't need a nudity clause. Just in case you're planning on including one.'

Ruby snorted a surprised laugh and shook her head. 'I'm easy on the subject of nudity. In fact,' – her insides squeezed – 'naked is part of the deal. I'm not so easy when it comes to my heart.' She rubbed a fist on her chest, realising how ridiculous it was: Gabe knew where that particular piece of her anatomy was. He just didn't know how important it was that she kept it safe. 'We keep this simple and light. No heavy feelings. I'm going home in two weeks, back to my real life, and I'm not looking for a relationship.' She wasn't looking to feed this side of herself.

Gabe stared at her for a moment. 'I understand,' he said quietly. 'Nothing complicated.'

'You also have to accept that I'm going to continue to look for the father of Anna's child. Who may or may not turn out to be Aaron.' She didn't add that she was 100 per cent certain it was him, but the subtext was clear. 'I'm not going to stop looking until I get proof.' Gabe had flinched when she'd said Aaron's name, but his expression didn't alter. 'If we spend time together, I'll expect you to let me get on looking without interfering. If it turns out to be your brother, I'll ask for your support.'

His lips pinched. 'I can do that,' he said softly. 'It's not Aaron, but I'll do everything I can to help you find out who it is.'

'Then let's do this,' Ruby said, leaning closer and ignoring the sensible, rational part of herself which was still begging her to run.

'In that case,' Gabe murmured, bending until his warm breath tickled her cheek, 'I suggest we seal our deal with a kiss.' Then he captured her mouth, making her knees wobble and her body heat until Ruby's mind blanked and any warnings or misgivings disappeared.

17

Ruby and Lila arrived early at The Oyster Bar on Sunday evening. Gabe had been caught up in a series of problems at the brewery over the last few days, so Ruby hadn't seen him, but he'd promised to be at The Marples meeting tonight. She'd worn her favourite pink lace underwear especially. Since their pact to spend time together with no strings, they hadn't had a chance to follow through and tonight was the first time she was going to see him. She brushed a hand over the silk dress she'd worn, which was both impractical and sexy, wondering if she was going mad.

The Oyster Bar was situated next to Indigo Cove's harbour, with amazing views of the seafront and boats which regularly moored in the tiny inlet overnight. It was only seven o'clock and a few tourists still pottered on the beach, enjoying the last of the heat from the sun. The restaurant was large for such a small village, and as they approached, Ruby could see a vaulted ceiling and gleaming multicoloured bottle-shaped lamps that dangled from the black rafters through the glass windows. Lila had told Ruby the restaurant was booked up for months in advance because Claude's Michelin star had been well earned.

Under the hanging lights she saw pretty black tables and elegant chrome chairs with high backs. All were laid with starched linen tablecloths, glossy silver cutlery, water and wine glasses. As they entered, Ruby felt a blast of icy coolness from the air-conditioning across her shoulders, a welcome contrast to the heat outside.

'*Bonjour, bienvenue!*' Claude appeared from the kitchen at the back of the large room to greet them as soon as the door opened. He wore his immaculate black suit, but his white shirt was undone at the collar, and he wasn't wearing a tie which made him look more relaxed. He peered over Lila's shoulder.

'We're the first.' Lila took pity on him when his face dropped. 'I know Ella had to sort some things out with the team who are cleaning the cafe. But she told me she was hoping to head here soon.' Lila beamed as she spotted a long table at the far end of the room, which was overflowing with white dishes of nibbles and tempting desserts. 'Looks like you've been busy.'

Claude shrugged. 'I like to cook when we're closed – it gives me a chance to experiment when the restaurant is empty.' He strolled over to the table, picked up a plate filled with treats and held it out. 'The results of some new petit fours recipes – please try some and tell me what you think.'

The door behind them opened again and Claude's eyes shot to the entrance. His cheeks flushed and Ruby turned to see Ella and Clemo. Ella wore an elegant, floaty white dress and looked almost fairy-like next to the large man. She paused after taking a few steps and picked up one of the menus at the desk where the maître d' usually greeted diners. She flicked open the menu as Clemo broke away to join them, pulling out a chair and immediately picking up a mini cheese croissant before swallowing the whole thing.

'That's a masterpiece,' he gushed, grabbing a square petit four covered in chocolate as he slumped down. 'Amazing,' he hummed, reaching for another as Claude strode up to join Ella.

'Did you want to try something especially?' he asked, ignoring the frown she gave him. 'I'm happy to make a dish just for you. It won't take long.' He sounded so eager to impress her Ruby felt sorry for him. This was why life was safer when you kept your feelings locked down.

'No, I'm just checking out the competition,' she said airily.

Claude gave her a half-smile and waved a hand towards the table where everyone was seated. 'Perhaps you'd like to check for yourself. I've been experimenting in my kitchen today – I'd appreciate your opinion. What you think is important to me.' He turned away and missed Ella's blush, then marched to the long table and pulled out a chair, turning to raise an eyebrow when he realised she hadn't moved. 'Are you staying or going?'

Ella shoved her handbag higher on her shoulder, then slowly approached Claude before sitting on the chair he was still holding for her. She frowned as she stared at the plates of food, finally picking up a small cake and nibbling at the edges. The room fell silent when she let out a low hum of pleasure as she chewed.

Claude's cheeks flushed and a ghost of a smile crept across his lips. He might have spoken then, but the door at the front of the restaurant opened and Gabe, Patricia and Ned walked in. 'Sorry we're late,' Patricia called out as they came to join everyone at the table. Gabe grabbed the chair next to Ruby and winked.

'Where are the dogs?' she whispered, as the others admired the food and Claude fussed around them, pouring glasses of sparkling water and offering coffee and tea.

'Aaron's got them,' he murmured as his eyes slid to her dress. 'You look amazing! I was going to ask if you wanted to come for a drive with me to Sunset Point after the meeting.' His green eyes met hers and tension flooded her belly. 'There's a gorgeous view over the cliffs – we can watch the sun set. I've not been for years.'

'I've heard of it.' Ruby's stomach performed a series of intricate somersaults. 'Sounds good.' She sipped a large gulp of water as the sensible part of her began to object. But she could do this, even feel good about it. She wasn't harming anyone and in a couple of weeks, they'd both walk away, proving she could let herself feel – even trust someone – without getting hurt.

Clemo pushed back his chair to reach for another dessert. As he did, Ella picked up one of the petit fours and bit into it, letting out a soft sigh.

'You like?' Claude asked, his features hawk-like as he watched her.

'It's...' Ella paused as countless emotions crossed her face. She put the remainder of the dessert on her plate. 'I want to say it's awful, but it's not.' She frowned. 'It's really good.'

'I can give you the recipe if you want?' Claude offered, eliciting another frown and a firm shake of the head. His shoulders drooped and his jaw tightened.

'You can give it to me,' Clemo joked as he picked up another petit four. 'Should we start the meeting?' he asked, shoving the whole thing into his mouth.

Lila nodded. 'I officially announce the commencement of The Marples – does anyone have anything to report? I know my granddaughter has news...'

Ruby sat up straight as everyone turned to stare at her. She cleared her throat. 'I went to the exhibition in Talwynn to see if I could find any photos that showed who my friend Anna spent time with at the Spring Carnival. Did anyone else learn anything?'

Clemo shook his head, scooping up another dessert. 'I've asked around, but I haven't had any luck. Did you find much at the exhibition?'

Ruby nodded. 'Anna was in one of the collages.'

'That's brilliant because no one I've asked has recognised

her yet either.' Ella picked up another dessert too, oblivious to Claude's look of elation.

Ruby frowned. 'Unfortunately, I couldn't see who Anna was with. Someone had an arm around her shoulder, but his or her face was obscured.'

'So what's your plan?' Clemo leaned back in his chair and tapped a hand on his belly.

'I'm waiting until the photographer is back in the country so I can get a copy of the original photo – she promised to send me a link once she's back,' Ruby said.

'Any idea when that'll be?' Patricia asked, and Ruby shook her head.

'In the meantime, we'll all keep asking around,' Clemo promised.

'Now that's settled, is there any other business?' Lila asked.

'I've got nothing to report.' Ella scanned her notepad as she absently picked up another of Claude's desserts. He watched intently as she bit into it, his lips tensing when she gave an almost indiscernible dip of the chin. 'Aside from the graffiti you told me about, and the sweet wrappers and signs of a bonfire Ruby and Gabe found at Smuggler's Rest.' Ruby risked a quick peek at Gabe and felt a shiver travel down her spine when she realised he was watching her.

'I have something.' Clemo raised a finger. 'A customer mentioned they saw a group of teenagers defacing the mural by the ice cream parlour. One of the boys painted a moustache on one of the seals.'

'I heard about that,' Lila said, looking amused. 'I'm guessing it's the same kids who painted on the rocks.'

Clemo nodded. 'The moustache has been cleaned off now and my customer didn't know the names of any of the so-called artists, but he thought he recognised their faces. They're definitely from around here. Maybe we should step up our patrols of the high street, see if we can catch them in the act?'

'We ought to ask Darren if he knows of anyone,' Ned said, and Lila nodded. 'In the meantime, Patricia and I can do most evenings. We're not busy. So count us in.'

'We'll catch them eventually.' Clemo frowned. 'It's only a matter of time.'

The sun was starting to set as Gabe drew up at the top edge of Sunset Point where it overlooked the cliffs that hooked over the shoreline, offering impressive views of the sea and horizon. They were the only car parked there for now – probably because it was early Sunday evening.

'It's usually much busier, or it was when I used to come here; people come from far and wide to see the views,' Gabe explained as he parked, and pushed back his seat so he could twist towards Ruby.

'Did you come a lot when you were younger?' she asked, undoing her seatbelt and moving her seat into a more comfortable position too, making sure she was within easy reach. The light was beginning to dim outside, but it was still warm, so she opened one of the windows to let a soft breeze blow through the car.

Gabe grinned. 'It's a very romantic spot and I brought a few special dates here when I was a teenager. Different car.' He frowned at a bitemark in the black headrest positioned next to his face, where foam had begun to poke through. 'Better car probably – which sucks because I was only about eighteen.' Amused, he shook his head and pointed at the car park. 'Once I passed my driving test, this was the go-to place for a hot date.'

'How hot?' Ruby asked, ignoring the twinge of jealousy that shot through her as she studied him. Gabe seemed more relaxed this evening. She ran her eyes across his broad shoulders; one of his hands was lightly clasped on the steering wheel, the muscles across his forearm bunched. The other was tapping a tune on his thigh.

He scrubbed a fingertip across his chin. 'If I were to compare what used to go on here to what happened on the beach with you, I'd say it was one step up from frigid. That includes the night I lost my virginity – which used to rank as the highlight of my entire life.' He smiled as his eyes drifted down to Ruby's mouth, releasing a flood of lust in her belly. 'What about you? Where did you go with guys?'

'I was more interested in pottery than dating when I was a teenager, then numbers took over from that.' She didn't elaborate. In truth, watching the disaster that was her parents' marriage had put her off. It was only after she'd decided to keep her liaisons brief and dispassionate that she'd allowed herself to go ahead. 'I made up for it in university, but a lady never tells.'

Gabe glanced out of the windscreen. 'I'd almost forgotten about this view. Do you want to take a walk? There's another beauty spot that's not far.'

'You want to *walk*?' The disappointment was clear in her voice, and Gabe leaned across the car to brush his mouth over hers.

'I plan to kiss you, Ruby, but it's not dark yet,' he whispered. 'I know I said I was an exhibitionist, but I lied.' He grinned before his eyes slid to her sheer, silk dress. 'Will you get cold outside?'

Ruby opened the door and hopped down. 'If I do, I suppose you'll have to find a way to warm me up, won't you?' She waited while Gabe wandered around the car and took her hand, then led her towards a small pathway that followed the cliff. She stopped when they were a few steps down the track to take in the view. 'It's beautiful. I'd forgotten this too.' Why did everything smell so much better here; why were the colours so much brighter too?

'Do you come to Indigo Cove a lot?' Gabe asked as he began to walk.

'Not often enough. I let things get in the way, but I plan to visit more often. Nanou's getting older and...' Ruby thought about the leak in the office and the trouble with the roof. She'd managed to contact a builder on Clemo's recommendation and he was supposed to be coming to check out the mess. 'She's not very practical. My father can't be trusted and I need to keep a better eye on her. No one else is around to do it.'

'I can visit more regularly if you like?' Gabe said. 'I like your grandmother – she's been amazing letting me use the Pottery Project to make the tankards.'

'That's okay.' Ruby shook her head even as her eyes pricked at the unexpected offer. They weren't meant to be forming bonds. She was supposed to be keeping Gabe at arm's length, not inviting him deeper into her life.

Gabe continued, oblivious. 'Going there each day has been fun. She's quite a character. Is your dad the same?'

Ruby grunted. 'He has a talent for pottery, but that's his only similarity to Lila. I don't know what my grandad was like; he died when Dad was ten.'

'That's tough,' Gabe said quietly, taking her hand again as they continued to walk. Ruby could see a bench under a tree in the distance and wondered if that's where they were headed. 'Must have been hard on your dad to suddenly become the man of the house. I found it hard enough, but I was almost in my thirties – *and* I had Aaron.'

Ruby frowned. 'I don't feel sorry for my father,' she said simply. 'Just because we lose our parents young, it doesn't mean we can use it as an excuse.'

'Sometimes, things that happen in the past can shape the way we see life.' Gabe's forehead crinkled and Ruby wondered if he was thinking about his brother.

'Being an arse isn't a foregone conclusion – it's a choice,' she grumbled. 'My dad chose to leave his family. Maybe not in the same way his father left him, but he must have known how much damage it would do to me and Mum, and he did it anyway. He didn't even have the decency to leave forever, he kept coming back.' She knew she sounded bitter but couldn't help it. 'He kept on reopening the wound over and over. Making sure Mum still wanted him because he was too selfish to let her love anyone else.' She rolled her shoulders, wishing he hadn't brought up the subject. There was no use discussing it. Nothing would change.

She just wanted Gabe to kiss her, wanted to get lost in the moment again. She didn't want to think too much. As if he'd read her mind, he encouraged her to sit on the bench beside him. The sun was still warm, but there was shade from a weathered beech tree and the view was magnificent. 'Are you going to seduce me now?' Ruby teased.

Gabe ran a fingertip across her lips, letting it float slowly down the curve of her neck. 'I'm sorry I talked about your dad.' He leaned down and skimmed his mouth across hers, setting off a torrent of shivers.

'I'm being grumpy and you're too nice,' she whispered as he continued to press his mouth to her collarbone, let it flutter across her shoulder as heat pooled in her centre. *This was what she wanted...* Gabe slipped a hand across her shoulder, dislodging one of the thin straps of her dress which drifted down her arm. 'I can kiss you as much as I want here and no one will see.' His eyes flickered back up the track towards the car park. 'Unless they get the same idea.' His lips curved as a seagull squawked overhead. 'We might attract some wildlife, though...'

'It's okay.' Ruby leaned into him as she pushed her hands underneath the bottom of his T-shirt, feeling the smooth skin on his chest. She felt reckless again, could feel the pressure releasing in her chest as she allowed herself to let go of the bonds she'd tried to live within for the last ten years. Gabe's body felt the same as a few days before, but somehow different. His skin was hotter and smoother without the cold water creating goosebumps on its surface. She lifted her head and their mouths met. She could feel the blood pumping through her body and pressed closer. Then a phone began to ring beside her and Gabe pulled back to search his pocket. His grabbed his mobile and held it up, but it wasn't ringing. 'Dammit,' Ruby grumbled, reaching for her bag as the ringing stopped, then started again. She pulled it out without checking the screen. 'What?' she snapped.

'Ruby?' Her Nanou sounded upset and she quickly slid the strap of her dress back onto her shoulder, trying to concentrate.

'What's wrong?' she asked as Gabe mouthed the same question.

'I just got back from The Marples meeting – I walked to the cafe with Ella so we could catch up, which meant I was a bit late.' She swallowed.

'What happened?'

'Someone broke into the Pottery Project while we were gone. I've called the police and they're coming now. I'm waiting outside. Ruby, I don't know what they've done. There are pieces of pottery everywhere. Someone smashed it all over the studio, but I can't tell what's been broken. I don't want to go in on my own...'

Ruby sprang off Gabe onto her feet and started to jog towards the car park without waiting for him, knowing he was following from the sound of his footsteps. 'Don't worry. Stay in the car, lock the doors, wait for me. I'm coming,' she promised.

18

Lila wasn't sitting in Beatrix when Gabe skidded the car into her drive, spraying pebbles at a police car which was parked beside it. Its blue light was still flashing, but there was no one in sight. Ruby ignored the thump of fear in her chest as she opened the door and jumped from the passenger seat before Gabe's car had fully stopped, hurling herself towards the Pottery Project. The door to the entrance was wide open and she stopped just inside, letting out a gasp as she took in the carnage. There were fragments of pottery on every surface – all over the floor and counters – although on closer inspection, none of Lila's equipment or paint pots looked like they'd been damaged. Ruby spun around to study the mess. All the pictures and pieces of pottery that had been carefully displayed on shelves, or in the pretty glass-fronted cabinets, hadn't been touched. She wandered a little further inside, taking care not to tread on the multiple shards as her Nanou appeared from the drying room, clutching one of her cats. 'Nanou, you're okay.' Ruby exhaled as Lila manically stroked Walnut, while a young male police officer made squiggly notes on a black pad.

'I'm fine, just a little shaken,' Lila muttered, frowning as she took in the disarray. 'I'm not sure about this place, though.' She scraped a hand across her forehead, looking weary.

Gabe half tripped over a piece of broken china as he burst through the door and ran up to join them, righting himself just before he fell. He bent to study the shattered piece that had almost derailed him. 'This looks like one of my tankards,' he said faintly, pinching his nose. 'Thankfully, it's not one I've painted.' He stood and followed Ruby as she joined her grandmother and gave her a hug. Lila looked dazed – her usually smooth skin was paler than usual, her eyes a lot less bright.

When Ruby pulled back, Lila shook her head. 'You've been telling me to lock up properly. I should have listened. I've always been too trusting. Until today I thought that was a good thing.' She stroked Walnut again as she glanced around the studio, her grey eyes wide as she took in the mess on the floor. 'I don't understand why anyone would do something so horrible. It makes no sense...'

'It's got to be the teenagers who've been vandalising the village,' Gabe said, sounding annoyed as he sidestepped Ruby and knelt to pick up another broken shard. 'This is another piece of tankard.' He sighed. 'I'm going to have to come to the studio for a few more hours so I can replace the broken ones.' He rose as the policeman stopped scribbling. Lila opened her mouth, but the officer interrupted.

'It doesn't look like anything's been damaged aside from some pottery, which is good,' the officer reported stiffly. 'We've checked the equipment, and I took a cursory look around the house – nothing's been touched, according to Ms Penhaligon. The damage is confined to some of the craft in particular.' He nodded to the chaos on the floor before pointing to the untouched paint pots and pottery wheels. Everything looked exactly as it had done when they'd left the studio on Friday.

'You're sure no one went into the house?' Ruby asked sharply, as a vision of her computer – which she'd left out in her bedroom – filled her head. How could she have been so trusting? All her customer accounts were on the laptop, her whole life. She'd been so distracted at the thought of seeing Gabe she hadn't even considered it. She was too caught up with being in Cornwall, her usual defences eroded to nothing.

'It doesn't look like it.' Lila patted Ruby's arm as Gabe rubbed her shoulder in an act of solidarity that made her whole body warm. 'We're guessing they were disturbed while they were here. It's why—' The older woman stared up at Gabe. 'It seems they only had time to break your tankards.' Her eyes widened. 'Which is odd because everything else the class has made over the last fortnight hasn't been touched.'

The policeman nodded. 'It is strange. All the unfinished pottery is stored in the same place, some on the same shelves. I can only surmise the culprits didn't see the other work, which...' He tapped his pen on his chin. 'Seems unlikely.' He levelled his attention at Gabe. 'Alternatively, it's possible they have a particular vendetta against you. Anything I need to know?'

Gabe opened his mouth and closed it as his eyes scoured the floor and his shoulders sagged. 'How many of the tankards are broken?' he asked roughly, taking in a pile of pottery shards by his feet – some of which had been painted in the colours of the Roskilly Brewery logo.

'From what I can see, pet...' Lila took in a deep breath, her face filled with sympathy. 'All of them have been smashed.' Her eyes widened. 'You don't think this was done by the same people who've been causing trouble for you with the car and at the brewery, do you?'

The police officer's head jerked up from his pad. 'You've been experiencing other issues?'

'I've reported them all to the police, but...' Gabe sighed. 'I thought all that was connected to the vandalism. I can't see how this would have anything to do with me.' He shoved his hands into his pockets.

'Can you think of anyone who might have done this?' the policeman asked.

'No,' Gabe said firmly. 'Honestly, I run a brewery. I'm not involved in anything sinister. I've barely had a life for the last few years. Everything I do is connected to the business.' His eyes slid to Ruby. 'Unless someone's taken umbrage with the way I cut my hair, I've not had a chance to upset anybody. This has got to be a very odd coincidence.'

'You need to let us know if you think of something – or if anything else happens to you. Meanwhile, I'll take a look at those vandalism reports at the station.' The police officer gave Gabe a card and turned to Lila. 'I'll send someone to check for fingerprints, although it's unlikely we'll find anything – whoever did this was able to walk straight in.' Lila's smile dropped. 'We can advise on security around the studio, and I'll put everything in my report, but from now on I'd suggest you lock your doors.' His tone turned stern. 'It's easy to be complacent when you live somewhere so idyllic, but unfortunately there's a chance of crime wherever you are. Best not to invite it – or make it so easy. You've got a lot of valuable equipment in this studio; you don't want someone to park up a van one night and steal the lot.'

'Yes, officer.' Lila sighed as she scoured the studio again, shaking her head as the policeman turned and left.

Gabe stood staring at the mess after he'd gone, then slowly bent to pick up another couple of shards and place them on the table. One of the pieces showcased half of the brewery's logo. Ruby remembered it had taken Gabe hours to paint the few tankards he'd done. 'I can't believe all that work is just... gone.' He blew out a long breath, scrutinising the floor. 'I've only got a week to remake and paint another hundred.' He looked crushed. 'I know they were a sentimental idea and not worth all the time, but we've advertised them on social media and to our mailing list. I've got pre-orders. Customers have been remarking on how much they love the concept. I don't want to let anyone down, but...' He shook his head, then straightened his shoulders. 'I can do it, I just need to... focus. See if Aaron can spare some time.' The words were uttered with an air of resignation.

'Don't fret. We can help,' Lila soothed. 'I could get Ned, Darren and Patricia to have a go at making tankards in one of our pottery classes.' She grimaced. 'Although I'll have to supervise them closely. Gryffyn hasn't been to a lesson since Wednesday.' She pressed her lips together, looking annoyed. 'But when he returns, and his granddaughter assures me he will, he's very handy with a pottery wheel.' She glanced at Ruby and winked, clearly not prepared to break the older man's confidences.

'I can make tankards. I've done it before,' Ruby found herself offering. She wouldn't turn her back on Gabe, but it didn't mean she was taking up pottery again beyond this one-off.

'No.' Gabe shook his head. 'I don't expect you to give up your time. This is *my* problem.' He grimaced. 'I just wish I knew who was doing this... If it's a coincidence or the police officer was right and it's something to do with me or the brewery. They were just tankards. I'm not sure why anyone would want to smash them.' He pinched the bridge of his nose again as he looked around. 'It is strange they left everything else, though. I don't know what to make of it.' He sighed, shaking off the mood. 'Do you have a bucket so I can tidy up?'

Ruby went to grab one from the back room. She could see the racks of drying pottery – Ned, Darren and Patricia's bowls from Friday, cups and saucers from the day before. As the police officer had mentioned, nothing aside from the tankards had been touched. Everything was exactly as they'd left it. Had someone come to the Pottery Project with the express purpose of destroying Gabe's work? *If so, why?* Could Aaron have something to do with it? She still didn't trust him and nothing she'd heard had changed her mind. But why would he hurt his brother? She headed back into the studio and put the bucket on the floor before gathering a handful of shards.

'I can do it,' Gabe said as he knelt beside her and began to pick up random pieces, checking each one and pulling a face as he threw it into the bucket.

'If I help, it'll be faster,' Ruby said, ignoring his answering grumble.

'Why don't I make us all a nice cup of tea,' Lila said, moving towards the door. 'I made chocolate cake earlier, that'll make us all feel better.' Then she headed outside.

Gabe didn't speak as they continued to clear up the shattered pieces. Ruby could tell he was angry because his shoulders were tense and he wasn't talking. There was no sign of the easy, warm man she was used to and a part of her wished he'd return. Getting involved made no sense, but she was drawn to Gabe, felt sympathy with his predicament, and the mere act of helping didn't mean she was letting herself care. They worked in silence until she heard the crunch of gravel from the drive and glanced up. Her Nanou was probably returning with the tea and cake now, anticipating that all could be fixed with a sugary snack and a quick shot of tannin. Ruby stood, searching around for a clear surface for Lila to put the mugs on, grabbing a couple of shards of tankard and throwing them into the bucket. She jumped at the sudden rap on the door, turned and sucked in a gulp of air which lodged in her throat, rendering her speechless.

Because instead of her Nanou's smiling face and treat-filled arms, Ross Penhaligon – her wayward father – was standing just inside the entrance, grinning.

19

'Rue!' her father exclaimed, dropping his battered brown bag onto the ground where it landed with a thud as he swept inside, holding his arms wide as if he expected a hug.

'No!' Ruby snapped, finding her voice, sidestepping him before he could touch her, practically skidding across the studio to put one of the worktables between them. Her heart was thumping hard with a combination of surprise, longing and fury. How dare he come. How dare he finally make good on one of his promises. 'It's too late,' she barked, aware that Gabe was standing too, staring at her, his head twitching back and forth between them. Her father's arms dropped and his features sagged. But she kept her resolve, even as the tiny chunk of the child inside her softened at that look. Her father had once been able to wrap her around his little finger, in the same way he'd done to her Nanou and mum. But those days were long gone and she wasn't about to drop her defences. 'Why are you here?' she asked, her voice toneless.

He looked confused. 'I told you I'd booked a flight. Didn't you get my email?'

Ruby pulled a face. 'I learned a long time ago not to believe what you promise in those.' Her eyes were drawn to the bulging bag he'd dropped at the entrance. 'If you're planning on staying in the house, then I'm leaving,' she said bitterly.

Ross's eyes widened at the vehemence in her tone. He looked older, she realised. He'd let his hair grow out and it was peppered with grey. The last time she'd seen him – at her mother's funeral – it had been cropped short and crow black. He'd once dyed it, a testament to his vanity – but wasn't the natural look in these days? And those grey flecks suited him, brought out the sky blue of his eyes. Then again, her dad had always been handsome – it was one reason why he'd been so good at taking them all in. Who wouldn't trust a good-looking stranger? Her eyes crossed to Gabe and she pressed her lips together.

'And you are?' Following the direction of her gaze, her father turned to the younger man, his face contorting into an expression that could only be described as suspicious. Ruby almost snorted with laughter. Years ago the idea of her dad being protective would have filled her with warmth. Now it just lit her fury.

'A friend,' she bit back. 'Nothing to do with you.'

'Gabe Roskilly,' Gabe answered quietly, holding out a hand. Ruby barely stopped herself from batting it away. Her father took it and shook, holding on for a little longer than necessary, probably gripping Gabe's knuckles in some kind of testosterone-fuelled warning, because it took the younger man two tugs to disconnect. It would have been amusing if it hadn't been so out of place.

He had *no* right.

'Are you visiting?' Gabe asked pleasantly, his eyes flicking back and forth between them in confusion – although he was too polite to let it show on his face. Ruby's animosity shouldn't have been a surprise. Then again, Gabe was the type of man to forgive and forget. Just look at the way he protected his brother. He was a million miles from the person she'd become. Yet another reason why she had to stop her heart opening for him.

'I...' Her father gazed at her as something shifted across his face. 'I'm not staying here with Nanou. I thought I'd pop in to... say hi. I've got a date with a friend later.' He pointed at his bag as if that would somehow explain everything. Ruby heard the crunch of gravel outside again and guessed her Nanou was coming. She shut her eyes.

'Pet, who's here?' Lila called from the driveway. 'There's a huge motorbike. Oh lordy, they didn't come back, did they?' She charged through the entrance, her cherry-red Doc Martens almost colliding with her father's bag. She righted herself just in time, carefully balancing a tray stacked with a large teapot, mugs and slabs of chocolate cake. When she spotted who it was, her mouth erupted into a spectacular smile. 'Ross!' In seconds, the tray was on the counter, and she'd been swept into his arms. They rocked back and forth as Lila hummed. 'I didn't know you were in the country.' She pulled away to study him, shaking her head. 'You look good, son. Tired but good. Are you here for a while?'

He glanced at Ruby. 'I'm not sure. I'm staying in the village, with a friend. I wanted to surprise you.' He gave her one of his trademark grins – the one with the single dimple in his left cheek that had divested many a woman of their senses. His eyes must have caught on a piece of broken pottery because he frowned. 'What happened – did you invite a posse of Greek waiters over for the evening? Where's the ouzo?' He bent and picked up a black shard before breaking away from his mother to pace the rest of the studio. 'Or is this something else?' His tone sharpened.

'We had a break-in while I was out earlier. The police have already been. Whoever it was smashed all the tankards Gabe was making for his business. Nothing else got damaged.' Lila kept her voice light. 'It's a bit of a mystery. There have been a few incidents at his brewery too.'

'It's probably not connected,' Gabe said, although it was obvious from his voice that he was struggling to convince himself.

'What kinds of things?' Her father's lips thinned.

'Oh, for goodness' sake,' Ruby muttered. 'This has absolutely nothing to do with you.'

'Slashed tyres,' Lila answered, patting Gabe's shoulder. 'His car got keyed and someone dumped manure on the steps of his family's business.' She counted the incidents off on her fingertips as if she were narrating a shopping list. 'You'll know of it – the Roskilly Brewery?' She turned to Gabe and beamed. 'Did I forget anything?'

'Um.' Rosy triangles spread across the tips of his cheeks. 'I think that's all of it.' He cleared his throat. 'Aside from the things that have been happening in the village, which may or may not be connected.'

Ruby frowned. 'Gabe's been having some trouble selling the field next to the brewery too.' She paused, unsure if he'd be happy with her sharing the information, but when she glanced over, he didn't shake his head. She turned to her grandmother, ignoring her father. 'The estate agent pulled out at the last minute and they were very strange about the reasons why. I was wondering if it might be linked to the vandalism too?'

'I'm pretty sure it's not.' Gabe pushed his fingertips through his hair, dishevelling it. 'Probably,' he added quietly.

'Our mystery keeps expanding. The Marples are working on tracking down whoever's involved.' Lila smiled at her son. 'We've been patrolling the area and asking around.'

Ross frowned, looking genuinely concerned. 'This is a matter for the police. You shouldn't get involved.'

'You don't need to worry. We're here to take care of Nanou,' Ruby snapped, wondering when she'd turned into such a shrew.

But her father always got to her; just being around him sent her hackles skywards.

'Do you want some tea and cake?' Lila asked in her sing-song voice. When Ross grunted and bent to pick up another piece of pottery, she grabbed a mug and plate and handed them to him before doling out the other two to Ruby and Gabe. Ruby didn't object; it was easier to just take it. She watched her father stand again and pace across the studio to look in the drying room, storage area and at the kiln. His expression was thunderous when he returned and he glared into the bucket they'd left on the floor, which was half filled with broken shards.

'I don't like the sound of what's been happening to you and —' He held up a sliver of pottery and waved it at Gabe. 'I don't like the look of this. Have you done something to attract the attention of the wrong people?'

Gabe gaped.

'Or anything at all to deserve this?' Her father's voice turned threatening. 'Because if you have – I'll tell you now, I'm not happy about my mother and daughter getting caught up in it.'

'Estranged daughter,' Ruby corrected, thumping the half-empty cup and plate onto the counter and glaring at him. 'And whatever Gabe's caught up in he's always welcome here.' She looked to her Nanou, who was nodding.

'We don't turn our backs on our friends, love,' Lila said quietly. 'Whatever Gabe needs, we're here to help. The whole village will stand by him, and as I said, The Marples are already investigating what's been going on. We're not children and we look after our own.'

'I don't like it, but I suppose I don't get a say.' Her father stared at them and his shoulders sagged. 'But if you'll let me,' he said to Ruby, 'I can help. I know people. People I used to deal with aeons ago when I didn't know better.' He dropped the piece of broken china into the bucket and sipped some tea before choking. '*Jeez*, that's strong. I think I'd prefer the ouzo.'

Lila grinned. 'I'll get you a glass in a minute. Tell us about these friends.'

'Not friends. Contacts.' Her father's dark eyebrows met. 'But these are the kinds of contacts who might know something about what's been happening. If they don't, they'll be able to find out.' He narrowed his eyes at Gabe. 'I'll ask around. Make sure whether all these events are just kids or a genuine coincidence. See if I can find out who's responsible. It might take some time, but if there's anything worth knowing, they'll find it out.'

'Thank you.' Gabe seemed to relax. 'I'd appreciate it. I really do think this is all just a case of bad luck, but it would be good to put everyone's minds at rest.'

Ross's gaze stayed fixed on the younger man for a few quiet moments until he tugged it away. Ruby frowned at her dad. She didn't want him here but perhaps having him around for a few days might be useful, after all? She just had to keep herself well out of his path while he was. She didn't care why he'd come. She'd turned her back on her father years before, and she wasn't about to let him into her life now.

20

Gabe walked behind the oak desk and sank into what he still thought of as his dad's chair in the small office at the back of the brewery. He shuffled for a moment trying to get comfortable, remembering his old man and how much he was missed – how much easier life had been when he hadn't been the one in charge. Gabe fidgeted again – the chair that had fitted his father like a glove felt too large, the arms were too high and the base dwarfed his behind. Evidence of his inadequacies and the fact that he didn't really measure up? He blinked, wondering what his father would have made of what had been happening. Then he poured himself a small glass of Deep Water Ale as Sammie sank to the floor under the desk and was immediately joined by Rex, who lolled over him like a limpet. Gabe drank deeply from his glass and pulled up the email he'd just read from one of the estate agents he'd spoken to in Talwynn last week. It had been sent earlier today. He scanned it again, feeling something in his stomach knot.

Dear Mr Roskilly,

Unfortunately, due to unforeseen circumstances we are unable to assist with the sale of the plot next to Roskilly Brewery. I'm sorry to be the bearer of bad news, but everyone here at Merit's wishes you every success. Please don't hesitate to get in touch should you require assistance with another sale.

Kind regards,

Mr R Dyson

Merit's Estate Agent, Talwynn

Gabe scrubbed a hand over his face and sipped his beer. He'd tried to call Mr Dyson as soon as he'd seen the email, but the phone had flipped to voicemail. Perhaps it was because he was calling on a Sunday, or maybe he'd blocked the number? A-Plus Services, the other estate agent he'd met with on the same day, was continuing with the listing so far, but this was bizarre, especially when he took the other rejection into account. He'd been ignoring the signs for a while now, but add this to the devastation at the Pottery Project this evening and it was clear it was time to stop and smell the roses – or in this case dung. Despite his protestations to the contrary, it was clear this was unlikely to be another coincidence. He pinched his nose. Someone obviously had it in for him or the brewery. He just didn't know who, or why. Aaron passed through his mind like a black cloud. The conversation they'd had about selling the business had been bothering him; he'd pushed it away at the time, surmising his brother hadn't really meant it. But what if he had?

Gabe sucked in a breath, exasperated with himself. He owed his brother trust, didn't he? Aaron had been through so much already without his only relative turning on him. At least Ruby's father was looking into the problem now, so there was some hope he'd find a reasonable explanation. Gabe had been holding out for it all being a coincidence – but it was becoming increasingly clear that was unlikely.

There was a knock on the door and Jago eased it open before taking in Gabe's open laptop and half-full glass of beer. 'Woman trouble?' he guessed, plodding inside still wearing his green steel-capped wellies, tugging off his cap and scratching his head. 'I'm hoping you're going to say yes because if that look on your face is anything to do with the brewery, I don't want to know. The heaters in the warehouse malfunctioned this morning and some of the ale has spoiled – which means production is way down again.' He puffed out an annoyed breath. 'I've worked here since I left school and I've never known the gear to behave like this – it's like a mechanical apocalypse.' He pulled out a chair, then must have changed his mind because he tramped over to the counter at the edge of the office to grab a glass and a bottle of the beer Gabe kept out to show visitors. He popped the lid and poured before sipping the top of the frothy liquid and letting out a satisfied groan. 'Okay, I needed that...' He slumped into the visitor's chair on the opposite side of the desk to Gabe and continued to sip, as the ridges in his forehead smoothed out. 'Oh wow, I've said it before and I'll say it again, I'm a genius.' He sank another mouthful and sighed before checking his watch. 'Dammit. I've got to leave in a few minutes. It's Sunday night and I shouldn't even be here, so lay all that misery on me now, but you'll have to be quick.' He finished the half and slapped the dirty glass on the table, then folded his arms over his dark overalls and gave Gabe one of his don't-mess-with-me stares.

'I'm fine,' he muttered.

'So it *is* woman trouble.' Jago angled a dark eyebrow and nodded sagely. 'It's been a while, but I can just about remember that far back. Did you even *try* buying her flowers?'

Gabe didn't smile. 'This has got nothing to do with Ruby.

We're just...' He waved a hand in the air because he wasn't sure he had the words to explain it. 'Having fun,' he finished limply.

Jago blinked his dark lashes and pressed his lips together. 'You haven't had fun with a woman since you split from Camilla. I think you've forgotten how. Besides, fun is more Aaron's speed. You're more the type who mates for life.' He held up a palm when Gabe started to protest. 'It takes one to know one, so that's not a dig, more of a "yes, I get it" male bonding moment.' His chest heaved. 'Appreciate it because I don't do them very often – and don't bother to disagree.'

Gabe didn't. There was no point. His friend was right. He'd been feeling lost for years, more than a little lonely. Every day felt like the same thing over and over, carrying the weight of responsibility with no one to share it. Watching the way Jago was with his wife and kids kept triggering flutters of jealousy, a tentative *what if*? Now Ruby was around, the *what if* had become a more definite question, although he didn't have an answer for it. 'It's not woman trouble,' he said evenly, taking another sip of beer. 'But you're right about one thing – you *are* a genius.' He offered the slightest tilt of his lips.

'So what is it?' Jago furtively checked his watch again before he frowned at the open laptop Gabe had set to one side.

Gabe sat up straighter and waved a hand. He didn't want to worry Jago – the burden of what was happening at the brewery and its financial consequences had to remain squarely on his shoulders. A problem shared wasn't always halved – he knew it could multiply like a fungus, infecting everything it came into contact with. And he wasn't about to lay this pain on anyone else. This was his problem – and Aaron's. Not that he'd had a chance to share it with his twin yet. 'Go home. Everything's fine. *I'm* fine,' he added as his friend's eyebrows met. 'It's nothing I can't handle.'

'If I didn't have to leave in two minutes, I'd make you tell me,' Jago growled. He rose from his chair and nailed Gabe with a scowl. 'Tomorrow you *will* share. You have to know you're not alone in...' He twirled his wrist. 'Whatever this is. Sometimes, it's important to talk.'

'I talk to Aaron,' Gabe said, even though they both knew that was a lie. It would be pointless because his brother never talked back, not about anything important, and recently – at least since Ruby had been on the scene – Gabe had suspected he only told him what he wanted to hear. 'I'm fine, really. I've just got a lot to think about.' He tried another smile and failed, distracted by the million things whirring around his mind – Ruby was just one of them, and in some ways she was the easiest. But the thing he was finding hardest to come to terms with was whether Aaron was involved in what was happening at the brewery. The thought had only started to occur to him when he'd seen all the pieces of broken tankard. Not many people knew about his trips to the Pottery Project. A handful of Lila's clients, Jago and a few brewery employees. But Aaron knew. Although what the sense in all that destruction was, he had no idea. But now the thought had taken hold, it was hard to dismiss. Had he spent the last few years covering for his brother, looking for the best in him, making excuses while all the while he'd been laughing at him? He swallowed. Did that make him an idiot? He wasn't sure he was ready to decide.

He rose and followed Jago to close the door behind him. Then he leaned back against the dark wood, taking in the sprawled dogs and their interlinked paws. The brothers were close and Gabe felt a pinch in his chest for the relationship he'd inexplicably lost, before he tracked back to the desk and peered at the laptop. He'd received a copy of the brewery's latest set of accounts almost a week ago and hadn't found time to look at them. That was supposed to be Aaron's domain, but now Gabe wondered if leaving it all to his brother had been such a good idea. He opened the email and attachment, then almost jumped out of his skin when someone rapped on the door.

'Come in,' he said, rising to his feet as Ruby walked in. She was still wearing the pink silk dress from earlier and something about her presence in the room instantly soothed him. The hair that she'd put up into a bun had started to come loose and he had a sudden urge to take the whole lot down – to run his fingers through those wavy locks as if they were some kind of stress toy.

'Your, um...' Ruby pointed behind her into the shop. 'Jago told me to come straight in. He said you'd be happy to see me.' She looked confused. 'You don't look happy. Am I disturbing you?' Her fingers knotted as she took in the laptop and beer. 'Working?'

Gabe shrugged as he watched her. The tight knot of tension between his shoulder blades had eased now she was here. 'I thought I might check the accounts, but I'd welcome some company. I suspect they'll be grim reading, so I've been avoiding them. Also, numbers aren't really my thing.' He didn't miss the shock that flickered across her face. Then again, numbers were Ruby's thing. For a moment, he considered asking her to look at them, before dismissing the idea. That would feel disloyal somehow. 'Fancy a beer?'

She took in his empty glass before nodding and he tracked up to pour her a half, putting it on the table where Jago's had been sitting a few moments before.

'I probably shouldn't have come,' she said, slumping into the chair and folding her arms in her lap. 'Dad decided to stay for a couple of hours so he could catch up with Nanou, and I didn't have the heart to...' She waved a hand. 'I wanted to make myself scarce.'

'Do you want to talk about it?' Gabe asked as her eyes traced his fingers, which were drumming on his empty glass, before her attention strayed up to his mouth. He swallowed.

'Not really.' She cleared her throat. 'In truth, I've got this feeling, this...' She made a hissing sound. 'I just had to get out of his way. He has a talent for getting under my skin, making me feel guilty for not giving him another chance.'

'Should you?' Gabe asked, leaning back in the chair.

Ruby shook her head. 'I'm not my mother. I don't believe in second chances. Do you have ouzo?' she asked, slamming the empty glass back onto the desk. 'Since *he* talked about it, I can't get the taste out of my mouth.'

'By *he*, I assume you mean your father?' Gabe asked, heading to the cabinet to check in the cupboard where his dad used to keep spirits.

'Tonight I'm sticking with pronouns. It makes it easier to pretend he doesn't exist.' She sighed.

'I've got tequila or white rum but no more clean glasses.' Gabe pulled out two half-full bottles and brought them back to the table. 'Choose your poison and I'll rinse some out.'

She looked up at him, her eyes sparkling. 'Suddenly I'm feeling reckless. Same glass is fine. I'll have one of each, let's start with tequila. It might just help me forget about *him*... Besides, I'm not driving.'

'How did you get here from the Pottery Project?' Gabe poured her a small shot, suddenly pleased she'd come. Spending time with Ruby was preferable to sobbing over his problems – or worse, the company accounts.

'I got a taxi. I walked into town and happened to see one by the harbour.' She smiled. 'I thought they were rarer than mermaids.' She shrugged.

Gabe chuckled. 'They usually are. I'd say this was your night, but...' He watched as she drank the shot in one, tipping her head backwards over the chair and exposing the soft white skin on her neck. He'd dreamed about pressing his lips to that exact spot, moving slowly downwards... Something thrummed in his belly, dipping below his waistband, and he picked up the bottle of tequila and poured himself a large shot. He could call Ruby a taxi, then walk home from here, leave the car. He was supposed to be relaxing more, wasn't he? Proving he wasn't just the boring twin. He swigged the spirit down in one, then thumped the glass back on the table, feeling the final knots of tension across his shoulders ease. He'd drunk shots with pretty women before, although he couldn't remember far back enough to recall the exact details or whether he'd been this drawn to his drinking companion. 'Another?' he asked when her eyes met his and any sensible thoughts evaporated. Because her pupils were now almost completely dilated.

'Rum this time.' She licked her lips, making the heat coursing through his body edge closer to boiling. 'Same for you...' She pointed to his empty glass. 'We're going to get drunk.' She reached up to pull the band out of her hair, and Gabe watched speechless as blonde curls tumbled down her shoulders, framing her face which was flushed from the rush of alcohol. 'And we're going to let our hair down.' Her grin was impish and he found himself smiling back. This was the other side to Ruby Penhaligon. The one he'd seen on the beach and again at Sunset Point before they'd been interrupted. This was a peek behind the rigid shield she hid behind. He liked it. Liked *her*, he realised. A lot. In another life their relationship might have become serious. But not in his. Not now. His eyes skimmed the laptop. He had too many other places he belonged and there was the small matter of Aaron... It was one thing for him to doubt his brother but quite another for someone else to do the same.

He poured Ruby a generous shot of rum and gave himself the same. Jago's words came back to taunt him as he gazed at her again, watched the delicate pulse in her neck as she picked up the glass, sipped a little and swallowed. *Fun is more Aaron's speed. You're more the type who mates for life.* But he didn't have the headspace for a mate, did he? He drank some of the rum, let it slide down his throat, but didn't finish the glass. He wasn't in the mood to get drunk, didn't have time for a hangover. He watched Ruby place her glass back on the table too. She looked over at him, a knot marring her forehead.

'The alcohol's not really working and I'm not up for a headache. I'm still not fully relaxed, though.' Her eyes dropped to Gabe's mouth and his mind blanked.

'Um... what else might help?' he asked roughly, even though he'd already guessed what she was going to say. Or maybe he was just hoping. She was here, wasn't she? It might be the whole reason she'd come. If it was, he wasn't complaining. Even if a small part of him wondered if it was such a good idea, if he could really hold his feelings in check.

She stood and began to walk around the desk, the silk of her skirt swishing around her legs. 'I've a few ideas.' Her voice was low and sexy.

'Like what?' he asked, knowing he was already sunk.

'You know.' Her eyes met his. 'In the interests of not being boring...' She gave him a half-smile.

'Heaven forbid,' Gabe said, his lips curving as heat and lust extinguished any remaining doubts. Then Ruby started to move again and he moved too, meeting her as she rounded the corner of the desk and practically leaped into his arms.

'Remember the rules,' she whispered as she leaned into him, wrapped herself around his body, shooting all of his senses into orbit. *What were the rules again?* he wondered as she pressed her lips into his, smoothing the crease with her tongue, encouraging him to open his mouth. He wasn't capable of holding back now, so he lifted her and placed her bottom on the desk, making sure the laptop wasn't going to get squashed. She wrapped her legs around him, slid her fingers into his hair as his heart thumped faster, sending a tsunami of blood rushing into his ears. 'We don't need this.' She eased back to push her fingers under the hem of his T-shirt and lift it above his head, exposing his torso which she lightly stroked with a fingernail, making the muscles across his stomach bunch.

'I should probably lock the door,' he ground out, starting to pull away as Ruby put his top on the table, but she didn't unlock her legs.

'It's Sunday evening, aren't we the only ones here?' she asked softly.

'Well... probably. Yes.' Gabe's gaze fixed on the entrance and he could almost hear his brother telling him he was boring again. He had to wonder if the assessment was right. What kind of man worried about locked doors when he had a woman like Ruby in his arms? He glanced down as her hands slid to the straps of her silky dress. She slid them slowly off her shoulders to her waist, obliterating any thoughts of locked doors or people wandering in from his mind. She wore a sheer pink bra which was exactly the right shade against her pale skin; it made her look almost luminous. He didn't get to study her for long because she fixed her mouth onto his again, then let her fingers drift under the waistband of his jeans. Gabe almost leaped up, had to grab her arms and make her stop. 'We should probably slow down,' he groaned, as his fingers wandered to the curve of her back to unclasp the hooks of her bra and let it fall from her shoulders. She pressed herself into him, and he moaned as their mouths met again. This time the kiss was hot and deep and took his breath away. 'Are you relaxed yet?' he asked, catching his breath as he pulled back an inch or two to undo the tiny buttons that secured the top of the long skirt, failing miserably because they were too small for his clumsy fingers. In the end, he gave up and pushed the silky cloth slowly up her legs, laying it onto the table to expose her thighs and matching pink pants.

'Almost,' she whispered, leaning in to nibble his earlobe. 'That doesn't mean we're slowing down.' He felt her hands dip to his jeans again and undo his belt buckle, unthreading it before placing it on the table by the soft folds of her skirt. She sighed as he pressed his fingers against the lace of her pants, leaning down to pull one of her nipples into his mouth.

'Glad to hear it,' he whispered as she sighed again, making his pulse thud.

'I've dreamed about this,' she murmured as he moved his mouth to the other nipple, making it pucker as she wriggled closer to the edge of the table. 'Sometimes, when I'm working on a spreadsheet, I imagine just letting go...'

'With who?' Gabe growled against her mouth as he kissed his way across. He knew he sounded jealous but wasn't capable of hiding it.

She gasped as he moved lower. 'No one in particular, but I'm guessing any fantasies will feature you from now on.'

Gabe grinned. The words shot through him, filled him with something he didn't want to name. He slid his hands to the sides of Ruby's hips and gently tugged off her pants, felt her reach into his. Before his jeans slid down his legs, he reached into his back pocket and pulled out a condom. He hadn't been expecting this, but after what had happened on the beach, he'd wanted to be better prepared. Ruby eased back and watched as he opened the packet. Then he moved closer again until their skin was pressed together and their bodies were touching.

It almost felt spiritual as they joined and began to move. Gabe could feel a spinning in his head, a crash of emotion as he kissed Ruby again, then let himself fall.

21

Ruby pulled out her laptop the next morning, ignoring the new aches in her body, trying to ease the memories of Gabe's kisses from her mind. Spending time with him was supposed to be fun, a way to relieve the tension in her chest which had once again subsided. But when he'd walked her the long way home to the Pottery Project in the early hours, holding on to her hand, she'd known she was beginning to develop deeper feelings. Feelings she didn't want to have. Ruby ignored her sense of anxiety and flicked through her emails. After responding to a couple of clients, she scanned down and recognised the name of the photographer from the exhibition in Talwynn. She opened the message; the woman explained she was going to be back in the country in the next few days and promised to send Ruby a link with all the photos she'd taken in Indigo Cove as soon as she arrived. Would things change between her and Gabe once she had the evidence to prove Aaron was the father of Anna's child? Something in Ruby didn't want to risk it, but she knew she had to proceed. Just having Ross in Indigo Cove was throwing up so many feelings from her childhood – she had to ensure Maisy never went through the same. Ruby checked her watch and got out her mobile to call Anna. They hadn't talked in a few days, and she wanted to catch up to see how the flat and job hunt were progressing.

Anna picked up on the second ring. 'Morning,' she said. 'How's the love life?'

Ruby almost choked on her coffee. 'Too complicated to talk about this early in the morning,' she said as Maisy gurgled in the background. 'How's the job hunting?' She changed the subject quickly, unwilling to confide in her friend about what was happening with Gabe. The sex was hot and devastating in its intensity. If anyone was in danger of breaking her contract or rules, it was her.

'I've had two interviews, but no news yet,' Anna confided as the baby giggled. 'Simon called...' She dropped the bombshell, sounding breathless.

'What?' Ruby gulped down her coffee, burning her mouth.

'We met up and talked. We... I don't know, we might give things another try.'

'You're getting back together?' Ruby's forehead scrunched. If Anna got back with her ex, what would happen when she proved Aaron was Maisy's father?

'I'm not sure,' Anna said vaguely. 'We miss each other. Simon acknowledged he's been stupid and jealous. He knows he needs to work through that. There are a lot of things we still have to talk about. I just... I don't know. I'd forgotten how much I loved him. How good he is to Maisy. He was so happy to see her, and she lit up when he walked into the restaurant, wouldn't stop babbling the whole time we were talking.' The line fell silent. 'I'm just wondering if we could make this work. But I don't want to move in with him again, not until everything's sorted. And you know how I feel about getting my independence back.'

'I do,' Ruby said softly. 'You need to know I'm getting closer to tracking down Maisy's biological father.' When Anna let out an irritated huff, she pressed on. 'I'm not going to force him on you both – I'm not sure you'd want him in your lives – but I do want you to have choices. For Maisy to have them when she gets older.' The kinds of choices she'd never had.

'I'm not interested,' Anna snapped. 'I know why you're doing this, Ruby, and I appreciate it, but it annoys me that you're not taking my feelings into account, that what I want doesn't matter.'

'Of course your feelings matter,' Ruby said, hurt.

There was a clatter and Maisy started to cry. 'I need to go. Let's talk some other time. I'm not going to change my mind about this. Maisy doesn't need a father, same as you didn't. When you stop obsessing over what you didn't get from Ross, you'll realise you were probably better off without him.' With that, Anna hung up. Stunned, Ruby stared at her mobile before she heard the patter of cats' feet in the hallway and quickly gathered her things – Patricia, Darren and Ned would be arriving for their lesson soon and she had lots to get ready. She tracked into the hall, stopping outside the study to open the door and check the damage. Nothing had changed since she'd removed the carpet. The builder had promised to visit and quote on the work in the next few days, but she had no idea how they'd pay for it.

Ruby didn't see her Nanou as she made her way out of the cottage and locked the door before heading to the Pottery Project. Music was playing in the studio – something soothing by Mozart – and the space felt tranquil, as if the atmosphere left by the break-in the evening before had somehow been eradicated. Lila was laying out cakes and scones in the kitchen when Ruby stepped inside, making the older woman jump.

'Pet, you scared me.' She twisted around and half smiled. Her hair was in its usual bun, but there were no implements poking from it, which suggested she hadn't done any pottery today, probably because she was still upset. 'You got home late last night?'

'I went to see Gabe,' Ruby admitted. 'Did you have a nice time talking with... my father?' She didn't feel comfortable calling him Ross, but 'dad' and 'father' felt wrong too. How did you refer to someone who had no place in your life?

Her Nanou nodded, her face brightening. 'He was telling me about the investments he's been making. He's doing really well and he promised he'll return all of my money before the end of the month, so you really don't have to worry about the office,' she gushed.

'Nanou, you know you can't trust his promises.' Ruby sighed as someone called out from the entrance. They stepped into the main studio to find April with a half-asleep Harriet in a buggy and Gryffyn standing by her side.

'Good morning!' April sang, guiding her obviously unwilling grandfather further into the studio, holding the crook of his arm. He looked so uncomfortable Ruby almost expected to see an iron buckle strapped to his heel and a heavy chain being dragged along behind. 'As you know, Grandad hasn't been feeling well which is why he missed so many classes, but despite that, he spent the whole time moping around the house and wouldn't go to bed to sleep off his mystery illness.' April glared at her grandfather as the baby let out a yelp from the pram. The young woman swiped a hand across a cheek, drawing attention to the dark circles under her eyes. 'Harriet's been up most nights, teething. I'm hoping a dose of Calpol will mean I get a few quiet hours to recover.' She fixed her grandfather with a miserable stare. 'It's hard getting sleep in the daytime when someone is stomping his own personal marathon around the sitting room. I'm sure Grandad will be far happier here. Until late last week I'd have said he's been having the time of his life. Did something happen?' Her head spun towards Lila.

Lila widened her eyes and pursed her lips. 'No, he's been

the perfect client. He picked up the pottery skills like he was born to it. If I didn't know better, I'd have sworn he'd tried it before.' Her lips curved, but her face was bare of any hint that she was teasing.

Gryffyn coughed loudly into his palms and April patted him on the back. 'I'm pleased to hear it. Let's hope he manages to get through the rest of the course without any more mystery ailments.'

Gryffyn shoved his hands in the pockets of his jeans as he studied the studio. 'Something's happened in here, I can smell it.' He sniffed. 'There's a lot of dust... Did something get broken?'

'I'll explain when Patricia and Ned arrive.' Lila pointed to the kitchen. 'Why don't you get yourself a slice of cake? It's good to have you back, Mr Brown.' She said his name without irony, but her message was clear – Gryffyn's secret was safe if he didn't want to share it. The older man pierced her with a surprised look before he nodded and headed into the kitchen.

'Thank you for being so discreet,' April whispered when he'd disappeared. 'But Grandad told me you'd guessed who he is.' Her eyes shot to the kitchen. 'He's always been such a hero to me, but after he had the stroke, he just...' She grimaced. 'Gave up.'

'Is that why you booked him onto the course?' Ruby asked.

April nodded, pushing the buggy back and forth when Harriet started to complain. 'I was desperate. I knew he wouldn't want to come along, but he had to get his hands back in some clay. I guessed once he had, he'd find it almost impossible to stop.'

'He seemed to manage fine staying away last week,' Lila grumbled.

April shook her head. 'He's been so miserable. I knew if I insisted, he'd come back. He just didn't want it to be his idea. But I promise, Grandad's been like a new man since he started your course. Now we just need to figure out how to get him to stay.'

Lila brushed her hands over her smock. 'I have a few ideas...'

April beamed. 'Thank goodness.' Her smile dropped as Gryffyn sauntered out of the kitchen.

'What are you gabbing about?' he barked.

'Nothing!' April began to pull the buggy backwards out of the exit as her grandfather started to protest. 'Have a good day – I'll pick you up at five o'clock. Have fun!' Then, with one last penetrating look at Ruby and Lila, she left.

The older man sniffed the air again. 'It really doesn't smell right. It's not just your fancy incense nonsense either.' He thumped his mug onto the counter and tramped across the room to peer into the drying room and then the storage area. 'All the tankards have gone,' he gasped. 'There's no way Gabe finished painting the lot in the few days I was gone. What happened?'

There were more footsteps on the gravel driveway and Patricia poked her head in. 'Good morning!' She swept inside with Ned following. 'Sorry we're late. Someone came to discuss putting a pond into our new garden. After Ned painted the fish on his bowl last week, we decided we didn't want to wait.' Her smile faltered as she took in the assembled faces. 'Is something wrong?'

Darren scooted into the studio behind Ned and his nose twitched. 'It smells funny in here – like when I go out and Mum dusts my bedroom.'

'We had a break-in last night.' Lila calmly folded her arms when Patricia let out a shocked gasp. 'Nothing to worry about. All your pottery is fine, but Gabe's tankards were smashed. If you get yourselves some refreshments, I made tea, coffee, scones and carrot cake this morning – I'll explain everything.'

'Do you think it was the people causing trouble in the village?' Ned asked, as Patricia headed into the kitchen and returned carrying hot drinks which she handed to Darren and Ned. She revisited the kitchen and appeared seconds later with plates piled high with chunks of cake before heading back to get herself a mug.

'Someone's causing trouble?' Gryffyn asked as he sipped his coffee.

Ned nodded. 'There's been a lot of petty crime recently.'

'Do you know who's responsible?' the older man growled.

'Not yet, but we think there are a few culprits,' Ned admitted. 'Could be teenagers. No offence!' he added when Darren made a snarling sound.

'It's always the teenagers who get blamed.' The young man rolled his eyes.

'If it's not kids, who is it?' Gryffyn asked.

Lila picked up a pottery tool and slid it into her bun. 'As Ned said, we've no idea, but a few of us are trying to find out – I suspect at least some of the issues are connected to Gabe and his brewery. The fact that it was only *his* pottery that got smashed last night suggests he's being targeted for some reason.' She pulled a face. 'I'm not sure he's ready to believe that yet, but my son popped in for a visit last night and he thinks the same.'

'Why didn't I know about all this vandalism?' Gryffyn asked.

Lila pursed her lips. 'You were a bit distracted.' Her eyes darted to his hands and the older man frowned.

Ned scratched his chin. 'Wasn't Gabe making those tankards for his brewery's centenary?' He searched their faces.

'They were supposed to be finished by next week – that leaves him no time,' Patricia gasped, calculating on her fingers how many days were left. 'How's he supposed to replace them all? Doesn't he need them for his customers?'

'They need to be thrown, dried, fired and painted. It's going to take hours,' Lila said softly as her eyes travelled around the room.

'It's an impossible task if he's working alone,' Patricia agreed, finishing her drink and walking over to the hooks next to the kitchen to tie on an apron.

'Then we'll help the boy,' Gryffyn snapped, as his attention rested on Lila. 'You can turn making tankards into a lesson, I assume?'

'Oh!' Patricia clapped her hands and bounced on her heels. 'I'd love that.'

'Me too,' Darren said, flushing when everyone turned to stare at him. 'At least it won't be boring.'

'They're not easy...' Lila looked unsure. 'The logo took us hours to get right. It took Gabe a few evenings to perfect it and he made a lot of mistakes – not just breakages but false starts.' Lila's eyes slid back to the older man.

'Are you chicken?' He quirked an eyebrow. Lila's shoulders stiffened and her eyes dropped to Gryffyn's hands. The challenge was clear, but instead of looking angry, his face lit up. Then again, how often did anyone challenge him these days?

'We'll need all hands on deck if we've a hope of getting them all done,' Lila said. 'Ruby's quick on the wheel but even with the six of us working flat out, it's likely we won't get them all finished.'

Gryffyn stared at Lila. 'We'll do it. I once finished a whole tea service in an afternoon. This will be a lot easier. Especially if we have a team working on it.'

'We'll have to involve Gabe. I know he wanted the tankards to be made by members of his family,' Lila said. 'Although in the end it was only him who ever turned up.'

'Well, we're part of his family now.' Patricia flashed a smile. 'His pottery family anyway. If it's a choice between letting us help and letting down his customers, I'm guessing he'll choose the former.' She blinked, her eyes skirting the room. 'Why don't we start straight away, we can make something before he arrives. Show him how much we want to help?'

Lila nodded. 'That's a good idea. Gabe is coming to the studio late this afternoon. We don't have much time, so we'd better get started. Ruby, can you put out some clay please? Set yourself up next to Ned and I'll work close to Patricia and Darren. That way we can show them how to make the tankards step by step.'

'Um, if you don't mind.' A wave of pink engulfed Ned's cheeks. 'Can I work beside Gryffyn? I mean, I do a lot better if I'm being...' He paused. '*Encouraged* by someone who's, well... a little bit mean.'

'Charming,' Gryffyn muttered, but his blue eyes sparkled. 'Why don't you move to my corner?' he suggested to Ruby. Then he picked up his coffee and mug and practically sprinted across the studio to the wheel closest to Ned. 'I'll not be giving you any encouragement, boy. You play by my rules, do what you're told, and remember everything I told you last week. I'll turn you into a potter – even if it kills you.' He began to wet the wheel, looking lively, and Lila took a moment to watch, her eyes bright with amusement.

'Looking forward to it, mate.' Ned barked out a laugh.

Darren stood by his wheel, seeming torn.

'Why don't you move over here too?' Ned suggested. 'Boys together?'

'Yep,' Gryffyn agreed. 'I'd like to see what you're capable of and this way I get to keep an eye on you too.'

The teen's cheeks flushed, and he jerked his head before pacing across the studio.

Ruby grabbed the wet clay from the storage area and cut slices for each of the potters, wrapping them in cling film so they didn't dry out, while Gryffyn lowered his stool and wriggled around trying to get comfortable.

'Do we have a template, or something we can copy?' Patricia asked Lila.

She shook her head. 'Every tankard got smashed, there's

nothing to work from – aside from the logo. We're going to have to create a design from memory.' She turned to Gryffyn. 'Why don't you start us off?' Her voice was all challenge. The older man stared at her, then looked down at his hands, his expression grim before he shucked his shoulders and nodded.

Ruby plucked the business card Gabe had given her from the pocket of her apron and handed it to the potter. 'I've got this, if it helps...'

The older man scratched a hand over his salt and pepper beard and stared at it. 'I'm not sure we can recreate what Gabe was doing exactly. But I made a set of tankards for an exhibition once.'

'I knew you weren't a beginner,' Patricia said.

'I think the design might work here,' he continued. 'It's got simple lines which would be easier for a novice to work towards – and we can just paint the logos on later.' His attention flicked up and his gaze rounded the room. 'I'm going to demonstrate. Watch me carefully because I'm only going to do this once. If you get stuck, ask. And!' His gaze shifted to Ned. 'There's no such thing as *can't* in my studio.'

Patricia coughed. 'I thought this was Lila's studio?'

'Oh, I'm more than happy to share it,' Ruby's Nanou said, giving Gryffyn an assessing look. 'I've been teaching here alone for a long time now – I suspect it would benefit from some new blood.'

'My blood is decidedly old,' Gryffyn growled as he flexed his fingers a few times and began to press them into the clay, manipulating it into a perfect globe. He set the wheel in motion before wetting it with exactly the right amount of water.

Lila gave him a sober look. 'There's no such thing as *old* in my studio – no *has-beens*, no *I can't* and no *I give up because I'm not as good – or as young and flawless – as I was.*' Despite her tone, there was a sparkle in her eyes Ruby had never seen. 'If you can work with that, you're very welcome. I've been thinking of hiring someone to help with the teaching for a while.'

Gryffyn coughed. 'There's nothing like your own words being thrown back in your face. You're giving me something to think about all right. At least the fact that I said them first means they're worth listening to.' Lila let out a loud burst of laughter and Gryffyn grinned. 'But I work for no one – never have.'

'Partner then?' Lila countered, looking surprised. 'With equal say in everything...' She paused when Lemon and Walnut scampered between her legs. 'Except for the cats.'

Gryffyn studied her for a long time, perhaps considering the idea, before he shook his head. 'I'm a loner when it comes to pottery, it's the way I like it. Besides, I *am* a has-been.' He turned back to the wheel. Lila frowned as he began to work on the clay, squashing it expertly in his fingers as he gradually worked the material into a funnel shape, pushing and kneading as his face tensed in concentration. Ruby watched transfixed as within a few minutes Gryffyn had created a perfect tankard shape with smooth sides, a fine ridge at the top and a rotund base. She'd never say it aloud, but it looked better than any of the tankards Gabe had made. 'This has to dry.' Gryffyn used a wire to cut the bottom of his creation, then moved it onto the table beside him. 'In a minute I'll show you how to make the handles. I hope you were all watching carefully?' He moved his gaze to Ned who bobbed his head, then to Darren who saluted. 'Then why are you all still watching me?' he snapped. Ned grinned and quickly threw water on his wheel, immediately moulding his clay into a slightly wonky imitation of the shape Gryffyn had made, while Darren got started too.

Lila watched them work before picking up another of the pottery tools and threading it into her hair. She dipped her chin towards Gryffyn's abandoned pottery wheel and stared at Ruby. 'Go on then, show us how many you can make.'

Ruby walked slowly across to the wheel and breathed in as she picked up the fresh slice of clay, relishing the feel of the material beneath her fingertips. She'd vowed she wouldn't do this again, but she could already feel the fast patter of her pulse as anticipation swept through her and her blood began to pound. She placed the clay onto the wheel and thrust her fingers into it, closed her eyes, and for the first time in years let herself feel...

22

Ruby stretched, easing herself away from the pottery wheel towards the kitchen and switching on the light, illuminating her workspace. She'd been working for hours – the rest of the gang had left an hour before, but she just wanted to finish the tankard she was making so it was ready when Gabe arrived. She pressed her fingertips into the clay again, smoothing the surface, letting her head fall back and closing her eyes so she could rely on her sense of touch. She'd not let go like this in years, but just one stroke of the pliable surface and she'd fallen head over heels. Better, the tension in her chest had eased. There was something so comforting about the texture of the clay and how she could manipulate it into whatever she wanted. Sure, it went wrong more often than not, but there were so many possibilities, so many outcomes just waiting to be found. Working with numbers didn't have the same unpredictability – you always knew what you were going to get. She frowned: that had always been one of the reasons she'd loved her career. No surprises, a series of checks and balances you could rely on, a safe conclusion to a day's work. But was it too safe, was she just masking all her feelings? She blinked at the odd thought before staring down at her hands.

A breeze whispered through her hair and she opened her eyes and checked the entrance. 'Sorry I'm late.' Gabe was standing in the doorway watching her, his green eyes bright and serious. 'We had an offer on the field via another one of the estate agents, and it looks like it might actually go through this time. All very last minute, and there was some toing and froing about the offer on the phone.' He wandered into the studio, his long legs eating up the space. and closed the door after checking for cats. Then he let the dogs off the lead and admonished Sammie as he wandered to one of the pottery stools and started to cock his leg. Rex scampered after and began to imitate his brother, but a sharp word from Gabe put a stop to them both.

'You must be relieved?' Ruby asked, taking in a deep breath, overwhelmed by her reaction to him. Her whole body seemed to be vibrating, as if it wanted to leap off the chair and throw itself at the man. A leftover from what had happened the night before? She pushed the feelings away and tried to fill her mind with numbers, but found her attention slipping to Gabe's hands instead, remembering how good his rough finger-pads had felt when he'd touched her.

He stopped beside her. 'It's good news. Especially since we had another problem today. A file of data corrupted.' He rolled his shoulders as his jaw flexed. 'Jago's frantic.'

'Why?' she asked, relieved at the change of subject.

'We've likely lost a load of casks in the system because we can't track them anymore – expensive, inconvenient, frustrating.' He shook his head as his forehead squeezed. 'I really don't understand what's happening.' He stopped suddenly and pulled a face. 'I'm droning again.' His lips thinned as he gazed at her, making her insides fizz. 'Everything okay? You look...' He continued to study her. 'Something's off.'

'I'm fine,' Ruby said, keeping her voice light, turning her

back – uncomfortable that he could read her so easily. 'I've got something that might improve your day. A surprise.' She grabbed his hand and led him to the drying room, where twenty-five newly created tankards were drying on the second shelf.

'What – how?' His jaw dropped as he gazed at the creations.

'The pottery gang. They wanted to help out, even Gryffyn. I know you wanted to remake the tankards yourself, but... well, we didn't think you'd have enough time. If we work together over the next few days, we should have all one hundred ready for the centenary. Everyone helped.' Ruby intertwined her fingers, disconcerted that she cared so much about Gabe's reaction. He said nothing as he bent to look at them more closely. 'Is it okay?' Ruby asked, wondering if they'd made a mistake when he remained silent.

Gabe scratched his chin. 'It's...' Ruby's heart clenched. 'Actually, it's great.' His mouth stretched into a broad grin. 'I mean, they're obviously not as good as the originals.' He puffed out his chest and snorted. 'But seriously, I've been worrying about this all day. We had one of our most important customers ask if he could increase his order because he wanted more tankards and I was wondering how I was going to tell him we had none.' He closed his eyes and scratched his fingertips across his lips. 'I've stopped asking for help since Dad died; I thought Aaron and I should be able to handle everything, but...' His chest heaved. 'Thank you.' He turned to gaze at her. 'You've honestly saved my life.'

Ruby put her hands in her pockets and stepped away, overcome by her reaction to the sweet words. 'It wasn't just me, everyone helped. Gryffyn especially. He's a good teacher, although you'd never know it if you listened to half the stuff that comes out of his mouth.' She quickly made her way out of the drying room and almost tripped over the dogs on her way back to the pottery wheel. 'Did you want to make some tankards while you're here? I assume that's why you came?' She swallowed, feeling the burn of embarrassment shift across her skin. She never lost her cool around men, had never let herself care. She deliberately turned away, then felt the warmth of his chest across her back.

Gabe leaned down and dropped a kiss on her shoulder, and she almost combusted on the spot. 'Sure,' he murmured softly. 'You might have to demonstrate. Jokes aside, those tankards are better than any I made.'

Ruby nodded without turning and went to grab some clay, laying it out on the wheel and wetting it before she got to work. She didn't look at Gabe as she pressed her fingers into the material, wetting it again and letting her hands absorb its ebb and flow – but she could feel him watching. 'You need to squeeze it here.' Her voice was husky and he dropped a hand on her shoulder as he moved so he could watch. There was something about the feel of Gabe's skin on hers that made it difficult to breathe. 'Get closer so you can see.' She sucked in a breath as he hesitated and then lowered himself onto the back of her stool. She wanted to tell him to back off, but found her throat closing up. 'Closer,' she murmured instead, scooting forward, giving him space to inch nearer to her back. She could feel him pressing against her now, feel the warmth from his muscles burning into her skin. What was wrong with her? In a couple of days, she'd have proof Aaron was the father of her best friend's child, and Gabe was bound to be angry – she should be keeping him at arm's length, protecting herself. Added to that, she was leaving, going back to her real world, where she got to control her feelings, where she didn't get hurt. But she found herself rocking backwards so her bottom connected with Gabe's groin, heard his sharp intake of breath as he pressed himself against her and dipped his mouth to the ridge of her neck. She shuddered, caressing the clay between her fingers, adding more water to the wheel until it was dripping wet. Then she watched transfixed as her hands pressed and slid as if they were somehow guiding themselves. The movements were erotic and something tightened in Ruby's chest as she let that side of herself go, let her creativity rise to the surface. Gabe continued to dab his mouth along her neck, moving to her jawline.

'Is this how all your lessons start?' His voice was low. 'Because if it is, I might book myself in for a course.' Ruby's breath rushed out as he slid his fingers underneath the bottom of her shirt, tentatively stroking the rough pads of his fingers across her skin, exploring as he gained confidence. She should be moving, pushing him away, but found she didn't want to. She held in a groan as Gabe glided his hands upwards while she hugged and rubbed the wet clay. 'That doesn't look much like a tankard,' Gabe joked, coming up for air to watch. Ruby pressed her fingers inwards, clutching the smooth surface. *This isn't me* – at least, this wasn't the woman who'd spent the last ten years trying to avoid strong emotions of any kind. She tried to pull back, but the tight feeling across her chest was getting stronger as she continued to hold in her feelings. Added to that, a pulse was beating between her legs. Ruby pressed her thighs together as Gabe undid her bra, loosening the material so his hands could explore.

'Oh...' Ruby's fingers shook and she suddenly lost control – the clay collapsed inwards, landing in a gloopy mess.

'I'm sorry,' Gabe whispered, sounding anything but as he slid his fingers to the waistband of her shorts, making quick work of the button. Ruby swallowed, wishing she could bring herself to move, as her head fell back onto his shoulder and she moaned. She knew she should stop him, jump up from the stool and finish whatever was happening, but couldn't stop herself from giving in. Her body was awash with sensation, the rigid control she was so proud of gone.

There was a knock at the entrance and Ruby jerked away.

'Is that Nanou?' she whispered, fumbling to fasten her bra as Gabe jumped off the stool, leaving her feeling oddly bereft.

He glanced at the doorway and strode towards it, looking back to check she was decent as Ruby jumped up and rearranged her clothes. 'It's your dad,' he said softly.

'You'd better go,' she murmured. She couldn't handle both of them being here at the same time. Not when her emotions were so heightened and she was feeling so confused.

Gabe frowned but nodded. 'I'll message you later.' Then he strode back to kiss her on the cheek. He grabbed the dogs and opened the door before Ruby could ask him to give her more time to gather herself.

'Um, I'll make a pot of tea,' she said to her father, disappearing into the kitchen without looking at him. When she returned, he was hovering by her wheel.

'It's good to see you potting again,' he said quietly. 'Did you know Lila put me on a wheel in this studio when I was three? I made a blob shape. It was terrible, but I think she still has it somewhere.'

'She told me. She keeps it in the sitting room with a mug you made.' It sat amongst Lila's favourite pieces, in pride of place next to Ruby's red bowl: relics from two talented potters who'd both walked away from something they loved. It was the first time Ruby had realised it and the thought made her uncomfortable. 'Nanou told me having your pottery there makes her feel like you're with her. I suppose she needs something since you so rarely are.'

Her father absorbed the jibe with a good-natured tip of the head. 'I know I deserve that,' he murmured, the corners of his eyes crinkling. He glanced around, then swept past her to look into the drying room. 'I heard from Nanou that you were making more tankards. The replacements look good. I used to love coming here when she was working. I still enjoy crafting here on my visits.' He sauntered back to admire the shape Ruby had created before Gabe had arrived. She'd left it drying on the counter. 'That's brilliant, you're a real chip off the old block,' he said, and she felt a rush of anger, a sudden desire to smash the fragile structure with her fist. She didn't need her father's approval, hated the way those kind words had warmed her insides.

'You said you used to love coming here, yet you gave it up,' she said carefully, trying to keep her temper in check.

He sighed, pulling up a stool. Ruby fought the flinch, the desire to escape. So what if he wanted to connect with her? She didn't have to let him and she should be able to share the same air as the man. 'I didn't give up. I paused, I suppose,' he said earnestly. 'It was hard, frustrating. In those days I was always looking for an easy fix.' The admission was a shock and Ruby gawked.

'Is that why you gave up being a husband and a father too?'

'You're mad and I get it,' he continued in a low voice, his eyes fixed on the pottery in front of them, perhaps because he couldn't bear to see what was etched across her face. 'I'm a crap father, and I was a worse husband. I wasn't ready to be either of those things when you were born.' The edge of his mouth twisted. 'I had no idea what to do with you when you came along and your mum was so much better at everything than I was. I suppose it became easier to just let her get on with it.' He let out a long sigh as the memory of her mother sat between them, an open wound neither of them had faced.

'I guess she didn't have much choice,' Ruby said, wondering why she was still here. She didn't want her father's confessions and his recognition of his inadequacies wasn't going to make up for anything. She was over him. All the way over. Had been since the last – and final – time he'd let her down. It's why she kept her heart safe, why she'd never allow herself to get close to a man again. But then she thought about Gabe and blew out a breath as she realised she was falling for him. She had no control over her feelings, despite all her best intentions. Would pulling away now, trying to keep herself safe, end up being more painful than just letting herself go?

'If it means anything, whenever I came home, I always meant to stay,' her dad continued, his face contorting. 'I wanted to be what you both needed, but I...' He frowned. 'I used to watch you and think you deserved so much better. Both of you. Being around you was a constant reminder that I wasn't good enough.'

'So you left and proved your point over and over again...' Ruby said, ignoring the shudder in her chest. His need for connection – she wasn't going to give him that. If she gave him anything, she'd be allowing him to manipulate her. Then how long would it be before he hurt her again?

His shoulders sagged. 'I thought we had all the time in the world. I believed one day I'd be ready. I'd make the money I kept promising, one of my deals would work out, then I'd come home for good and make you both proud.'

Ruby glared at him. 'Instead, you broke all your promises, left us high and dry. Smashed any chance we had of being a family. As good as killed my mother.' At her assessments their eyes met. Her father's were the same shape as hers, but it was the only similarity they had. The only similarity she'd allow.

He shrugged but didn't protest. 'I let her down. I let you both down.'

'And you can't make up for it,' she said quietly, lifting the tankard from the counter ready to move it into the drying room before turning towards him – steeling any feelings she could feel leaking out. 'You're still the same man doing the same things. There's no redemption for you here, whatever you think you want. If I let you in – even an inch – I know I'll live to regret it.' His face paled, but she ignored it. 'Leopards don't change their spots – even if they think they can.'

'Are you sure?' he asked softly.

She nodded, but for the first time the jerk of her head was more out of habit than certainty. Her father's eyes stayed fixed on hers for a few moments, and Ruby saw his chest heave before he nodded. He opened his mouth and closed it before nodding again, lifting himself off his stool. Then he turned and walked slowly out of the studio, as Ruby fought the desire to follow him. She had to stand firm, she had to stay safe, which meant she not only had to avoid her father from now on, she had to do the same to Gabe.

23

'I need money – from the brewery.' Aaron swigged from a mug of coffee and swiped a hand through his sandy hair without looking at Gabe. His voice was croaky, as if he had something stuck in his throat. 'It's my business too,' he said accusingly. Gabe glanced at the door of his office and stood to shut it, blocking any chance of their employees overhearing.

'I know that, but we haven't got any money,' he said softly, tracking back to the desk. 'The accounts are grim reading.' He frowned at his brother. 'You must know that, you see them every month?'

Aaron shrugged, his expression blank.

'There are more outgoings than I'd usually expect and a lot's been going wrong with the equipment recently – it's hit our bottom line.' Gabe's stomach clenched and he fought the fear of letting his family down, of failing everyone. When Aaron didn't respond, he slumped into his dad's chair, avoiding Sammie and Rex who were asleep under the desk. 'Why do you need it?' he asked more gently.

Aaron shook his head. 'Nothing much, just... you know, things for my design course.' He avoided Gabe's eyes as he drank from the mug again, then tracked across the carpet, tracing the perimeter of the small room like a caged animal. Had he lost more weight? Gabe hadn't been paying attention, too caught up in the broken tankards and his worries about the business – not to mention his complicated feelings for Ruby. He frowned, wondering what his dad would think of that.

He stared at Aaron's face, noticing the pale skin and bags under his eyes. 'Are you ill?' he asked as fear punched his solar plexus.

'I'm fine. I don't know why you'd even say that. It's like you want me to be sick again,' Aaron bit back.

'What?' Gabe's head snapped up.

'It means you get to be the big hero all over again, to bail out the poor weaker twin. Don't think I didn't notice how Dad was always telling you to take me under your wing. I'm a grown man and I don't need rescuing,' he ground out, his eyes lit with a vehemence Gabe had never seen. 'I'm doing a course, trying to be the person Dad wanted, to make a success of myself. I helped with the brewery logo, worked on the counter, took your meeting with the estate agent. What else do I need to do to prove myself?' His tone was bitter. 'I'm just asking for a helping hand.'

Gabe swallowed. He'd been doubting Aaron when his brother had only been trying to finally stand on his own two feet. How had he missed it? Guilt swamped him and he did some fast sums in his head. 'I can give you a thousand – a loan against the sale of the field now we've got an offer.' He couldn't afford it, but he'd find a way of raising the money. When the land was sold, he'd be able to pay it back. If the estate agent was right, the whole thing would go through in weeks, giving them a welcome influx of cash.

Aaron nodded, the relief on his face tangible. Sammie woke and trotted out from under the desk, then sniffed his brother's shoes, begging for attention. Aaron ignored him, his eyes already on the door. 'I've got to go, I've an... online meeting with one of my tutors. If you can transfer the money today...' He glanced back at Gabe. 'Hang on, I almost missed what you just said. We've got a buyer for the field?'

'Yep, the offer came through last night, which is why I haven't mentioned it. The sale should go through quickly. After we get the money, we'll be able to look at expanding. Maybe we should celebrate with a few beers tonight?' Gabe stood and strode around the desk to get closer to his brother.

'I'm busy.' Aaron stumbled backwards taking a long, wide step, his mouth forming a grim line. There it was again – that distance, the hint of annoyance. No matter how hard he tried, Gabe couldn't breach it even after all these years. Was it because his brother thought he'd somehow stepped in and taken over? Had Aaron been mad at him for years? He swallowed a wave of hurt and shook his head as his brother turned and grabbed the door handle, then looked round. 'You'll have the money in my account before the end of day?'

'Sure,' Gabe murmured, watching Aaron ignore Rex as he trotted up to stand beside Sammie before he slammed the door in the dogs' faces.

It was oddly quiet at the Pottery Project as Gabe sat at one of the wheels and rotated it slowly, immersing his fingers in the clay, remembering how it had felt when he'd last been with Ruby, his fingers tracing her skin. He hadn't heard from her since they'd been interrupted by her father; he'd texted a couple of times last night and again this morning, but there'd been no response. Was she having second thoughts about seeing him? She was leaving in less than two weeks so that was probably for the best. He didn't have the time for a relationship – especially considering all the problems at the brewery and his recent revelations about

Aaron – but he'd still been thinking about her, wondering if there might be a way for them to continue seeing each other when she was back in London. He frowned at the shape forming between his fingers – it was off centre, wobbly, and nothing like the template he was supposed to be working from. An imitation of his life? He shook his head as Ned, Patricia, Darren and Gryffyn wandered into the studio, talking loudly.

'You're here, boy!' Gryffyn muttered, stooping beside him and frowning at the creation on his wheel. 'Did your hand slip?' he asked, sounding amused before he went to grab one of the aprons from the hook beside the kitchen.

'I—' Gabe cursed as the shape wobbled and collapsed. 'Got distracted.'

'No mind,' Lila sang, walking into the studio beaming. 'I'll make us some tea – a gulp of that and you'll find your mojo again. Where are the dogs?'

'With Jago,' Gabe muttered, wondering what he'd do if his head brewer ever decided to leave. His whole life would probably look like his lump of pottery... The others grabbed their aprons and began to get their equipment ready too.

'Remember, not too fast!' Gryffyn barked, as he started up his wheel and splashed on water, narrowing his eyes when Ned did the same. 'Slower,' he growled, before his attention shot to Gabe. 'You need to concentrate: we've got seventy-five more of those to make, dry, fire and paint.' He watched Darren work until he saw a perfect tankard begin to emerge. 'Good work,' he said softly. 'You remind me of... well, me, from a few years back. There's a raw talent in those fingers waiting to emerge. You just need the right teacher.'

'Were you good at pottery once then?' Darren asked bluntly. 'I guess you're too old to get better now.'

Gryffyn chuckled. 'I was okay. You'll learn a lot from Lila, though.'

'Well, I think you're *both* brilliant,' Patricia muttered. 'You make a good team.'

Darren nodded. 'Yep. You're like good cop, bad cop – only with clay and a pottery wheel. You're better than any of my teachers at school.' The teen harrumphed and continued to mould his clay, so he didn't see the flicker skip across the older man's face.

Lila slid out of the kitchen and grabbed a couple of tools to jab into her hair. She glanced around the room and frowned. 'No Ruby?'

Gabe shook his head, swallowing disappointment.

'She's in her room, she told me she had some work to catch up on,' a man's voice rang out, and when Gabe turned, Ross Penhaligon strode into the studio, pulling up his shirtsleeves. 'I heard you needed all hands on deck?'

Lila went to pat him on the shoulder. 'This is a treat. It's been ages since I had you in my studio. Why don't you set up at my wheel?' She wandered to the counter and dragged out her sound system and some vinyl. 'It's shaping up to be a Dolly Parton day,' she said as she put on a record and '9 to 5' began to play loudly.

Darren groaned and rolled his eyes at Gryffyn, who snorted but didn't object. The older man seemed more relaxed; was there even the tiniest hint of a smile at the corner of his mouth?

'I'll do a couple of hours of tankards, then I'll have a look at that problem in your office,' Ross said, setting himself up. He had the same easy flow of movements as Lila, and Gabe could see the similarities to Ruby in the shape of his eyes. 'The money's still coming.' He held up a palm when Lila looked worried. 'It's just going to take a bit more time and I... I'd like to help. Maybe I'll stay in Indigo Cove a little longer than originally planned.' Lila pressed a hand to the edge of his face and beamed.

'Any more problems with the vandals?' Patricia called out,

and Gabe saw a tankard shape began to emerge in the clay she was crafting. It was smooth and even – everyone in the class was coming on leaps and bounds. Unlike him – Gabe frowned at the chaos on his wheel and began to clear it up.

'Nothing's been reported,' Lila admitted. 'That's looking great.' She smiled, walking up to join Ned, her eyes scouring the room as she kept a careful eye on the potters – although Gabe noticed they rested on Gryffyn more often than not.

'I saw something,' the older man barked. 'I've been seeing it for a while, but I didn't connect the dots until you mentioned all the shenanigans. I just now realised it might be important.' He skimmed his fingers over the tankard he'd just finished before cutting it off the wheel and guiding it to the counter, grabbing more clay. He started to shape it and they watched mesmerised, waiting for him to continue.

'And?' Lila probed, when it was clear Gryffyn had got caught up.

He glanced at her and his blue eyes fired. 'April and I are staying in a house which overlooks the eastern end of the beach. I don't always sleep, or Harriet wakes me when she's teething.' He shrugged. 'Sometimes at night, I get up and look out of the window. I keep seeing the same bunch of teenagers milling around.' His eyes slid to Darren who shrugged.

'Nothing to do with me.'

'I've no idea if they're connected to the vandalism, but Ned mentioned some chairs had gone missing from the harbour and...' Gryffyn's forehead wrinkled. 'One of the kids was carrying one, they were playing catch with it.' He pushed out his bottom lip. 'They looked harmless enough, but I was thinking of walking down after we finish today. I'll talk to them, find out what they're up to.'

'I'll come.' Ned stretched up from his wheel, his usually amiable expression more serious. 'I used to be in security – you shouldn't go to the beach alone.'

'I want to go too,' Darren said. 'See if I know them.' His lip curled. 'They won't talk to any of you. You're too old.'

'I think we'll all go,' Lila said firmly. 'Let's call it a Pottery Project outing.'

'I'll see if I can find time to come,' Gabe promised. If the kids Gryffyn had seen were connected to what was happening at the brewery, he wanted to know who they were and why they were targeting him.

24

'Simon and I are back together,' Anna said to Ruby the minute she picked up her mobile. 'I know you'll think I'm crazy, but he's really changed. That doesn't mean we're moving in together yet. I've got a place of my own now, we're going to take it slow.'

'You've got a flat?' Ruby asked, stunned. 'That was quick.'

'I've not moved in, we're still in the hotel.' Maisy giggled in the background and a man's voice rang out. 'Simon helped me find a place close to where he lives – he's here now.'

'Well... wow,' Ruby floundered. 'That's...' She wasn't sure what to make of the change of heart and was instantly suspicious.

'Simon told me the break made him realise what a jealous idiot he's been,' Anna said quietly. 'He spent so much time focusing on whoever Maisy's father was, he forgot that it was him. He got completely freaked out, which is why he didn't want to adopt her anymore.'

'Are you sure you can trust him?' Ruby asked, keeping her voice low.

'Can we ever be sure about anything?' Anna let out a long

sigh. 'Sometimes, you've just got to take a leap of faith. You're so hung up on the way your father behaved, you've forgotten there are good men out there, Ruby. And you've started to expect everyone to let you down. That leaves no room for people to make mistakes.' She paused. 'But people make them, get confused, go down the wrong path. That should be okay... as long as they learn from them and find their way back.'

'I know,' Ruby murmured, thinking of her dad. He was here now, although she wasn't sure for how long. Was Anna right? Was she just waiting for him to mess up?

'Simon wants to adopt Maisy, he says he's ready.'

'And you're thinking about it?' Ruby asked, moving away from the small desk she'd set up in the corner of her Nanou's spare room. She'd been working all morning, avoiding Gabe, her mind filled with a million emotions and fears. Was she waiting for him to let her down too? 'What about Aaron?'

Anna snorted. 'Even if he is Maisy's biological father, I've told you already, I don't care.'

'I know you deleted the photos from Instagram, but I'm going to have different proof soon. I can talk to his brother, ask him to make Aaron get involved,' she pleaded.

'He's a sperm donor, Ruby, nothing more,' Anna said quietly. 'I told you, I'm not interested. Nothing's changed and it's not going to.'

'I get that's how you feel now,' Ruby murmured. 'But what if Aaron can change too?'

'Maybe he can, I don't know him well enough to say,' Anna said. 'What I can tell you is that even if he does, I don't care. You choose the people you want in your life. Some of them fit – if they do, they become your family – and some of them you have to leave behind. I'm choosing Simon, I've already chosen you. Who are you going to choose?'

'I don't know,' Ruby whispered, continuing to stare at the mobile long after her friend had said her goodbyes and hung up.

. . .

Ruby opened her laptop again and stared at her emails. She'd been waiting to hear from the photographer in Talwynn, but now the email had arrived, she wasn't sure what she wanted to do. Anna didn't care if Aaron was Maisy's father, so she wasn't sure why it was so important that she expose Aaron as the liar he was. Perhaps she just wanted to protect Gabe. It was clear that even if he was Maisy's father, Aaron wouldn't be welcome in his daughter's life. Then again, what if Simon suddenly let Anna down? She stared at the email for almost ten minutes trying to decide before she clicked on the link and loaded the page. The blank screen filled with a gallery of tiny pictures and she checked the first, expanding it in all its multicoloured glory. She leaned on her elbows and started to scroll, getting caught up in familiar faces and locations. Many she'd seen at the exhibition. After ten minutes, she spotted her Nanou standing by the harbour, staring out to sea with a hot drink in one hand and a slice of chocolate cake in the other. Gabe featured a few pictures on, his rugged frame braced against a pillar. Ruby guessed it was him because his battered Volvo had been parked in the background and his expression was too nurturing for it to be Aaron. She let her eyes scan his profile and felt something inside her click – made herself ignore it.

She continued to scroll, carefully examining every face, pausing to study them and checking for the photo of Anna. The photographer had spent hours capturing people on the Ferris wheel, and there were lots of colourful shots of the mural and beach, plus a few outside The Pasty Place. Her finger suddenly stopped its slow glide on the trackpad as she saw the edge of Anna's face, a pink T-shirt she recognised. She stared at the photo, then flicked to another, recognising it as the one from the collage. Ruby sat back in her chair, slowly nodding because the owner of the mystery arm swung around Anna's shoulder was who she'd suspected – Aaron. It definitely wasn't Gabe. She knew his clothes, the way he tilted his head, the almost imperceptible contraction of his eyes when he was thinking. It was inconceivable now that she hadn't been able to tell them apart at first.

Ruby's stomach knotted as she imagined Gabe's reaction when she confronted him with the evidence. She'd been working towards this moment since she'd found out Simon wasn't Maisy's father, but now she felt more confused than justified. Gabe trusted Aaron, and she was about to break that trust. She leaned forward as she continued to search through the photos, finding more of the couple together. It was obvious from the way they were holding hands and kissing that they were more than friends. When she'd finished, Ruby sent three of the pictures to her Nanou's printer, wishing she hadn't found anything, after all.

A series of loud bangs erupted from Lila's office when Ruby wandered down the corridor to pick up the photos from the printer. She swung the door open and stopped just inside, her breath catching when she spotted her father taking a mallet to the plaster on the furthest wall where the rot and mould had bedded in. He'd moved the furniture to the far corner of the small room and thrown a white sheet over it in an effort to protect it from the mess. Ruby wandered further in and peered under the edge of the sheet, locating the printer which had already produced the colourful photos of Anna and Aaron. She grabbed and checked them before shoving them into her handbag, feeling a twinge of regret when she imagined Gabe's reaction. Would he believe her, or find some other way of protecting his brother? For the first time, doubt prickled across her skin. What should she do? Let a father walk away from his child like Ross had done to her? Listen to Anna and leave it be? Torn, she frowned at her father as he put the mallet down and turned, spotting her. 'What are you doing?' she asked.

'Nanou told me about the leak, so I thought I'd see if I could help,' he said, staring at the patch of plaster he'd been working on which was now back to bare brick. 'It's not as bad as I expected. With a bit of luck, I might be able to fix it myself.'

'Meaning the money isn't coming?' Ruby snapped, shaking her head.

Flames crept up her father's cheeks. 'The money is coming, Rue. I spoke to my partners this morning.' He held her eyes. 'I'm expecting dividends to be transferred into my account any minute now.' He pulled his mobile from his pocket and checked the screen. 'It isn't here yet, but they promised. I know I have no right to expect you to believe in me, but I'm going to prove myself to you.'

Ruby had heard the same words a thousand times before, but for the first time in years, she felt a twinge of optimism. She chewed her bottom lip as Anna's words filled her head. Could people change? Was there hope for her father, after all? She blew out a breath. 'I have to speak to Gabe.' She turned and dismissed him.

'Wait!' he said, gently taking her arm. 'We need to talk. I heard from my contact earlier. I know who the vandals are and it's not good news.'

25

'I saw them loitering there,' Gryffyn growled, pointing to a series of rocks as he tracked along the empty beach close to where he was staying with April and Harriet. Ruby glanced around but could see nothing except seagulls and a scatter of black rocks poking out from the sand. The sun was high as it was still late afternoon, and she could feel the warmth on her face but took no pleasure from it.

'There are footprints,' Ned shouted, pointing towards the sea where the waves were drawing in and out, erasing the edges of the telltale tracks. Darren scampered ahead, then bent to examine them more closely. He stood suddenly and pointed right as if he were a bloodhound catching a scent. Ruby followed the others, holding herself back. She didn't know why she'd come, but after speaking with her father and burying herself in work for a few hours, she'd found everyone in the Pottery Project making plans to meet the rest of The Marples. They were preparing to hunt for the mystery vandals, and she'd been packed up and hauled along, while her dad had opted to stay and guard the studio. The group had been expecting Gabe to show up too, but he'd been caught up in a problem with the phone lines at the brewery. Ruby hadn't minded; she wasn't ready to confront him about Aaron, or the things her father had discovered. She was too worried about how he'd react. She knew she'd have to tell him eventually, but she was putting it off. She hadn't confided in anyone – it wouldn't feel right before she'd talked to Gabe.

'I see something!' Clemo yelled, pointing to a clear area in front of some dark cliffs that jutted over the sand just before the beach curved around a sharp bend. Ruby saw three small shadows in the distance, then they disappeared. Seconds later, Claude started to gallop towards them, with Clemo and Darren bringing up the rear.

'There are caves down that way that would be perfect for hiding in!' Clemo bellowed, beginning to sprint, his muscular legs powering over the ground.

Lila came to tuck Ruby's arm into hers as they followed, with Gryffyn, Ella, Patricia and Ned flanking them both.

'You okay, love?' her Nanou asked quietly as Clemo, Claude and Darren drew closer to where the shadows had been standing.

'All good,' Ruby murmured, feeling bad for holding back but knowing she had to. Darren suddenly shouted as three figures emerged from the mouth of one of the caves and began to run in the other direction, away from them.

'We need to catch up!' Darren shrieked, storming ahead. His youthful legs ate up the space as the rest of the men were left in his wake. Even Gryffyn and Lila started to trot, and within a few minutes, the group had reached the top edge of the beach just before it curved around. There was a chair slung in the sand just a few metres ahead. Claude jogged over and bent to pick it up, dusting off a leg.

'*Merde.* This is from my restaurant,' he growled, as he glared down to where the three figures were now hovering, their heads snapping left and right as they frantically searched for an escape.

'We only want to talk!' Darren yelled, stepping forward, but as he moved, Clemo went too and what looked like three teenagers scooted back. Darren twisted around. 'You need to let me go on my own,' he whispered. 'They won't talk to you, but I might be able to convince them to come back.'

'But they're surrounded,' Gryffyn growled, rolling up his sleeves and pointing to the sea. The tide had been drifting in while they were on the beach, cutting off all access further down. The only direction the teenagers could safely head in now was towards them.

'There are more caves down there,' Ella said. 'We don't want to scare them.'

'True, they might run inside and get themselves lost,' Lila said quietly. 'What if they got trapped?'

Gryffyn huffed. 'Fine,' he grumbled. 'Let the boy try.' He turned to Darren. 'Tell them it'll be better for them if they just come clean. Not just that, it's the right thing to do.'

The teen snorted. 'Yep, that'll work.' He rolled his eyes before turning back towards the trio who were standing a little further away, tentatively glancing at the narrow entrance to the caves on their left. 'Don't move. I just want to talk,' he shouted, gesturing with his arms. 'The olds will wait here, you've got nothing to fear.'

'Charming,' Gryffyn grunted, and Ned put his hands on his hips while Claude continued to brush sand from his chair. They all watched as Darren slowly approached the group of teenagers, still holding up his hands. Then they waited as the young boy talked earnestly, waving his arms and pointing in their direction, pulling wild faces and shaking his head.

'What are they saying?' Patricia stepped forward and cupped a hand to her ear.

'No clue. We need to wait. We know from our own kids they're more likely to open up to someone of their own generation.' Ned pressed a gentle hand on her shoulder. 'Darren will be able to talk to them at their level. He's our best bet.'

'I don't like it,' Gryffyn protested, but he didn't move. After a few more minutes of discussion, the group slowly turned and began to tramp in their direction. As they drew closer, Ruby could see there were a couple of boys and a girl, all dressed in black.

'You want to talk to us?' one of the boys asked belligerently, stepping forward. His skin was pale and he looked around sixteen. Ruby could see he was holding a packet of sweets – the same brand as the ones she'd found on Sunbeam Moor and at Smuggler's Rest. It suggested they were responsible for at least some of the vandalism, which tied in with what her father had found out.

'I know you from the cafe,' Ella said, sounding annoyed. 'You're from the village?'

'No comment,' the boy said, his expression hostile.

'This will go better for you if you talk. Did you steal that chair, boy?' Gryffyn demanded, pointing to where Claude was standing.

'No, he did.' The boy pointed to a teenager with white-blond hair and smirked. 'We'll take it back.' He shrugged. 'It was just for fun. It's not damaged.'

'Fun?' the older man snapped. 'What about the one you did break?'

'That was an accident,' the girl with long black hair and heavy make-up murmured, glancing at her boots. 'We were playing catch—'

'Catch?' Patricia sounded surprised.

The girl shrugged. 'There's not much else to do around here.'

'So scratching cars, slashing tyres, smashing pottery and dumping manure is fun, is it?' Ned snapped.

'Um—' Ruby began to speak out, but the girl shook her head vehemently.

'We just told him.' She stabbed a finger at Darren. 'We didn't do any of that! We took the chairs for a laugh.'

'We were going to bring them back.' The blond boy kicked his foot in the sand without looking at them. 'We've made some fires, done some stuff on the moors and around the beach and high street, but we didn't do any of those other things.'

'You expect us to take your word for it?' Clemo asked, spreading his legs and glaring.

The pale boy shrugged. 'I don't care.'

'I do,' the girl whispered, swiping hair from her face as a gust of wind caught it. 'It wasn't us. We didn't mean to break the chair and we'll pay for it.' She widened her eyes, and despite the layers of make-up, Ruby could see she was really quite young.

'I believe them,' Darren said quietly and the teens nodded, gathering around, absorbing him into their group.

'So do I,' Ruby said, wondering if she'd have to come clean before talking to Gabe.

'I don't know,' Clemo growled.

'I think we have to give them the benefit of the doubt,' Lila said softly, glancing at Gryffyn. 'People do silly things sometimes, but I have to say what's been happening to Gabe is a long way from the petty vandalism in the village.'

'I don't know if I believe them either,' Ned said gravely. 'They could have easily broken the tankards on Sunday night.'

'I don't think—' Ruby started to explain.

'But we couldn't,' the girl squeaked, suddenly searching the pockets of her jeans. 'We went to watch a *Matrix* movie marathon in Talwynn on Sunday – see, here's my ticket.' She thrust it triumphantly under Ned's nose. 'It was on for most of the evening, we couldn't have been in two places at once.' The men frowned as the two boys searched their pockets and produced the same bunched-up stubs.

Lila studied them before nodding. 'Did you paint on the rocks by Sunbeam Moor and on the mural outside the ice cream place?' she asked. 'Be honest, you're going to have to fess up.'

The pale boy puffed out his chest. 'So what if we did? I'm an artist and everyone says we should express ourselves. Besides, that moustache was good. Took me ages, then someone cleaned it off.'

Darren shrugged. 'It *was* good.' His eyes flicked to Gryffyn. 'Wrong but...'

Lila nodded. 'Makes you think. With the right tools, maybe a decent teacher, who knows what he could do.'

The older man considered her words. 'You like to paint?'

'Dunno.' The boy shrugged.

'Yes, he does,' the girl said shyly, earning herself a sharp look.

'I heard the youth club shut. Must be hard to find things to do now?' Patricia took a tentative step towards the teenagers, her expression kind.

'We didn't go all the time,' the girl said.

'Do you like pottery?' Lila asked, her face brightening.

'Why?' Gryffyn asked, still glowering at the teens.

'Because I have an idea.' Lila suddenly smiled.

'Oh, I see.' Patricia started to grin too. 'That might just work!'

'What?' Gryffyn and Ned both demanded, their heads bobbing back and forth between the two women.

Patricia and Lila put their heads together and began to chatter excitedly until Clemo put his hand in the air. 'Hang on,' he yelled and the crowd quieted. 'If these kids aren't responsible for the things that have been happening at the brewery and the Pottery Project, then who's been targeting Gabe?'

Ruby looked down at her bag, realising she couldn't put it off any longer – it was time to tell all. She just hoped Gabe would listen to what she had to say.

26

Gabe rearranged the kegs at the front of the brewery shop, then headed behind the counter, jerking around as he heard foot-steps approach, hoping Ruby had finally decided to pay him a visit. He'd been jumpy all day – he had no idea why, but there was a prickle across the back of his neck, an odd foreboding that something wasn't right.

'We need to talk.' Jago folded his arms across his chest. He wore his usual steel-capped wellies, a green boiler suit and a bone-deep frown.

'What?' Gabe asked, suddenly afraid his head brewer was going to resign. He couldn't even contemplate the possibility of running the brewery without him so ignored the feelings of dread as they sank in.

'Someone's been switching the labels on the bags of hops,' Jago said soberly. 'I spotted it while you were speaking to the phone engineer earlier, thankfully before we used any.' He shoved his hands into his pockets, his spine stiffening. 'I think it's time we agreed there are too many things happening in this place for it to be another coincidence.'

'Vandals again?' Gabe asked, glancing around. 'There's no way they'd get access. It must just be a mistake.'

Jago's Adam's apple bobbed and he gazed at the floor before looking up and deliberately meeting Gabe's eyes. 'We have to consider the possibility of an inside job – maybe even sabotage.'

'That's, what... who?' Gabe asked as his whole body turned icy, shaking his head before Jago uttered the name he knew he was thinking. 'It's not Aaron. He loves this place as much as we do,' he implored, remembering their conversation from the day before, feeling another wave of guilt that he'd ever suspected his brother. 'Aaron might be a bit unreliable but—'

Jago sighed heavily and looked down at his wellies without answering. Gabe could read his mind, though – the thoughts had been etched in his voice, the doubt brimming from his eyes.

'I know my brother can be irresponsible.' Gabe cleared his throat. That was an understatement, but his dad's words were ringing in his head – *You need to take care of Aaron.* Couple that with the things his brother had said in his office and Gabe knew he had to protect him. 'He wouldn't do anything to jeopardise the business. It's his future and he's happy here.'

'Would he tell you if he wasn't happy, though?' Jago asked softly. 'Because from where I've been standing, your brother barely speaks to you about anything important at all.'

'That's probably my fault.' Gabe bristled and started to shake his head. 'Siblings don't always share everything,' he grumbled. 'Your kids are young, things will change when they get older.'

Jago's forehead bunched. 'I'm not trying to tell you I know better.' He planted his calloused hands on the oak counter and leaned forward to look into Gabe's eyes. 'All these problems – it's not normal. Add them to the vandalism and broken tankards: mate, you've got to wake up and smell the roses before this whole place goes down.'

'It's not going anywhere.' Gabe ran a hand through his hair, feeling weary. 'We're going to be fine. We've got a buyer for the field, the whole thing should go through before the end of the month. There's really nothing to worry about.' At least that's what he was telling himself. And he believed it, most of the time.

Jago huffed. 'Don't treat me like an idiot. I know exactly how much trouble we're in.' Gabe's head jerked up. 'Suppliers talk – I know we've been paying our invoices late.'

'We have?' Gabe choked. It was news to him. 'It'll just be a blip in the payments, nothing to worry about.' Unsettled, he made a note to call their accounts company later.

'Stop being a fool and shutting me out.' Jago grimaced. 'I work here too. I loved your dad and I care as much about the brewery as you. Stop taking the whole damn place on your shoulders – there are people here who would be happy to share the load.' His eyes flashed bright blue, and he shook his head when Gabe gaped at him.

'It's not that,' he started, even though the brewery *was* his responsibility – Aaron's too. 'It's just—'

'None of my business. Sure.' Jago's voice was clipped. 'Look, I've got to get back.' He swallowed and ducked his head in the direction of the office. 'See if I can do something to fix this latest... *mistake*.' With that, he turned his back and strode out of the shop, leaving Gabe staring after him, ignoring the insistent prickle across the back of his neck.

'Are you free to talk?' A voice Gabe hadn't been expecting piped up behind him an hour later and he felt an answering warm arrow in the centre of his chest. When he turned towards the counter, Ruby was standing there, her father flanking her. They were both frowning.

'Everything okay?' Gabe asked, feeling that tingle of foreboding ratchet up, moving forward as Sammie and Rex bounded under the counter to greet them. 'Is there a problem with the tankards?' His heart sank. When he'd left the Pottery Project, everything had been fine. Had something happened since?

'It's all good,' Ruby soothed, reaching out to pat his arm but jerking it back before it landed. 'We're well on our way to replacing them. It'll just be the painting and glazing to go soon.' She nodded. 'Don't worry. They'll be ready in time.' Her eyes dimmed. 'We're here because I need to tell you something.' She grasped the handle of her bag and tapped her palm against it, wincing. 'About Aaron.'

Gabe shook his head as his hackles rose. On the heels of his conversation with Jago, it felt like everyone was out for his brother's blood. 'What about him, and why are both of you here?'

Ruby flushed. 'My father spoke to his contacts – he thought it would be better if you heard what they said from him. In fact, he insisted.' She tipped her head towards Ross and gulped when Gabe didn't respond. 'We need to talk about the things that have been happening. You need to know who's really responsible for them.'

'We know it's probably just vandals,' Gabe said firmly, putting his palms flat on the counter, knowing already he wouldn't like what Ruby was going to say. 'Gryffyn said that he and some of the pottery gang were going to track them down.'

'We were at the beach just now; we spoke to the teenagers he saw. Darren got them to admit they stole the chairs from Ella's and Claude's. They lit the fires too, sprayed graffiti and did some stupid things along the high street.'

'Like painting a moustache on the mural,' Ross said, his expression sober.

'So it *was* them who dumped the manure, attacked my car and smashed all the pottery?' Relief flooded Gabe's chest. He *knew* he'd been right to trust Aaron. 'Is that why you're here?' If it was, why weren't they smiling?

'It wasn't them,' Ruby said, her grey eyes wide. 'I'm sorry, but—'

'It's not Aaron,' Gabe snapped, his temper rising as he read her expression. 'I know what you're thinking. But the kids – whoever they are – were obviously lying.'

'It *was* Aaron,' Ruby interrupted, pressing her lips together as if she couldn't bear to say the words.

Gabe's chest heaved as he felt the blow; it was almost physical. 'You have to know you have no right to hurl a lot of unfounded accusations at my brother because you don't know who else is responsible.' Ruby was just like Jago. Could no one cut his brother some slack? 'The other day you were accusing him of fathering your best friend's child. What are you going to blame him for next?' The words were unkind and for a moment he regretted them, but he had to be strong, had to protect his brother. Loyalty and family demanded it.

Pain slid across Ruby's face, and she glanced at her handbag, looking conflicted. 'I know you won't want to hear this,' she whispered when he started to shake his head. 'I understand why. But Dad talked to his contacts and—'

'For the first time in your life you're going to listen to him? Is that the same man who walked out on you weeks after you were born?' Gabe bit back furiously, hating himself when her eyes rounded.

'There's so much you don't know,' Ruby pleaded.

'Fine,' he snapped, looking back at Ross. 'Tell me, what's Aaron supposed to have done now? Is he plotting to steal the Crown Jewels, has he hijacked a plane, did he make a pass at you?' His eyes swivelled back to Ruby, wondering if this was just her way of severing their connection, by trying to drive a wedge into his relationship with his brother – wasn't that exactly what Camilla had done? As Aaron had surmised at the time when his ex had accused him of making a pass, she simply couldn't cope with how close they were. Surely Ruby knew by now that accusations would spell the end of their... affair, or whatever this thing humming between them was. Maybe she just wanted it to be over? Pain seared deep inside, but he shoved it away. 'Because you have to know, I've heard it all before.'

'Aaron's been gambling and he's in debt,' Ross said calmly. 'I don't know all the details, but you need to take a step back and face some hard facts. To think about the things that have been happening in the brewery and to you.' He paused, glancing at Ruby. 'My daughter's not responsible for any of this, there's no reason to be angry with her.'

Ruby's eyes widened and brimmed with tears as she turned to stare at her father.

'I understand all about letting people down – I know how hard it is for them to finally give up on you,' Ross said softly, turning away from her. 'It took me years to get it.' His lips thinned. 'Too many years – and by the time I did, it was too late. I'm only happy Ruby saw through me before I ruined her life. I'm telling you this so you understand you need to let your brother go too.'

'Dad...' Ruby said, her voice hoarse.

'The truth is...' Ross leaned onto the counter and looked into Gabe's eyes. The gesture was protective and for a moment Gabe felt irritated. Ruby didn't need shielding from him. 'Your brother is in debt to some very bad people.'

'Who?' Gabe snapped, fighting the fear expanding in his throat. 'If that were true, he would have told me.' *Wouldn't he?* He blew out a breath. If he stopped believing in Aaron now, it would be the end of their relationship. The end of everything he'd promised his dad.

Ross blinked. 'Perhaps Aaron didn't want to burden you – maybe he thought he could solve it himself. I will tell you he needs to pay back the money he owes. If he doesn't, well...' The man's eyes bored into his and his silence said it all. 'Aaron wants – needs – you to sell the business, and he's doing everything in his power to make that happen.'

'That's utter crap,' Gabe snapped. 'Don't forget, most of this stuff has been happening to me. Does that mean I'm somehow guilty?' On firmer ground now, he straightened, looming over them.

'Sabotage, vandalism... those things are very common for these people to get involved in. They like to threaten and scare. You look exactly like your brother; chances are you've been mistaken for him,' Ross said.

'Which would explain the damage to your car, the tankards,' Ruby added softly.

'I'll wager the latest offer on that field next door will fall through soon. Isn't it the one thing standing between you and financial ruin?' her father asked.

'You seem to know a lot about things that are none of your business,' Gabe said calmly. 'The sale is going through fine, the contracts should be signed by the end of this week. How could the people my brother's supposed to know be able to stop that?' He considered the two estate agents who'd already pulled out and dismissed them – sure, it was odd, but it wasn't proof that what Ruby and her father were saying was true. 'You're both wrong.' Gabe glared at Ruby, but she jerked her eyes away.

'These people have long arms and a wide reach, and people in the area are terrified of them,' Ross explained. 'Just one word from them and you'll lose your buyer – or estate agent.' He lifted a brow, making his point. 'It's only a matter of time. They're going to do everything they can to make you sell the whole place instead – to get their money and all the interest Aaron owes.'

'Who are these mystery people?' Gabe folded his arms as his throat tightened. 'Because from where I'm standing, you could be making them up.'

'You won't have a clue unless you move in the same circles or know someone who does.' Ross folded his arms too. 'I did once. I was clever enough to get out, but all those years of chasing dreams meant I lost a lot in the process.' His eyes tracked to his daughter and he winced.

'This isn't about you and Ruby,' Gabe snapped, swiping a hand across the back of his neck as it prickled again. 'I know you turned your back on your family, and living through that has coloured everything Ruby thinks and does.' He gazed at her, shaking his head. 'You know what I'm saying. This is just an excuse, a way for you to retreat because it's far too terrifying to feel anything – just another withdrawal in a long line of them. I'll grant you, it's a good one. But I guess it's what you do. Leave and lock yourself down?'

'That's not true,' Ruby said softly, her face reddening.

'Isn't it? How come you gave up pottery, which you love? How often have you been to see Lila in the last year?' Ruby flinched and Gabe felt a corresponding pain in his chest, fought to ignore it. 'My brother has been through enough without having to put up with a load of lies. I'm supposed to protect him.'

'By believing in him, no matter what?' Ross asked, as Ruby put a hand on her father's shoulder and tilted her head towards the door.

'Please can you let me talk to Gabe, alone?' she asked.

He looked surprised, a little wounded, but then Ross jerked his chin and turned towards the door, taking a moment to look back and glower at Gabe. 'You hurt my girl and you'll deal with me,' he murmured, before heading out.

Ruby stepped closer to the counter, placed her fingertips on the wood. She looked so pretty Gabe had to fight the catch in his breath. 'I'm sorry,' she said quietly. 'I didn't come to hurt you. But you had to know what we heard.' She glanced at her bag again, fiddled with the clasp.

'And *you* have to know, I don't believe a word of what you've said.' His voice was gruff. 'You've had it in for Aaron since you arrived.' He stared at her. 'You accused him of being Maisy's father and you've not managed to prove that yet.'

Her face paled and she glanced at her bag again, her lips quivering. 'That doesn't mean he's not guilty.'

'And it doesn't mean he is. My brother's a lot of things, but he's not a cheat. He doesn't get women pregnant and walk away. He's not responsible for what's been happening here.' He glanced around the room, feeling desperate. 'I know someone is, I get that this isn't just coincidence. But it's not Aaron. You need to look at why you're blaming my brother, you need to search inward. Because as I said before, this isn't about him – it's about your need to find fault in relationships you don't seem capable of understanding.' He rubbed a hand across his chest. 'Unconditional love, trust, the ability to open yourself up to love. You need to learn those things, Ruby.'

She lowered her head and he saw her eyes fill, had to fight the desire to take it all back and apologise.

'Is that so?' she whispered, as a single tear slid down her cheek.

He dug his fingertips into his palms so he wouldn't stroke it away. 'You should leave,' he said, forcing out the words, ignoring the pain that almost eviscerated him.

He was doing the right thing, walking away from a woman determined to come between him and his brother. Blood was thicker than water – and blood was thicker than love. He swallowed, watching as another tear leaked from Ruby's eye. Then she turned and retreated, clutching her bag against her side.

27

Gabe blinked and read the email again as someone knocked at the front of his house. He strode through the kitchen, remembering to duck under the low beams, then pulled the door open to find Jago scowling at him from the porch.

'You're an idiot,' Jago said mildly.

Gabe let out a hollow laugh. 'I'm going to agree with you, but first I'd like to know why.' He signalled to his friend to follow, leading him through the hallway into the wide open rustic kitchen, grabbing a glass and filling it with beer without asking. Then he pointed to the breakfast bar. Rex popped his head up from where he was sleeping under the large table, but one look at Jago's face and he laid it back down.

Jago swigged some of the drink. 'I heard you talking to Ruby and her father in the brewery shop earlier. It's taken me this long to work out what to say. I thought I'd pop in on my way home to share.'

'And idiot's all you came up with?' Gabe murmured. 'Because I'd have gone with imbecile. I'm thinking about getting it tattooed here.' Disgusted, he stroked a fingertip slowly across his forehead, frowning at the laptop sitting on the breakfast bar before flipping it around so his head brewer could see. 'Read the email – out loud,' he demanded.

Jago bent to see the screen. '"Dear Mr Roskilly. I regret"...' His eyebrows met. 'I'm guessing this isn't good?' He glanced back at the computer when Gabe didn't respond, scanning ahead. '..."to inform you that the buyer of the field adjacent to your property has dropped out of the sale." Oh *sh—*' Jago grimaced, glancing up momentarily before continuing. '"This is an unexpected development, but I'm sure you'll be able to get the sale back on track. I'm afraid we're unable to proceed with representing you, but no doubt you'll find another estate agent who'll be happy to pick things up. Yours truly, Tilda Walker, A-Plus Services."' Jago straightened. 'That's...' He puffed out a breath and slumped onto one of the chrome stools, leaning his arms on the breakfast counter and cupping his chin. His blue eyes met Gabe's and he frowned. 'So Ruby and her father were right?'

Gabe nodded. He was still reeling, his stomach in knots. 'Looks like it,' he said gruffly. 'I think on some level I knew – I just didn't want to face it. It's still hard to believe Aaron would do any of what they accused him of, even with all the evidence piling up.' But it was clear his brother had, and Gabe had hurt Ruby by rejecting her version of events, ruining any chance he had of being with her. Imbecile wasn't a good enough word – nitwit, moron, simpleton all worked but none of them quite cut it. None summed up just how badly he'd messed up. He put his elbows on the counter, then leaned his head onto one of his hands. 'I talked to the accountant when I got home from the brewery today. Without the money from the sale of the field, we're—'

'Screwed?' Jago finished. 'Tell me...'

Gabe nodded, swallowing a wave of regret. He'd been so determined to see the best in his brother he'd missed all the signs of his deception and pushed everyone away. 'Looks like

Aaron's been creating dummy invoices from a fake hops supplier using a logo and letterhead he designed.' His laugh was hollow. 'The accountants paid all of them – he's literally been bleeding the company dry. I was too stupid and distracted to keep an eye on the books, and I felt like I should trust him.' His voice was toneless. 'Seems that design course taught my brother a lot more than I realised, he's very talented. He's obviously responsible for all the problems we've been encountering in the brewery too.' He scratched his head. 'Ruby said he's been gambling, Ross told me he has huge debts, but Aaron never said a word. If anything, he made me feel guilty for not trusting him. Dad always told me blood was thicker than water.'

'It's not,' Jago growled.

Gabe winced as Sammie appeared from the hallway, holding a half-chewed wellington boot before offering it to him. 'I've only had those a week,' Gabe grumbled. 'I left them by the back door.' He glanced to where one shiny boot stood, alone. It should have made him laugh; instead, he groaned. The beagle dropped the ruined welly at Gabe's feet, barked and trotted up to join Rex, who was still curled under the kitchen table looking angelic.

'If that doesn't prove my point,' Jago said dryly, 'nothing will.' He leaned forward to look into Gabe's eyes. 'Sometimes, you have to *choose* who makes up your family,' he said, his voice kind. 'Find the people you know you can trust.'

Gabe nodded and swallowed just as his mobile went off. He grabbed it from his pocket, feeling his heart leap when he saw it was Ruby. Maybe by some miracle she was calling to forgive him?

'You need to come to Lila's,' she gasped before his brain could form an apology. 'Now!'

'What's happened?' He straightened, his eyes meeting Jago's as he registered the fear in her voice.

'It's Aaron,' Ruby said. 'He's been hurt.'

. . .

'Where is he?' Gabe shouted, charging into Lila's house with Jago bringing up the rear. He was out of breath, both dogs were off their leads, and the instant they entered the hallway, they began to scramble up and down, searching for cats and signs of life.

'Here!' Ruby yelled and Gabe followed her voice, turning right into a huge sitting room. Patricia, Darren and Ned parted and Gabe saw Aaron lying flat on a fluffy pink sofa. His face was red with bruises and he held his arm awkwardly by his side.

'Ouch,' Aaron groaned, as Lila cleaned a patch of blood from the dark bruise forming at the edge of his mouth. Ruby, Ross and Gryffyn were hovering over him, but Ruby didn't look up.

'What happened?' Jago gasped, skidding to a stop beside Gabe.

'Clemo found your brother on the road by the beach earlier – someone had just dumped him there,' Ned said, his eyes bright. 'Clemo's not here,' he added when Gabe skirted the room, searching for him. 'He had to drive Claude and Ella back to the harbour.'

'Why did he bring him here?' Gabe asked gruffly.

'He didn't know what to do,' Ned explained. 'Aaron didn't want us to call you or the police – he insisted, so Clemo chose Lila's because it was closest and we knew she'd have a first aid kit.'

'Why didn't you want them to call me?' Gabe asked Aaron, his eyes fixed firmly on his brother. It was like he was seeing him for the first time, reading the lies in his eyes, the shield he used to hide behind.

'Because, I dunno...' Aaron muttered, groaning again as Lila dabbed more blood from his bruises. 'You wouldn't understand.'

'Who did this?' Gabe strode forward with the dogs hopping

at his heels. 'Is it the people you owe money too?' At Aaron's shocked expression, he nodded. 'I know all about what you've been doing.'

'I don't know what you mean.' Aaron's expression shuttered.

Gabe bent to look into his face. His brother seemed different, pale, unhappy – gone was any eagerness to please, any of the connection he'd imagined. All those feelings he'd thought were buried under the surface – he'd just been kidding himself. 'I know everything. About how you've been creating fake invoices, sabotaging the brewery because you want me to sell up.' He swallowed. 'It's why you weren't keen on selling the field next door, because you knew we'd make more money if we sold the whole lot. It had nothing to do with sentimentality, nothing to do with me – or Dad.' Gabe saw Ruby jerk around, saw the groove in her forehead. 'You owe money to some bad people. Did they do this to you?'

Aaron coughed, trying to sit up. 'You've got no idea.'

'I think I do,' Gabe said. He didn't feel angry now, just hollowed out. He glanced at Ruby again, acknowledging the stab of guilt. She'd tried to tell him about Aaron and he'd pushed her away, put his brother before his own feelings and hers. Rejected her just like her father had done a million times. She'd never speak to him now, and he knew he deserved it.

'You've never understood. You were the golden child, the one who got it all,' Aaron spat, his tone low, the dislike palpable.

Gabe shook his head. Two pictures, two stories, both so different. Why hadn't he seen it before now? 'Why did they hurt you?' he asked softly.

'They're angry you keep trying to sell the field. They want the brewery on the market so I can pay them what I owe.' Aaron sighed. 'They want their money and interest, but it's taking too long.'

'How much do you owe?' Gabe asked, and waited while his

brother considered the question. His eyes were expressionless as Lila helped him slowly sit up and lean back on the sofa. He groaned softly, clutching his arm which looked like it had either been badly sprained or broken. Gabe wanted to get closer – on the one hand to offer his brother comfort but on the other to shake some sense into him. When Aaron named the figure, he almost choked. 'Well, that's...' Gabe's eyes widened. 'We'll have to sell the brewery, we'll never be able to pay that off.'

'I've got money,' Jago said quietly, pacing forward. 'At least, I can raise it.' He turned to Gabe. 'I want to be a partner in the brewery. I'll buy Aaron out – give him enough to clear his debts. We'll be able to sell the field, expand like you wanted. We'll run the place together.'

'I can't ask you to do that,' Gabe said, wishing he could, looking at the man who'd been more of a brother, a partner, a friend to him than his own sibling. *Damn*, he'd been so blind. 'The place is a mess, there's so much to sort out.' He looked down at Aaron again and shook his head, wondering how he could have allowed himself to be so thoroughly duped.

Jago sighed. 'Remember – sometimes, you have to choose your family, find the people you can trust. That applies to partners too.'

'Well...' Gabe looked at his brother for some acknowledgement of what he'd be giving up. When he didn't so much as show a glimmer of regret, he jerked his head. Without Jago's money, the family business would go under and he didn't want that. Added to that, the brewer was a good man, someone he could trust. He glanced at Ruby, then back at Aaron as a thought occurred to him and his stomach sank. 'Did you make a pass at Camilla?'

His brother pouted. 'She was being nosy, kept asking about my course.' He cleared his throat, looking embarrassed. 'I had to get her out of my hair. I figured if I made a pass, she'd either say yes and I'd tell you she was cheating, or—'

'You'd say she made it up and I'd finish with her...' Gabe trailed off, feeling a twinge of regret. He'd have to apologise to his ex at some point, but he couldn't regret the fact that they weren't together. If he was still with Camilla, he wouldn't have got close to Ruby – and she meant so much more. He shook his head. He really was an imbecile: why hadn't he seen all this before? His father's voice skipped through his head and he grimaced – what would his dad say now? He was almost grateful he wasn't here to see the truth.

'Glad that's settled,' Gryffyn grumbled. 'So what's going to happen to him?' He speared a finger at Aaron.

'We should call the police,' Ned said. 'He's caused so much trouble for everyone.'

'But won't that cause trouble for Gabe too?' Lila asked. 'If you pay these people off, surely they'll just go away?'

Aaron shook his head. 'It doesn't matter if we pay them,' he said quietly. 'They'll never leave me alone now.'

Ross nodded. 'He's right. Your brother's a meal ticket with dubious morals – their favourite kind of fool.' He sighed long and hard. 'I know some people in Spain – they'll take care of him for me.' When Aaron gasped, he gave him a toothy grin. 'I mean they'll find you a job – and keep you far, far away from Indigo Cove.'

His brother jerked his head. 'Okay.'

'Thank you,' Gabe said, glancing back at Ruby. She was staring at her father with a strange look in her eyes. She turned and saw him watching, but when he opened his mouth to apologise, she shook her head and spun away – and Gabe realised in that moment he might have lost her for good.

28

'Are you sure you have to go back to London?' Lila asked, hovering over Ruby in the Pottery Project studio as she worked on the wheel.

'I'm sorry, Nanou, but I've booked my train.' Ruby's heart was heavy, but she didn't want to stay in Indigo Cove a moment longer. Her father had promised to assist in the studio until Morweena returned from Hawaii, so she didn't have to feel guilty. Not that Lila needed much help; the whole thing had clearly been a ploy to get her here, away from her dull, safe life. But now a door had opened in her heart, she wondered if she'd be able to close it. Ruby pressed her fingertips into the clay as her wheel spun, crafting another tankard. The gang had been working hard over the last two days and there were only a couple left to make. She ignored the way her chest pinched when she thought about leaving, smoothing her fingertips over the pliable material, moulding the ridge, letting herself feel. But it was scary.

'I always said it. You're a natural,' Lila said quietly, watching Ruby as she worked. 'I hope you're going to find somewhere to do pottery when you get home? Or at least visit here more regularly?'

'I promise to do both,' Ruby murmured. She'd already found a pottery studio in London where she could rent a space, and it was only a short journey from her flat. She might not be prepared to let anyone into her heart, but she'd let herself craft. Giving it up had been a mistake.

'Have you heard from Gabe?' her Nanou asked, gliding gracefully around the studio in a pair of canary-yellow DMs, bending to kiss each of her tomato plants in turn.

Ruby could see her grandmother out of the corner of her eye, and took a moment to appreciate the way the older woman embraced life, how she let everyone and everything into her heart. The thought of doing the same still terrified her. 'No,' Ruby said quietly. Gabe had left soon after the revelations, supporting a limping Aaron to his car with barely a backward glance. It was for the best. She knew that, but it still hurt.

'The money's here!' Her father suddenly bounced into the studio, wearing a pair of shorts and a bright T-shirt, waving his mobile in the air before dipping it under Ruby's nose. She had to stop the pottery wheel as she read the screen and her mouth dropped open.

'That's a lot of money,' her Nanou gasped, coming to join them and taking the mobile from his hand. 'I always knew you'd do it in the end. Well done, love.'

Her dad flushed. 'I appreciate that. I'm not sure I've deserved all your confidence, but I hope to really earn it now.' Ross's eyes strayed to Ruby. Their relationship wasn't fully healed, but there was an ease now which hadn't existed since her mother had died. Perhaps in time they could build on it? Ruby knew she wouldn't ignore his emails anymore, at least. 'I'm transferring all of the money to you,' her father promised Lila. 'That's everything I borrowed over the years, with interest.'

'I don't need that much money,' the older woman gaped,

looking around the studio. 'I've got everything I want right here. If we can fix the damage to the office, then I'll be able to stay in my house and the studio – with my pottery, cats and tomato plants.'

'But it's yours,' Ross said firmly. 'I've got broken promises to fix. Maybe you could use it to expand the Pottery Project.' His eyes widened, filling with big plans. 'Or take on another member of staff? You do good work here, it's important.'

'You could advertise, go head to head with that competitor you talked about – you said you'd like more clients,' Ruby suggested gently.

'Ah, I already have a plan for that.' Lila grinned. 'An ace up my sleeve, a partner who'll draw in crowds of eager potters.'

Gryffyn? Ruby mouthed, but her Nanou tapped a finger on her nose. Before Ruby could ask more, her mobile vibrated. She jumped up and grabbed it from her pocket, hoping for a message from Gabe. Instead, Anna had sent a photo – a picture of Simon, Maisy and herself with a series of emoji hearts. Ruby messaged back a thumbs up, staring at the trio. Her eyes drifted to her handbag which was hanging on a hook beside the kitchen door and she tracked over to it, dug inside and drew out the photos of Anna and Aaron. She stared at them for a moment before ripping the pictures in half and throwing them in the bin. Gabe didn't need to see them. Maisy didn't need another father – especially one like Aaron. Her eyes drifted to her dad. Perhaps Gabe's brother would come good one day; maybe leopards could change their spots, after all? But in the meantime Maisy had all the love she needed. For the first time, Ruby realised she knew how that felt. In many ways she always had.

There was buzz of voices from the entrance and Gryffyn, Patricia, Darren and Ned wandered in, all chatting loudly. 'We're here to finish the tankards,' Gryffyn said, taking a seat on the stool closest to where Darren and Ned worked.

'Don't forget Darren's new friends are coming later for their first lesson.' Lila grinned.

'Lesson?' Ruby asked.

'Yes – Ned, your grandmother and I plan to start a youth club here on Thursday afternoons,' Patricia explained. 'For teenagers who've got nothing to do... It'll be just like having my own kids around again, and I think they'd enjoy doing pottery. It's a lot more interesting than vandalising the village, after all. What do you think, Darren?' she asked tentatively. 'Will it work?'

The teenager's brow furrowed as his eyes drifted around the room, taking in the tomato plants, record player and various pieces of half-finished craft. 'You'll need a bad-cop potter to keep them under control,' he said, his eyes shifting towards Gryffyn.

'It would help.' Ned nodded. 'I'd do it, but...' He shook his head and grimaced. 'My heart wouldn't be in it, I'd be too nice.'

The older man folded his arms. 'I'll be leaving Indigo Cove soon, boy.' His eyes clouded before they flicked to Lila.

'To do what?' she asked, folding her arms. 'To sit in your house and remember all the things you can't do, all the things you've had to give up?' Gryffyn frowned. 'I've said it before, you're a good teacher,' she said. 'Perhaps with time you'll be able to mould someone's talents as well as you used to mould clay?'

The older man waved his crooked finger. 'I told you, I'm not what I was,' he growled.

'That wouldn't stop you,' Lila muttered. 'You just need what's in here and here.' She tapped a finger on her head and heart. 'Mix in a healthy dose of mean and you've got the perfect ingredients to shape a talented potter.'

'I'd come to a youth club if you were helping to run it,' Darren said eagerly, flushing when everyone turned to stare at him. 'Sure you're old, but...' He jerked a shoulder. 'There's not much else to do around here. Besides, I'll bet you'd play better music and you wouldn't burn those awful incense sticks.' He wrinkled his nose.

Lila chuckled. 'So what do you think?' She walked towards Gryffyn, her grey eyes fixed on his face. 'Stay. Work in the youth club. Help me to run this place – be my bad cop. It sounds like I need one.'

'I already said no.' Gryffyn's eyes widened. 'It's a big leap from taking pottery lessons.'

'Not for a man like you,' Lila said, reaching out and brushing a finger down his cheek, triggering a blush. 'You've bloomed since you've been here, and it's not just because of the tea and cake.' She pointed to her tomato plants, which were heavy with fruit. 'This is a good place to grow, and there's space for you if you want it. I'd like a partner in the Pottery Project – someone to argue with.' Her lips pursed. 'I think you'd fit right in.'

Gryffyn swallowed. 'I... I don't know. It's—'

'Scary?' Lila asked. 'Yes, pet, putting yourself out there always is. But what you've got to ask yourself is, will going home, back to the life you weren't really living, be even more frightening?' Ruby squeezed her lips together as her Nanou's question hit home.

The older man's expression darkened before he jerked his chin. 'We'd need a dog – and I prefer biscuits.'

Lila's face glowed. 'We can talk about it.' She moved closer, her eyes twinkling. 'I'm sure there'll be a lot of things we'll talk about in time.' With that, she blew him a kiss.

Ruby finished packing her suitcase, her heart heavy as she zipped it, turning around in her Nanou's spare room before her eyes fell on the small photo frame beside the bed. She'd righted it and had spent long hours staring at the picture of her and her mother, wondering how things might have been. She knew it was time to move on. It wouldn't be easy, but sometimes you had to learn to forgive and forget.

'Can I talk to you?' Aaron asked from the doorway, making Ruby jump. He looked better today; the blood had been washed from his face, and the bruises around his eyes and mouth were a garish mix of yellows and purples.

'Sure,' Ruby murmured, putting her hands on her hips, blocking him from entering her bedroom. If they were doing this, he was staying where he was. 'I thought you were leaving for Spain?' Her eyes flickered to the hallway behind him, and her skin buzzed in anticipation as she wondered if Gabe was going to appear.

Aaron nodded at the brown holdall by his feet. 'It's why I'm here. Your dad offered to drive me to the airport. Gabe's...' He winced. 'Busy.' She swallowed the wave of disappointment. 'There's a lot to sort out with Jago and... the people I owe money to. Also, he wanted to speak with another estate agent.' He dipped his chin, looking embarrassed. 'I'm here to apologise and explain. Well, my brother asked if I would and...' He let out a long exhale.

So this was Gabe's idea. Ruby felt hollow. He hadn't even come to see the apology for himself. Was he that determined to avoid her? The rejection almost made her knees buckle. 'Go on,' she croaked.

He jerked his chin. 'I started gambling when I was sick. I was young, but it was easy and—' He shrugged. 'I was brilliant at it. I wanted to be amazing at something. Gabe was so...' He shook his head. 'Good. I used to call him that behind his back, "Good Gabe", because he was. He got everything and...' His cheeks flooded. 'I was jealous, I see that. It wasn't fair – he was the same as me, but he wasn't ill. I hated him for it.' His voice turned icy. 'Really hated him. I guess everything grew from there.'

'You wanted to take everything from him too?' she asked quietly.

He shrugged. 'I suppose. If I couldn't have love, a life, a job, why should he?'

'But the brewery belonged to both of you.'

He nodded. 'It never felt like it. Besides, by then I didn't care. I was gambling, making so much money. More than Gabe could ever dream of. Then it got out of control. I lost and then I lost again and again. I started borrowing to cover my losses and ended up owing so much.' He puffed out a breath. 'The brewery didn't matter, only winning did. I got in over my head and...'

'You're sorry now?' Ruby asked, tilting her chin.

He pulled a face. 'I'm sorry for the mess I made. I want to make a new start, see if I can do better, be a better person.' He let out a long exhale. 'I thought maybe, perhaps, if you think it's a good idea...' His body stiffened. 'I should contact your friend about the baby.' He looked at his feet and swallowed. 'I... well, I admitted to Gabe that I met her at the Spring Carnival last year and that she'd called me afterwards. He said it would be the right thing to do.'

Ruby sighed; of course he had. The man believed in doing the right thing always. His steadfastness, loyalty and faithfulness were just a few of the reasons why she'd fallen for him. 'I'll talk to Anna and give her your number. Perhaps one day Maisy will want to get in touch, but...' She shook her head. 'She's got a father now. Whether she wants anything to do with you will be up to her. But if she does get in touch...' She stepped closer and looked into his eyes. They were like Gabe's but so different too. 'Make sure you deserve her. Use this chance you've been given. I never thought people could change, but...' She sighed, thinking about her father. 'Maybe some can. Try to be one of them.'

. . .

Ruby tugged her suitcase along the platform of Indigo Cove station, past the multitude of oak barrels filled with pretty red, pink, green and yellow summer flowers. She'd insisted her Nanou drop her at the entrance to the station rather than walk her inside. The parking inspector's face had lit up when he'd seen Beatrix whizz into the front bay and he'd pulled out his ticket machine, his eyes glinting. Ruby hadn't wanted her Nanou to get a ticket, but she also hadn't wanted Lila to see her expression when she climbed onto the train. For the first time in years, Ruby didn't know where she was headed. She felt numb, alone, and her life suddenly seemed so empty. Even the numbers she loved and trusted – the job she could always rely on – didn't feel like enough.

'The 12.32 train to London will be arriving on platform one in three minutes,' a loud voice boomed, and she dropped her suitcase on the ground, turning to see the train pull in. She watched it grow larger and larger, feeling her heart thump hard and the tension in her chest tighten until she could barely breathe. What was she doing here? Gabe's words rang in her head. *This is just an excuse, a way for you to retreat because it's far too terrifying to feel anything – just another withdrawal in a long line of them. I'll grant you, it's a good one. But I guess it's what you do. Leave and lock yourself down.* Was he right? Was that what she was doing now? She blinked and suddenly spun round, ignoring the train as it pulled up beside her. Instead of getting on when the doors slid open, she started to walk down the platform, dragging her suitcase behind her. Her legs began to speed up as if they had a mind of their own, then suddenly she was trotting, her case spinning and bumping on the ground. She wasn't going anywhere, not without talking to Gabe. She had to tell him how she felt.

Then suddenly Ruby wasn't running anymore; her feet were tangled in something and she was falling forward, diving towards the platform face first. Then a set of arms caught her just before she crashed. They lifted her gently onto her feet and just like that, she was gazing into Gabe's green eyes.

'Sammie!' he admonished, glaring down at the beagle who'd almost tripped her. The dog's lead was caught around her ankles, trapping her. Gabe knelt to untangle it. 'I'm sorry,' he said, standing again, brushing his hands against the sides of her arms. 'I know the train's here, I know you're leaving, but... please don't.' He looked serious. 'I'm an imbecile.' He shrugged. 'Actually I'm a lot of things – *was* a lot of things,' he corrected, flushing. 'Mostly I was wrong. I'm sorry I didn't believe you when you told me about Aaron, I'm sorry I pushed you away.'

Ruby shook her head slowly as relief flooded through her. She cupped the edge of his face, stroking a finger across the stubble on his chin before leaning up and brushing her mouth over his. The breath whooshed from Gabe's chest as the kiss deepened and his arms moved around to press against her back. 'I'm sorry too,' she croaked, easing herself closer to him, feeling the life seep back into her bones. 'You were right about some of it. I didn't want to open myself up to love, I wasn't ready to trust you. I had a lot to learn. Perhaps I used Aaron as an excuse. I didn't believe people could change. Perhaps the truth is that *I* had to change before I could.' She heard the sound of the train doors closing behind her and tugged backwards to look at Gabe, listened as the carriages pulled away, clattering on the tracks. 'I was coming back.'

Gabe's eyes shone and he beamed down at her, blinking in surprise. 'I thought you were going to make this difficult. I was prepared to kidnap you. Your grandmother's outside in Beatrix, ready to help.' He ducked his head towards the exit and grinned, and Ruby chuckled as the tightness across her chest eased, leaving her feeling lighter than she had in years. Then Gabe gazed at her. 'I don't know what the future holds, I know we've only just met, but perhaps together we can figure things out.' Sammie and Rex both barked and Ruby felt the whack of their two tails hitting her shoes.

'I'd like that,' Ruby murmured as warmth flooded through her, and she went up onto her tiptoes to slowly kiss and hug him tighter, thanking her lucky stars that she'd returned to Indigo Cove. In just a few short weeks, her whole life had changed and she'd learned to open herself up to love, family and even pottery again – and whatever happened, Ruby knew she wouldn't look back.

A LETTER FROM DONNA

I want to say a big thank you for choosing to read *The Little Cornish House*. If you enjoyed it and want to keep up to date with all my latest releases, just sign up at the following link. Your email address will never be shared and you can unsubscribe at any time.

www.bookouture.com/donna-ashcroft

The Little Cornish House took me to a whole new area of the country! I spent a wonderful week in summer 2021 with my family travelling around Cornwall getting a feel for the area and scenery, and wow, it's beautiful! I really enjoyed writing about and meeting all the new quirky characters in Indigo Cove, from Ruby, Gabe, Lila and Gryffyn to the Pottery Project students and The Marples. I tried to create a community of characters who took care of and watched out for each other because I think that's something we could all do with these days.

Ruby had a lot to come to terms with in order to allow love into her world – the arrival of her wayward father and the understanding that sometimes people can change, even after many years. Gabe, on the other hand, had to learn that you can't always blindly trust your family and that sometimes blood isn't thicker than water. The two of them had many challenges to overcome in the story so they were ready to let love into their lives, and I hope you loved their journey as much as I adored writing it.

If you did, it would be wonderful if you could please leave a short review. Not only do I want to know what you thought, it might encourage a new reader to pick up my book for the first time.

I really love hearing from my readers – so please say hi on my Facebook page, through Twitter, on Instagram or on my beautiful website.

Thanks,

Donna Ashcroft

www.donna-writes.co.uk

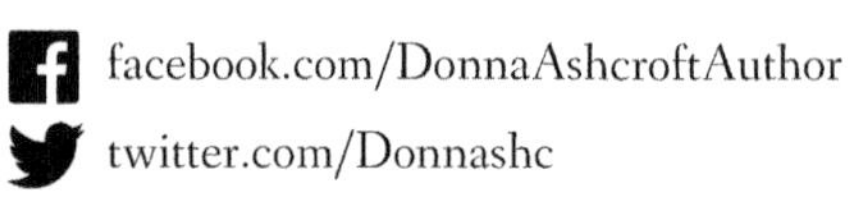
facebook.com/DonnaAshcroftAuthor
twitter.com/Donnashc
instagram.com/donnaashcroftauthor

ACKNOWLEDGEMENTS

Being published has been a lifelong dream, but the genuine good wishes and support I've received on my journey has been the most incredible bonus. I won't ever take it for granted and I just wanted to say a few special thank yous!

My first go to Mel and Rob Harrison who run the agency Goodman Fox – they built me the most wonderful website and have given me valuable advice on so many aspects of marketing. They are lovely, generous people with huge hearts and I'm very grateful to have met them.

I'd also like to say a huge thank you to Tring Brewery, in particular to Jared, Sam and Andrew. I approached the brewery to ask for advice on all kinds of things, from what brewers wear to the ways in which someone might sabotage brewing equipment. They spent a lot of time corresponding with me and brainstorming ideas which helped to make this story more plausible. I'd like to say thanks and to take this opportunity to recommend their wonderful beers and brewery tours.

On a day-to-day basis I'm fortunate to have the support of Jules Wake, my writing buddy who is always on hand to brainstorm, or reassure and advise me when I'm feeling stuck or despondent. To Chris, who puts up with me however grumpy I get, makes untold vats of tea and coffee and reads all my books. To my oldest friends Jackie Campbell and Julie Anderson, who break out the champagne, send me flowers, and are on hand to celebrate all my achievements. It really does mean a lot, especially when they both do such important work themselves. Thanks also to Hester Thorpe who helped to inspire some of Lila's quirkiest qualities, to Kirstie Campbell for the fabulous celebration cakes, to Christelle Ashcroft for the French language advice, and to Katy Walker for the introduction to pottery speak!

As always, thanks to my fabulous editor (without whom I wouldn't be here) Natasha Harding, and to everyone at Bookouture. I'd love to name them all, but special thanks to Aimee Walsh, Kim Nash, Noelle Holten, Jess Readett, Sarah Hardy, Peta Nightingale, Richard King and Saidah Graham. Also to Caroline Hogg, Catherine Lenderi and Claire Gatzen for their work on this book. Thanks also to the other Bookouture authors for your enduring support.

To wonderful friends, bloggers and readers who support me by buying and reading my books, letting me know they've enjoyed them, reviewing, blogging and cheering me on. Thank you! In particular to Katy Walker, Karen Spicer King, Ian Wilfred, Amanda Baker, Sue Moseley, Gillian Rogers, Ellie Hammond, Hester Thorpe, Alison Phillips, Tricia Osborne, Claire Hornbuckle, Cindy L Spear, Em the Bookworm, Anne Winckworth, Jan Dunham, Masha Rixon, Leigh Anderson, Paul Campbell, Julianne Benford, Donna Smedley, Helen Neaves-Wilde, Linda Heath, Lynda James, Amy Stockley plus Northumbrian Libraries and Staffordshire Libraries who have hosted me at virtual events. Also thanks to Laura Lovejoy for the inspiration from her fabulous surname.

To the wonderful bloggers who took part in my last book tour! They include Captured on Film, @wendyreadsbooks, Page Turners – Reviews by Caroline, Lu Reviews Books, @iheartbooks1991, @rachel.fox.14224, Star Crossed Reviews, Bookworm 86 and Stardust Book Reviews. Thank you so much for giving up your time to support me.

Thanks to my family – Erren, Charlie, Dad, Mum, John,

Peter, Christelle, Lucie, Mathis, Joseph, Lynda, Louis, Auntie Rita, Auntie Gillian, Tanya, James, Rosie, Ava, Philip, Sonia, Stephanie and Muriel.

Finally, to the readers who have been there with me throughout my journey – I wouldn't be here without you xx.